Praise for the Sloa...

"Distinctive characters and fun anecdotes about beer and brewing help make this a winner. Readers will want to keep coming back for more."

—*Publishers Weekly* on *Beyond a Reasonable Stout*

"Exciting and irresistible . . . This absorbing mystery will not let you leave it unfinished. Ellie Alexander is a formidable mystery novel writer."

—*Washington Book Review* on *Death on Tap*

"With its beautifully described small-town setting and seamlessly entwined details about brewing beer, this cozy will appeal to beer lovers everywhere as well as readers who enjoy mysteries highlighting family relationships and independent female m...   ...list

"Likeable characters, an atmospheric small-town setting, and a quirky adversary for the amateur sleuth. The engaging premise and pairings of beer and food should appeal to fans of Avery Aames's 'Cheese Shop' titles."   —*Library Journal*

"A delight for foodies, craft beer fans, and lovers of twisty mysteries with a bit of humor."

—*Kirkus Reviews* on *Without a Brew*

"Charming . . . featuring a clever protagonist and a talented brewer whose knowledge of the science and art of brewing beer is both fascinating and fun. The cozy village and the quirky characters who inhabit it are a delight, and the intriguing mystery will keep readers enthralled to the very end."

—Kate Carlisle, *New York Times* bestselling author of the Bibliophile and the Fixer Upper Mysteries

"Ellie Alexander's prose bubbles like the craft beers her protagonist Sloan Krause brews—a sparkling start to a new series."

—Sheila Connolly, *New York Times* bestselling author of the Orchard Mysteries and the Cork County Mysteries

"A concoction containing a charming setting, sympathetic characters, and a compelling heroine that kept me turning pages way past my bedtime."

—Barbara Ross, author of the Maine Clambake Mysteries

"*Death on Tap* is an entertaining sip of the world of brewpubs and tourist towns. Sloan, a foster child turned chef, brewer, and mother, is an intriguing protagonist. Pour me another!"

—Leslie Budewitz, two-time Agatha Award winning author of the Food Lovers' Village Mysteries

"A 'hopping' good cozy mystery ... Readers will enjoy listening to local gossip and tracking a killer along with her in the charming German-style 'Beervaria' setting of Leavenworth, Washington."

—Meg Macy, author of *Bearly Departed*

"Delightful! Brewmaster Sloan Krause is the perfect cozy protagonist: vulnerable enough to keep her heart guarded, yet capable enough to brew ales along with the big boys, whip up beer-inspired treats, and, of course, solve a murder."

—Cindy Brown, Agatha Award-nominated author of the Ivy Meadows Mysteries

ALSO BY ELLIE ALEXANDER

THE SLOAN KRAUSE MYSTERIES
Death on Tap
The Pint of No Return
Beyond a Reasonable Stout

THE BAKESHOP MYSTERIES
Meet Your Baker
A Batter of Life and Death
On Thin Icing
Caught Bread Handed
Fudge and Jury
A Crime of Passion Fruit
Another One Bites the Crust
Till Death Do Us Tart
Live and Let Pie
A Cup of Holiday Fear
Nothing Bundt Trouble

WITHOUT

A BREW

ELLIE ALEXANDER

St. Martin's Paperbacks

This is a work of fiction. All of the characters, organizations, and events portrayed in this novel are either products of the author's imagination or are used fictitiously.

Published in the United States by St. Martin's Paperbacks, an imprint of St. Martin's Publishing Group.

WITHOUT A BREW

For information, address St. Martin's Publishing Group, 120 Broadway, New York, NY 10271.

www.stmartins.com

Library of Congress Catalog Card Number: 2020021892

ISBN: 978-1-250-80215-6

Our books may be purchased in bulk for promotional, educational, or business use. Please contact your local bookseller or the Macmillan Corporate and Premium Sales Department at 1-800-221-7945, ext. 5442, or by email at MacmillanSpecialMarkets@macmillan.com.

Printed in the United States of America

Minotaur hardcover edition published 2020
St. Martin's Paperbacks edition / September 2021

10 9 8 7 6 5 4 3 2 1

WITHOUT
A BREW

ELLIE ALEXANDER

St. Martin's Paperbacks

This is a work of fiction. All of the characters, organizations, and events portrayed in this novel are either products of the author's imagination or are used fictitiously.

Published in the United States by St. Martin's Paperbacks, an imprint of St. Martin's Publishing Group.

WITHOUT A BREW

For information, address St. Martin's Publishing Group, 120 Broadway, New York, NY 10271.

www.stmartins.com

Library of Congress Catalog Card Number: 2020021892

ISBN: 978-1-250-80215-6

Our books may be purchased in bulk for promotional, educational, or business use. Please contact your local bookseller or the Macmillan Corporate and Premium Sales Department at 1-800-221-7945, ext. 5442, or by email at MacmillanSpecialMarkets@macmillan.com.

Printed in the United States of America

Minotaur hardcover edition published 2020
St. Martin's Paperbacks edition / September 2021

10 9 8 7 6 5 4 3 2 1

This book is dedicated to the real community of Leavenworth, Washington. Thank you for making me feel welcome, sharing your stories, and allowing me to use your little slice of Bavaria as the inspiration for the series. *Prost!*

A BITING JANUARY WIND BLEW into the taproom as the front door to Nitro opened and a group of skiers traipsed inside. They were loaded down with gear—expensive puffy parkas in an array of bright colors, ski goggles, boots, and poles. A slightly overweight guy with a pinched face and an entitled sneer glanced around the bar and scoffed. "This is where they sent us? Dude, it's going to be a long weekend."

His buddy laughed. "We're not in Seattle anymore, Kev."

They were followed in by two younger women dragging hot pink Prada suitcases behind them.

The first guy approached the bar, where Garrett, my boss and fellow brewer, and I had been pouring pints for locals and brainstorming our spring beer line. In the world of craft beer, we always had to think a season ahead. Despite the fact that we were deep in the throes of winter in Leavenworth, Washington, we were already dreaming up sunny, fruit-forward ales and sweet strawberry pilsners.

"Hey, who do I talk to about getting a couple of rooms?" The guy with the pinched face interrupted our conversation. He was tall with a slightly receding hairline. I put him in his early thirties, and judging by his smartwatch with its platinum band and his designer ski gear, I'd have wagered a guess that he worked for one of the many tech companies headquartered in nearby Seattle.

I gave Garrett a look to let him know that I had this, and turned to the guy. "We don't have any rooms."

His tightly wound face squeezed even harder. Big blue veins bulged across his forehead. "That's not what I heard. I was told you have the only rooms left in town, and we want them. I'll pay you cash. Hard money, right now, for them." As if to prove his net worth, he dug a leather wallet from his ski jacket and proceeded to flash a bunch of hundred-dollar bills.

Garrett stepped forward. "Who told you we had rooms available?"

The guy pointed in the direction of Front Street. "That cheap-ass property management company down the street. I rented a ski chalet from them for the weekend, but apparently the pipes froze, and it's flooded. That worthless woman tried to rebook us in a hotel, but everything is full. She told us to come talk to . . ." He paused for a minute and read a note jotted down on the back of a business card I recognized. It belonged to my friend Lisa Balmes, who owned a high-end vacation management company in the village.

"I need to talk to Sloan or Garrett—stat. The name's Kevin Malcolm. You may not be aware, but I'm a VP and I have high expectations when it comes to customer service."

He tapped his watch. "My friends and I are freezing our butts off here, so go get one of them for me."

"You're looking at them." Garrett pointed to his chest. As usual, his slightly disheveled hair was held back by a pair of the chemistry goggles he used when brewing.

"Great." Kevin snapped. "Then what do we need to do to get a couple of rooms ASAP?" He took five hundred-dollar bills out of his wallet and proceeded to stack them on the bar, one at a time.

"Technically we don't have any rooms ready," Garrett replied.

That was true. If Lisa had sent them our way, she must be in dire straits. We hadn't advertised the fact that we were about to open a craft-beer-themed B and B. Beer tourism was becoming big business, and we were sitting on a little gold mine. We had converted four bedrooms above the brewery into guest rooms in an attempt to pull in another revenue stream in the form of beer travel. Each room design was inspired by the four elements of beer—hops, grain, yeast, and water. We had started renovations in November, but then the holiday season hit and put us behind schedule. Our goal was to officially open next weekend, just in time for Leavenworth's annual Bavarian IceFest, but we had decided to start with a "soft" opening in advance of officially launching our new project. Just yesterday we had welcomed our first guests, a young couple in town celebrating their anniversary. It seemed like a good idea to test the waters before we made the space available to more guests.

"Look, I don't want to play games with you, man. Is this a money issue? Consider that a deposit." He nodded at the

3

stack of hundreds. "There's plenty more where that came from. I'm willing to fork out more even if this is a glorified Airbnb, because I'm not having my ladies sleep out in the cold." He glanced behind him and shot a lewd look at the two women waiting near the front door.

I shuddered at his condescending use of "ladies."

"Look, I'm a VP. A VP at a major ad agency that works with all of the tech giants in Seattle. You've probably heard of Screamtime."

Everyone in the PNW had heard of Screamtime. The irreverent ad agency was known for in-your-face ad campaigns that pushed every moral boundary. It was no surprise that Kev worked for the company.

He puffed out his chest and took out a vape pen. "I'll make it worth your while to have us stay. I know powerful people in the digital industry. A review of this place from me will get you noticed by the jet set."

The jet set? Who was this guy?

"Hey, there's no smoking or vaping in here." Garrett held up a finger to the pompous VP.

"Lame." He stuffed the vape pen back in his pocket.

"Give us a minute, and we'll see what we can do about rooms." Garrett pulled me over to the far corner of the bar. "What do you think, Sloan?"

I shrugged. "It's your call. I can get the rooms ready. They're basically done. I just need to get some linens and towels. I'm sure Lisa must be in a jam if she sent him to us, but remind me to thank her later." I rolled my eyes. "He sure seems like a *gem*."

"Trust me, I know the type. He's one of three thousand

4

VPs. We used to call them VPs of ass kissing. Guys like that are the reason I live here now." Garrett had recently moved to our Bavarian utopia after working in Seattle for decades. He had ditched city life to run a nanobrewery in the remote Northern Cascades. It had been quite a lifestyle change, but one that he had adapted to seamlessly.

I chuckled. "If nothing else, we can take his money."

"My thoughts exactly. And in some ways, if we can put up with Mr. VP and his pals for the weekend, we'll really have an official soft opening test. As much as I hate to admit it, we're going to have to learn how to handle his type once we open the guest rooms. It's not like we can ask people if they're entitled jerks when they make a reservation."

"I don't know. Maybe I should formulate some of kind of screening test." I was hopeful that guys like the one waiting impatiently at the end of the bar wouldn't choose Nitro's rustic guest rooms. One of the things I liked most about working in the brewery was the low-key vibe and relaxed atmosphere. The space was casual, welcoming, and a good spot to savor one of our signature pints for an afternoon. But Garrett raised a fair point. We were about to branch into the hospitality business, and that meant interacting with a variety of customers. I was a professional. I could deal with the VP.

"Why don't you get them beers to tide them over, and I'll go check on the rooms?" I retied my long black ponytail and rolled up the sleeves to my Nitro hoodie.

"What would I do without you, Sloan?" Garrett patted my shoulder. "You're one of a kind."

"Don't forget it." I winked and left Garrett to deal with the skiers.

5

Nitro is the smallest brewery in the village, with a tasting room and bar in the front, a commercial kitchen and our brewing operations in the back. It originally belonged to Garrett's great-aunt Tess, who used the space as a diner and guesthouse. Upstairs, each room had its own bathroom and fireplace. Garrett currently lived in a converted suite. He took the walls down between a couple of the rooms to create his own apartment. The other large suite was occupied by our first employee, Kat. In addition to the apartments and guest rooms, the upstairs included a shared reading room, which we had outfitted with comfy couches, bookcases stacked with plenty of fiction and an assortment of beer titles, and a snack area with a small fridge, self-serve coffee and tea, and late-night munchies.

As I walked past the reading room, I spotted Ali and Brad, our first soft-opening guests, curled up on the couch. They were leafing through a cross-country trail map and drinking cups of tea.

"How's everything going?" I stopped to check in with them.

Brad rested his arm around his wife's shoulder. "Good, good. We're mapping out our ski route for this afternoon. When do the lights come on?"

The lights that Brad was referring to were Leavenworth's winter showpiece. Over a million twinkle lights adorned every tree and storefront in the German-inspired village. They lit up our little alpine town from the day after Thanksgiving until March, casting a perpetual winter glow on our cobblestone streets. Visitors descended on our otherwise sleepy town every weekend in the winter to experience

6

the magic of the colorful light show and ski and snowshoe in our nearby mountains. Next weekend's Bavarian IceFest would include fireworks, ice carving, snow sculptures, and winter games like the penguin shuffle, ice cube scrambling, the snowball toss, smooshing, and a local favorite—Frisbee sweeping, where contestants sweep a Frisbee on a sheet of ice from one end of Front Street to the other.

"The lights come on at dusk every night. You have plenty of time to hit the trails this afternoon." I looked at the antique cuckoo clock, one of the pieces left from Garrett's great-aunt Tess. It was just after one. The sun wouldn't set until after five. "I'm glad I found you two. We have some unexpected guests staying." I explained the situation. "We weren't intending to book any other rooms this weekend, but we can't leave these guests out in the cold."

"Don't give it a thought." Ali rubbed Brad's hand as she spoke. "We're happy to share this space, and we are absolutely in love with our room, aren't we, honey?"

Brad agreed. "For sure. The hops theme is awesome. Especially the dried hops to put under our pillows. Nice touch."

Hops have a naturally calming effect. We decided to offer our guests the same immersive experience, by stringing dried hops along the ceiling, placing hop vines in small mason jar vases throughout the room, and leaving hop-filled sachets under the pillows. "I'm glad you're enjoying it so far. Don't forget to stop in the tasting room to get your free pint later." Guests who stayed with us would receive a special beer tasting, personal brewery tours, and homemade breakfasts.

"Oh, we're here for the beer! Don't worry, we plan to

7

camp out in the tasting room tonight and try everything you have on tap." Ali grinned. "I told Brad maybe we should skip skiing today and just go straight for the beer."

Brad squeezed her hand. "We have the entire weekend for beer, hon."

They were clearly celebrating their anniversary. His left arm massaged her shoulder as his right hand was entwined in hers. Their easy show of affection made me think of my soon-to-be ex-husband, Mac. I had caught him cheating on me with a young barmaid. At the time I had been furious, embarrassed, and totally unclear about what to do next, but like many things in life, sometimes the hardest struggles lead to new discovery. If it hadn't been for Mac straying, I probably wouldn't be at Nitro now. In some ways I felt grateful for his infidelity. Not that I condoned it, but we had been unhappy for a while. If I was being honest with myself, I didn't think I ever would have left him if it hadn't been for that fateful day when I walked in on him. A part of me would always love him. He had introduced me to the world of craft beer and given me my son, Alex. I was hopeful that in the days ahead we would be able to find a new way of being friends or at least co-parents, without the baggage that came from decades of an unhealthy marriage.

The hardest part of our breakup for me had been the thought of losing my connection with Otto, Ursula, and Hans, Mac's parents and brother. They were the only family I had ever known. As a product of the foster care system, I had no baseline for what it was like to have a family support you unconditionally. The Krauses had given me that, and I couldn't bear the thought of losing them.

The problem was, it wasn't solely Mac's infidelity that had put a strain on things with my in-laws. Our relationship was complicated and made more so by Ursula's revelation a couple months ago that she had known my birth mother. I had been sitting with that knowledge, unsure how to proceed. Learning that Ursula had known details about my past and kept them from me had left me feeling completely unsettled. Why had she withheld such important information? Her revelation had left me feeling like I was walking around in a daze. Everything I had thought I knew about the Krause family was in question. The situation was made worse by a phone call around the same time with my former case worker and only confidant, Sally, who had warned me that Otto and Ursula might not be the sweet couple I had always believed them to be. Was there another reason Ursula had lied to me all of these years? Could she somehow be involved with my parents' disappearance?

I shuddered at the thought. Sally was coming in a couple days, and until then, my only coping strategy was to keep busy and to push any thoughts of the Krauses to the side for the short term. Initially, Sally had intended to come to Leavenworth right away, but her plans changed after she had uncovered more information about my past. She had asked for more time to compile as much as she could before we met again in person. I had waited this long, so another day or two wouldn't kill me.

I turned my attention to the happy couple snuggled together on the couch. They even looked alike. Both Brad and Ali had dark hair and deep brown eyes. Ali's was twisted into a messy bun, while Brad's was trimmed short. Their dewy gaze made me wistful for young love. "Enjoy the skiing, and please don't hesitate to let us know if you need anything. We'll look forward to seeing you in the tasting room later."

I left them and went to the supply room to get towels, sheets, and toiletries. I planned to put the VP and his friends in the water and yeast rooms respectively, as both of those had two queen beds. They could figure it out from there. I wasn't going to insert myself into their group dynamic. We had arranged the hop and grain rooms for couples' retreats, with king beds and claw-foot tubs. If fully booked, Nitro could accommodate a total of twelve guests. Hopefully, that number would bring in some extra cash without inundating us with tons of extra work.

The highlight of our brewery lodgings would be custom beer-infused breakfasts. I loved to cook, so I had agreed to take on breakfast preparation in addition to the small menu we had for the bar. With nearly every room booked, tomorrow morning should be a good test.

I prepped the rooms and tried to push thoughts of Ursula and my past from my mind. The rooms had turned out better than I had anticipated. The water room was a sensory retreat with stunning photographs of Icicle Creek, the Wenatchee River, and Leavenworth's snowcapped mountains lining the walls. We had painted the room in soft, calming blue tones and adorned it with matching blue and white linens and an indoor water fountain. Yeast had been harder to visualize, but Kat, our newest addition, had had a stroke of genius when she found a quote about yeast and how every loaf of bread could have become beer but—tragically—didn't. We rolled with that idea by showcasing collections of photos from every step in the brewing process. The yeast room was painted in creamy beige tones with pops of orange, and had yellow accent pillows, a small loveseat for reading, and a stack of chemistry and science magazines.

Once the guest rooms were sparkling clean, with fluffy stacks of towels, chocolates on the pillows, and pint glasses ready for filling, I returned to the bar. Garrett was chatting with a local at one of the high-top tables. Kat was updating the chalkboard menu with two new guest taps.

Kat was in her early twenties with a mound of curls, dimples, and boundless energy. She had ended up in Leavenworth in a less-than-fortunate situation, and Garrett and I had taken her under our wing. In exchange for free room and board, she was our girl Friday. Kat might be young, but she was a quick study. She had learned how to pour a perfect pint, was developing her knowledge base of the craft, and was always ready to dive in wherever we needed her, whether that meant washing dishes or making beds.

I waved to Kat and ducked behind the bar. "Okay, the rooms are ready," I said to Garrett.

"Good." He handed me a gold-embossed business card. "Kev, a.k.a. Kevin Malcolm, VP of ass kissing, and his cronies are all paid up." He looked to Kat. "You'll both be happy to know that there's a big, big tip coming our way if he and his friends are happy with their stay."

"Gag." Kat stuck out her tongue.

"If they give you any problems, come talk to me or Garrett." I felt protective of Kat. "I know how to deal with guys like Kevin—don't let them intimidate you." I glanced to the front. "Oh, and don't let him vape."

"No worries." Kat brushed me off. "Those women are like their groupies. They hang on every word 'Kev' says. I don't think he'll mess with me when he has a vapid fan base drooling over him."

Kat was a bit younger than Kevin and his friends, but she was wise beyond her years.

"Here's to launching the bed-and-breakfast." Garrett gave us both high fives.

After working on the concept for months, I was excited to kick off our new endeavor. But I couldn't shake a nagging feeling that Kevin and his friends were going to be trouble.

CHAPTER

TWO

MY FEARS ABOUT KEVIN AND his pals were confirmed as the afternoon wore on. They camped out in the tasting room, ordering multiple rounds of pints and talking loud enough for everyone in the pub to hear their conversation. I knew it was intentional. Kev was the kind of guy who thrived on attention. His friends might not have picked up on it, but I noticed that each time he told a story about firing his personal assistant or how much he paid for his Tesla, he would do a quick survey of the room to make sure our other guests were listening.

They weren't.

At least they were trying not to. One table of regulars moved away from Kevin's group and came to sit at the bar.

"What's the deal with that guy, Sloan?" a doctor who worked at the village hospital just around the corner from Nitro asked. "Is he trying to impress us? Because here's a news flash—it's not working."

"Don't ask. They were supposed to be staying up at one of the ski chalets, but apparently the pipes froze, so Lisa sent them to us. Lucky, huh? Aren't you jealous? Maybe we should send them to the hospital. You have visitor rooms there, right?"

"No way. If that guy shows up at the hospital, I'm turning in my doctor card."

Garrett poured frothy new pints. "This round is on the house, Doc."

The doctor raised his glass. "Unnecessary, but thank you. If either of you need a sedative to help you sleep tonight, come find me."

I knew he was joking, but I did feel bad for Garrett and Kat. At least I would get to escape any annoying guests at night. For the moment, I was still living in the vintage farmhouse that Mac and I had spent years restoring to its original glory. Lately, though, I'd been toying with putting the house and acreage up for sale and making an offer on a sweet cottage in town. I had even gone so far as to tour the new property with my nemesis, April Ablin. She's Leavenworth's self-proclaimed ambassador and one-woman welcome wagon. To help solidify her position in the village, she dresses in outlandish barmaid outfits and somehow manages to butcher any attempt at speaking German, much to Otto and Ursula's delight.

A woman with long, silky blond hair swept into the bar. With her stylish black slacks and gray cashmere sweater, she didn't look like our typical winter ski tourist stomping around in heavy boots. She made a beeline for the bar and dropped her Italian leather purse on an empty barstool.

"Can I get you a drink?" I asked, sliding a Nitro coaster toward her.

"Yes, please. I could really use a drink." She sounded frazzled.

"Do you have a particular style of beer you prefer, or would you like me to make some suggestions?" Educating our customers on flavor profiles and hop varietals was the best part of my job. I loved being able to share my knowledge on the craft and help people find the perfect beer for their palate. We had an ongoing challenge at Nitro that we could match every customer's preferences with one of our custom craft beers. Thus far we hadn't missed. It was especially rewarding when a customer sat down at the bar and claimed they "hated beer." I took those words as my personal mission to introduce them to a variety of styles. Hops overwhelmed many palates, so I would often start with a pilsner or wheat beer. On the other hand, we had plenty of customers who refused to drink our malty offerings—for them, I went straight to our hoppiest brews, like our Pacific Northwest line of IPAs.

"Anything. Whatever you like best is fine." The woman made a sound like a half moan and twisted her straw-colored locks around her index finger. I could tell that blond wasn't her natural color, since her eyebrows were as dark as our winter stout. The contrast between her nearly black eyebrows, bittersweet chocolate eyes, and honey highlights was striking.

"Our most popular beer at the moment is our winter ale—it's a nice balance of hops with fifty IBUs and hints of pine and citrus. Do you want a taste?" IBU—International Bittering Unit—is a term brewers throw around, but for the novice drinking crowd, it's a great way to gauge a beer's hop profile. The lower the IBU, the less hoppy or bitter the beer will be.

"That sounds fine. I don't need to taste it. I'll take a pint."

"Great." I went to pour her a glass of our newest winter ale. Garrett and I had tweaked a holiday recipe for the hoppy brew. We had tapped it on New Year's Day and would have it on as our seasonal until mid-to-late February.

I returned with the pint and handed it to the woman. "Here you go. Is there anything else I can get you? Would you like to see a food menu?"

She scrolled through her phone. "No. I'm not hungry. I'm trying to find a place to stay tonight, though, and every hotel I've been to is booked. I had no idea Leavenworth was so popular during the winter."

"Only on weekends," I replied. "You're here with the Friday crowd. Monday through Thursday is pretty quiet. But today everyone rolls in for the weekend—skiing, sledding, shopping, and of course, checking out our annual winter light display."

The woman took a large gulp of her beer. Craft beer is made for sipping, not chugging. When I give tours of the brewery and tastings, I always encourage our customers to savor the experience. Our beer is best when you take the time to smell the hops, swirl the first sip in your mouth, and then close your eyes and take a minute to really absorb each distinct flavor. Sure, you can chug a beer to get a buzz, but you'll miss the nuances and subtle aromas that we spend weeks and months perfecting. Watching her knock back the pint made me sad. It was kind of like someone walking past an artist's painting and saying, "Oh, pretty," without bothering to stop and take note of the brushstrokes and layers of color.

"Great. Just my luck." She set the half-empty beer on the bar. "You don't happen to know of any hotels with availability?"

"Where have you checked?" I had a feeling she was going to be in the same predicament as Kevin and his friends from Seattle.

She rattled off the name of basically every boutique hotel and bed-and-breakfast in the village.

"That's pretty much it."

"I'm screwed." She pressed her thumb into her temple. "I don't want to drive back to Spokane in the dark. Getting through the mountain passes in the daylight was stressful enough."

"Yeah, that's a long drive. What is it, like, three and half hours?"

"Longer with the snow right now. I followed a snowplow through the pass. That was fun." She picked up the beer again.

I knew I had to offer the last empty room upstairs. Obviously, the universe was conspiring against our soft launch. "Hang on a minute. I might have an idea for you." I went to find Garrett. He was in the office checking on inventory numbers. To call it an office was an exaggeration at best. The tiny room had just enough space for two desks and a filing cabinet. Garrett had painted the far wall with whiteboard paint. He used it to work out new beer recipes. Today there were early sketches of our brainstorms for the spring line on the wall in purple and green dry-erase pen. Honey wheat,

17

a lavender sour, lemon and orange citrus, and a strawberry blonde were beers we were considering.

"Hey, so how do you feel about having another guest tonight and going all in on our not-so-soft launch?"

"What?" He set a stack of papers aside.

I told him about the woman at the bar.

"We can't win, can we?" His eyes held a touch of bewilderment. "I guess they weren't kidding when they said that we wouldn't have a problem keeping the place booked."

"I know. It's like, be careful what you wish for." I grimaced. "What do you think? Should we offer her the room and go for it?"

"Why not? What's one more guest?" He clicked the top of a ballpoint pen. "What about breakfast?"

"I'm going to work on that next. I'll see what we have in the kitchen. Since we knew that Ali and Brad were going to be here, I had already planned for tomorrow and Sunday. I'll probably need to grab a few extra things at the grocery store, but I can make it work."

"Let's do it, then." He flashed me a thumbs-up.

I left him to finish the inventory sheets and returned to the bar. "Good news," I said to the woman, who had finished the beer. "We have a room here if you're interested."

Her face lit up. "Really? Yes, please—I'll sleep right here on the bar if I have to."

I told her about our guest rooms and how she wasn't alone in her predicament.

"Thank you so much, you are a life saver, and I'm in desperate need of saving right now." She reached out her hand. "I'm Liv, by the way. Liv Paxton."

"Sloan, brewer turned innkeeper." I returned the handshake. "What brings you to our village?"

Her face blanched. She looked at a loss for words. "Uh, business."

"Oh." Leavenworth wasn't exactly a mecca for big business. I thought about asking what line of work she was in but didn't want to pry. "You're here at a beautiful time of the year. Be sure to check out the lights tonight."

"Okay, yeah." She didn't sound overly enthused. "I saw a flyer about that. This is my first time in Leavenworth."

"I'm sure you'll love it. There's so much to do. Do you ski?"

She frowned. "No. I hate the snow."

"Well, in that case, enjoy the shopping. There's a great spa just outside of town." I pointed to her empty glass. "Can I get you another?"

"Yes. Please."

I refilled her glass and came back to find Kevin and his pals gathered at the bar for another round. He smelled like strawberries and chemicals. I guessed it was from the vaping. "Hey, bartender, get this pretty little lady a beer as ice-cold as her ex-boyfriend's heart." Kevin winked at Liv.

Liv rolled her eyes and placed a perfectly manicured hand over her beer glass. "I'm fine."

Kevin was invading Liv's personal space with his thick arm propped on the bar. "Check out the watch. Have you ever seen anything like this baby? Solid gold Gucci band meets state-of-the art tech. This watch can do it all, order Chinese food and take photos under water when I'm diving. It can even start my Tesla."

19

"Good for you." Liv was less than impressed. She didn't bother to look up from the beer I had handed her.

Kevin proceeded to take the massive gold watch off his wrist and hand it to her.

"I don't need to see your fake watch up close."

One of the women in Kevin's party gasped and threw her hand over her mouth.

"Fake?" Kevin's face burned with color. "This isn't fake. It retails for over a thousand dollars. I make more than that in a couple hours at my company. I'm a VP."

"Yeah, he's a VP," the young woman chimed in. She was dressed in head-to-toe pink. A pink ski suit, hat, and scarf. Even her eyelids were dusted in a glittery pink shadow.

"Shut it, Jenny, I've got this." Kevin kept his attention focused on Liv. Jenny recoiled at his dismissal.

Liv turned her body away from them, using her leather purse to block the empty stool next to her.

Kevin thrust the watch at her. "Take a good look. You've probably never had a chance to hold a real Gucci, have you?"

"I don't care if your watch is from Target. I'm doing my thing. You do you." Liv tried to shift in her chair to move away completely.

"No, you called this fake, and that's a bunch of crap. Take a good look at it. It's solid gold." He reached for her wrist and tried to force the watch into her hand.

She threw her hands in the air and the watch landed on the floor. "Don't touch me."

"Hey, you broke my watch!" Kevin screamed.

Jenny picked up the watch and cradled it like it was an infant.

"Everyone calm down," I said with authority.

"She broke my freaking watch." Kevin yanked the watch out of Jenny's hand and held it up for me to see.

"You tried to assault me," Liz retorted.

Jenny rushed to his defense. Her cheeks flushed with color as she shook her finger in Liv's face. "Assault you? You don't even know who he is. He's one of the most powerful men at one of the most powerful companies in Seattle, and you just threw his watch on the ground."

Liv rolled her eyes and looked to me for support.

"Listen, I want all of you to go back to your table." I motioned for Kevin and his group to step away from the bar. Kat and Garrett must have heard the commotion, as they both appeared on either side of me at the same time. At least we had safety in numbers. Nitro wasn't the kind of pub where bar fights took place. I wasn't about to let that change now.

"What's going on?" Garrett immediately clued in on my body posture and stood between the groups.

"That witch broke my watch." Kevin glared at Liv.

"No, you tried to assault me," Liv repeated. Her face was stoic.

Garrett ushered Kevin and his friends to their table. "Look, guys, we're going out of our way to accommodate you, but if you're going to make a scene, we're going to have to ask you to leave."

"It's cool, it's cool," Jenny chimed in, tugging Kevin by the arm. "We'll have some beers, and chill, right, guys?"

"What the hell was that?" Liv glanced over her shoulder and shook her head. "He's still living the frat guy dream."

"I know. We get a handful of his type every now and then. Sorry about that." I lowered my voice. "Here's the thing. Kevin and his friends are also staying the night. Is that going to be a problem?"

"No. Not unless I sneak into his room and kill him." She laughed.

"That's dark."

"I've been told I have a dark sense of humor. Maybe because I've seen plenty of darkness in my life." She removed a tube of lip gloss from her purse and expertly applied it. Then she looked up at me. "I'm kidding. Don't worry. I'll avoid that group of frat boys and sorority sisters like the plague."

This wasn't exactly how I had envisioned our bed-and-breakfast guests would interact. I had imagined guests happily chatting over breakfast, strangers meeting and becoming friends, gathering in the tasting room for late-night games and pints. Never had I pictured guests fighting or threatening one another.

If we couldn't figure out a way to keep Kevin and his crew under control, our venture might sink before it had even started.

CHAPTER

THREE

GARRETT, KAT, AND I TOOK turns keeping an eye on Kevin and his group. Around dinnertime Kevin made a point of announcing loudly that they were going to have to venture into the village in search of more substantial fare. We serve small plates, bar snacks, and a daily soup at Nitro, but if guests are looking for a heartier dinner, we send them to one of Leavenworth's plentiful restaurants. In a town with only two thousand permanent residents, the world-class dining scene in the village often surprises visitors. From authentic German Wiener schnitzel to traditional steakhouses, and European bistros featuring locally sourced meats and produce to Mediterranean, Indian, Mexican, and Italian, there were ample options for every palate and price point. Visitors could grab a brat and beer at the Brat Haus, with its outdoor grill, or experience fine dining at one of the village's five-star restaurants.

"Unless you girls want greasy bar snacks, we're going to

have to head out in the cold in search of something better," Kevin announced. He stood and grabbed two suitcases. "Swagger, grab a bag. We'll be back down for you ladies in a few. Bundle up."

Garrett and I prided ourselves on our artisanal approach to traditional pub fare. Nothing we served would be classified as greasy. As much as I wanted to respond with a snarky comment, if Kevin and his friends took off for the night, that was all the better for me and the rest of our customers.

After they were gone, I went to clean their table, where the two women were waiting for Kevin and his friend to return from putting their bags upstairs.

"Can you believe her?" Jenny said to her friend as she gave Liv serious side-eye.

"Jenny, let it go." Her friend tried to appease her. "Kev was being an ass."

"What? Mel, how can you say that?" She ran her fake hot pink nails through her dirty blond hair and stared at her friend in disbelief.

Mel rolled her eyes. "How long are you going to do this? You and Kevin have been textbook dysfunctional for three years. You always end up hurt. I told you it was a bad idea to come this weekend. He treats you like crap, Jenny."

"No he doesn't." Jenny's bottom lip quivered slightly. She clicked on her phone and scrolled until she found a photo. "Look at this. It's us in Napa for Thanksgiving. Why would he invite me on a wine country getaway if he wasn't into me?" Next she tapped her index finger that sported a giant fake cubic zirconia ring. "He gave me this as a token of his affection. If he wasn't into me, why would he do that?"

Mel sighed. "Because everyone else turned him down. Face it, the only time he texts is when he wants to hook up." She placed her hand on Jenny's arm in a show of support.

Jenny's jaw dropped open. "That's so rude. He invited me for this ski weekend. I'd say that's more than a booty call."

I could tell that Mel wanted to say more, but instead she nodded. "Maybe you're right. Just be careful. I don't want to see you hurt."

I wondered about their relationship. They appeared to be about the same age. Mel wore expensive ski gear as well, but hers was more sophisticated than Jenny's hot pink.

"Don't worry. I have a plan. I'm going to do something that will get Kevin to really notice me." She shot a glare at Liv that made me step back.

Kevin showed up before she said more. "Ladies, let's go get wined and dined. You ready, Swagger?"

His other friend's name was Swagger? How fitting. Swagger had to be a nickname, because who names their child Swagger without an expectation that they won't end up the villain in a bad sitcom?

Swagger wrapped his arm around Mel. "You bet, Kev."

Kevin looped his arm through Jenny's. She looked triumphant.

I tended to agree with Mel, but I was hardly qualified to share relationship advice. My marriage to Mac had been rife with problems from the start. Not that we hadn't enjoyed good times, too. We had had our fair share of happy memories, but I knew at my core that I had loved the idea of Mac more than I had loved Mac. One of the reasons I had fallen for him so fast was that he came as a package deal. Mac had given me an instant family, and for that I would be forever grateful.

I loaded a tray with empty pint glasses and took them to the kitchen. There was a lull in the taproom. That often happened this time of day when our happy hour crowds moved on and the post-work crowd hadn't snuck out of the office yet. I decided to use the brief reprieve to finalize the breakfast menu. Garrett and I had been intentional in our use of our line of beers in all of the food we served in the pub. From bright citrus cupcakes made with our Pucker Up IPA to individual shepherd's pies infused with our dark stout, I enjoyed creating food that was sourced with local produce and that showcased our craft. I intended to do the same with the breakfast menu. Since we were deep in the winter season, I wanted our breakfast to reflect the rich flavors of our signature stout and bright notes of our winter ale.

After perusing a number of cookbooks, I had finally landed on stout French toast stuffed with a blueberry compote and maple ale cream cheese frosting. I could serve it with thick slabs of crispy bacon and fresh fruit. I scoured the industrial kitchen with its stainless steel counters and multiple refrigerators. We had bacon, eggs, cream cheese, and frozen blueberries on hand. I just needed to pick up a couple loaves of brioche from the bakery and swing by the market to grab some fruit. The thought of Liv and Kevin sharing the same breakfast table gave me a moment of pause. I wondered if there was a way I could seat them as far away from each other as possible. We didn't have assigned seating for breakfast, but maybe I should rethink that.

Since we would be housing no more than twelve guests

at any time, we had decided to serve breakfast at nine every morning. That would allow our guests to have a leisurely cup of coffee, but also give them plenty of time to hit the slopes or venture out into one of the many nearby alpine lakes. I glanced at the clock above the eight-burner stove. It was only a few minutes after five. The bakery and market would be open for another hour, and Garrett and Kat had the bar under control. If I loaded up with the rest of the supplies I needed for breakfast now, I could save myself a trip in the morning.

I tugged on my black ski jacket, a pair of gloves, and a red and black striped wool hat that Ursula had knitted for me. "I'm going to run to the store. Need anything else for to-night?"

Garrett shook his head. "We're good."

"I'll be back shortly." I braced myself for the cold. Leavenworth winters are notoriously snowy, and today was no exception. A brisk cold hit me as I stepped outside. I sucked in the icy air and paused for a moment. In my humble opinion, there was no place more spectacular than our little slice of Bavaria. The village was nestled in the alp-like mountains of the Northern Cascades. There was something so comforting and peaceful about being surrounded by the gentle giants with their pristine peaks and dense evergreen forests. The mountains took my breath away in every season, but seeing them buried in fresh white snow always brought a smile to my face.

I was careful to watch my footing on the slick sidewalk. The city kept the roads plowed and the sidewalks cleared, but even so, it was always tricky to navigate the piles of snow and icy walkways. A cold wind brushed my cheeks as I turned onto Front Street. This was another view that I never got tired of.

Front Street was lined with three- and four-story buildings designed to resemble a German village. The baroque architecture and twinkling lights that were just beginning to turn on brought a smile to my face.

There was a festive vibe in the air. Skiers trudged on the sidewalks, carrying heavy ski boots, and shoppers stopped to admire window displays of nutcrackers and buy steaming pretzels from outdoor vendors.

Our town gazebo was illuminated with hundreds of golden lights and hanging paper lanterns. Kids sledded down the small hill in Front Street Park while parents watched them, sipping warm cups of cocoa and hot cider.

"Sloan! Oh, Sloan, over here!" I heard April Ablin's familiar nasal voice calling me.

Great.

"Wait up, Sloan."

I thought about breaking into a sprint but knew that April would track me down anyway. That's one of the major cons of living in a small town.

April was breathless when she reached me. Her red hair was drawn into two braids that peeked out from under a knit hat. She wore a traditional red-and-white-checkered barmaid dress with a gray wool shawl around her shoulders.

"Aren't you freezing, April?"

"No, I'm wearing tights." She twirled. "Obviously you don't understand the depth of my responsibilities. People expect to see us dressed like this. It's all part of the mystique of visiting the village. The vast majority of business owners know this, but for some reason, you and Garrett want to be different." She sounded exasperated.

April and I had had this same discussion at least a dozen times. I wasn't about to stand out in the cold and debate the merits of decorating Nitro with German kitsch. "Did you need something?"

"Ja. Ja." April laid on a thick fake accent. Of course she pronounced *ja* with a *j* sound rather than the German *y*. "I need to talk to you about IceFest. You haven't responded to any of my emails. Can I count on Nitro to sponsor ice fishing? The maps are being printed tomorrow, and I need confirmation." She tapped on a nonexistent watch on her wrist.

"April, you've been by the pub five times this week. Garrett and I have said yes every time."

"I know, but I need your official confirmation. Everything must be in writing this year."

"Why?" Leavenworth's resident population had stayed steady at about two thousand people for as long as I could remember. April knew everyone's name, birthday, and most likely our bank account balances. Having us email her our "confirmation" was simply a way to bolster her importance.

"There was a major issue last year with the sled pull and the mug relay. My assistant was supposed to invite Valley Bank to sponsor the mug relay and Der Keller to sponsor the sled pull, but she got them mixed up and Der Keller ended up sponsoring the mug relay while the bank sponsored the sled pull. Total disaster." She threw her fake nails that were painted like icicles to her forehead. "It's all I've heard from both of them for the entire year. We are not making such a disastrous mistake again. I have made it crystal clear to my assistant that if she botches it again, she's going to be out of a job."

I pitied April's assistant. And I had never heard a word from Mac, Otto, Ursula, Hans, or any of the staff at Der Keller about being upset over the blunder. I was sure it was all in April's head.

"Fine. I'll email you when I get back to the pub." I started to move away from her.

She grabbed my arm. "Not so fast, young lady. You haven't responded to my messages about the new house either. If you don't make a decision soon, someone is going to swoop in and buy it out from under your feet."

Another classic April tactic. Leavenworth, as Kevin and his friends had made clear, wasn't exactly Wall Street. Most residents owned and operated small businesses centered on the tourist trade, and the real estate market reflected that.

"If you don't make an offer soon, you're going to miss out on a golden opportunity." April waved to a group of kids lugging bright red sleds toward the sledding hill. Then she stared at me for a minute. "My goodness, Sloan, is that an authentic German hat? Are you feeling all right?"

She leaned in to try and feel my forehead. "I never thought I would see the day when our very own Sloan Krause would wear something authentically German. Be still, my beating heart."

"It was a gift from Ursula." I glanced across the street at Der Keller. Its majestic entrance reminded me of a ski chalet. Flags with the Krause family crest, along with a red, yellow, and black German flag, waved in the wind. Giant bundles of white lights shaped into balls hung from the rafters. The outdoor patio was open year-round. Tonight each table was packed with happy beer lovers, staying toasty warm in front of Der Keller's gas fireplaces. A waiter wearing the traditional uniform of a red-checkered *Trachten* shirt and black suspenders passed around giant overflowing steins to the revelers.

I had spent most of my adult life at the brewery. It was still strange not to be involved in day-to-day operations. A familiar feeling of unease washed over me.

"But of course! The mother-in-law knitted a true German *Hut* for you."

I'd had my fill of April for the day. "You mean hat, right?" I started to move on. I'd been successfully avoiding the Krause family for a while now. I wasn't about to let April ruin that for me.

"Sloan, wait. Call me! Let's get this deal going, okay? *Kuss, kuss, kuss!*" She blew me three kisses and pranced off toward a group of unsuspecting tourists.

"Velcome, velcome," I heard her call to a pack of skiers as I hurried away in the opposite direction.

It didn't take long to pick up a few shiny loaves of buttery brioche and apples, bananas, oranges, and melons for tomorrow's breakfast. I was back at Nitro in less than fifteen minutes. That was certainly one of the pros of living in a small village.

After I put away the breakfast supplies, I returned to the bar to find Liv still sitting in the same spot.

"How's it going?" I asked, taking note of the beer in front of her. How many had she had? I would have to check with

Garrett and Kat. At some point (potentially soon), we might have to cut her off.

Before she could answer, Taylor, a local mechanic, came up to the bar. He ordered a round of pints for his buddies. "Hey, Sloan, how's tricks? Can I get a round for my guys?"

"Sure. The usual?" I asked. Taylor was one of our regulars. He and his crew often stopped in for a pint at the end of the workday. His grease-stained coveralls made me think they had come straight from the auto shop.

"You know us too well." He handed me a twenty. "Best beer and best service in Leavenworth," he said to Liv.

She looked up from her drink.

Taylor stumbled backward. "Oh, hey."

"Hey." Liv's tone was cold. Did they know each other?

"Sorry, you look like someone I used to know." Taylor took another step backward. "Hey, Sloan, can you bring those drinks to the table when you have a sec?"

"No problem." I had already poured the first pint and was about to hand it to Taylor, but he was halfway back to his table.

"Do you ever feel like nothing in your life is going right?" Liz asked. Her words slurred together as she spoke.

Yep. My intuition was correct. It was time to encourage her to switch to coffee.

"I think everyone feels that way sometimes. It's the human condition." I poured two more pints.

"Human condition. Yeah. I wish." She ran her fingers through her bleached hair as if trying to force away a painful memory. "Can I confess something? I have to tell someone, and you seem trustworthy."

"Bartenders are known for our listening ears and our sealed lips." I pointed to my right ear and then my lips. "What you say at the bar stays at the bar."

Nitro was quiet for the night. Taylor and his fellow mechanics sat at one of the larger tables, but otherwise there were only a few couples in the tasting room. The soft glow of Edison bulbs above the bar and the flicker of votive candles placed on each tabletop gave the space a welcoming vibe. The front windows were frosted and dripped with sweat.

Her shoulders loosened. "It's bad. It's really bad. I mean, if I tell you this, you're probably not going to want me to stay here. You might ask me to leave, and I really need a place to crash tonight."

What could be so bad that I would ask her to leave? "No, of course not. The room is already reserved for you. I'm sure whatever you're struggling with seems worse in your head than it will to me."

She looked up from her drink. Her eyes were wide with fear and something else—regret? "No, it's bad. You see—"

Before she could continue, Brad and Ali came up to the bar. They wore matching black ski parkas and hats with the words *Mr.* and *Mrs.* outlined in yellow thread. Liv and Brad locked eyes with each other. Brad looked as if he might be sick. Liv buried her face in her hands.

Ali stepped up to the bar, then turned to her husband. "Should we get a tasting flight, hon?"

Brad met my eyes and shook his head. He tugged off his hat. "Is it just me, or is it warm in here?"

I stood there not knowing what to do.

33

Ali appeared to be oblivious. "I don't think it's warm."

"You know, on second thought, I'm really hungry. Let's do dinner first and then come back to taste some beers." Brad pulled the hat on his head again and put one hand on Ali's waist.

"I thought you wanted to do the tasting flight now." Ali sounded confused.

Brad laced his other hand through hers. "I do, but suddenly I'm starving. Let's go see the lights and get dinner." He pulled her away from the bar.

Liv kept her face buried in her hands. "Are they gone?"

I watched as the door shut behind them. "Yeah, they're gone."

She wrapped her hand over her mouth. I could barely hear her as she spoke. "I can't believe they're here. This can't be happening."

"You know Brad and Ali?"

"Huh?" She turned to the door. Then she reached into her purse, handed me two twenties. "Keep the change. I have to go."

I wanted to ask her more. Did her confession have something to do with Brad? How weird that she would know two people in town—Brad and Taylor. She squeezed past a couple of full tables and went straight for the door. Was she following them? I was already worried about breakfast with her and Kevin in the same room. Now I was going to have to worry about her with Brad and Ali. Tomorrow might prove to be a complete disaster.

CHAPTER

FOUR

THE NEXT MORNING I AWOKE to the sound of snowplows. Alex was still crashed in his bedroom when I tiptoed down the hallway. Lazy winter Saturday mornings were made for sleeping in, especially with a teenager in the house. I left him a note along with a box of his favorite cereal on the kitchen counter. Mac was due to pick him up at lunchtime. We had worked out a temporary kid swap. I hated having to share Alex and, more importantly, making him hop back and forth between our places. It triggered painful memories of my foster care years, but Alex appeared to be handling the change with ease. I worried that he was putting on a brave face for us. He had mastered the art of concealing his feelings. He came by it honestly. The only person I had to blame for his closed emotional vault was me.

I knew I couldn't force the issue, so instead I had been trying to make space for him to talk. Simple things like our drives to and from school every day and chatting while spending an afternoon cross-country skiing. My singular focus was to make sure that he didn't suffer.

I wasn't sure I was succeeding on that front, but I had to keep nudging my son to be honest about his struggles.

Snow blanketed the organic farmland and buried the mountains in a deep layer of powdery white as I drove into the village. A handful of early risers strolled along the sidewalk in search of morning coffee and pastries, but otherwise our little Beervaria sat in a restful slumber. I passed life-sized murals depicting bucolic German village scenes. Many of the white stucco buildings with their wooden roofs and balconies had paintings of overflowing keg barrels and dancers in lederhosen and *Trachten* shirts. Each mural told a story, and the tradition dated back to the 1960s, when the town transformed from a dying logging and mining community to a thriving tourist destination. A local artist had painted a mural on the town hall building, and it was so well received that murals spread throughout the village. They became legendary. I often saw tourists spending hours taking in all of the murals, snapping pictures, and posing for selfies. Since Leavenworth's public art displays were so popular, residents enacted a policy where everyone had to vote for a new mural to be approved.

In a few hours Front Street would be alive with activity—kids making snowmen and sledding in the park, shoppers perusing our boutiques, and the Saturday artist market, and outdoor adventurers fueling up for a day on the slopes.

I breathed in the pine-scented air, parked the car, and went to unlock Nitro. When Garrett had first moved to Leavenworth from Seattle, he had insisted on locking every room inside the brewery every night. Garrett was especially concerned with making sure our office was locked, even during the workday. He was paranoid about the possibility of having our recipes stolen. It had taken some getting used to. In Leavenworth, we tend to trust our neighbors.

The taproom was dark. I left it that way and continued on to the kitchen. Garrett and Kat were both late sleepers. It worked well for our routine. I liked to be home on school nights when I had Alex. He would be off to college in a few years, and I was acutely aware that I needed to savor our time together. We would usually make dinner and recap his day before he had to do homework. I loved curling up on the couch with him to watch his favorite shows. Alex liked to tease me about falling asleep halfway into any show. The sad truth was that his teasing was justified. Most nights I found myself drifting off before ten. On the flip side, Garrett claimed he brewed best after midnight. He typically took the late shift at the pub and stayed up after closing to experiment with small batches.

Once in the kitchen, I started on breakfast prep by brewing a strong pot of coffee and heating water for tea. Then I spread the thick-cut bacon onto baking sheets lined with parchment paper and set them in the oven to broil. Next I chopped fruit and arranged cups with vanilla yogurt and a drizzle of honey. I wanted to make the stout French toast last so that I could serve it hot once our guests were up and moving.

I filled carafes with coffee and hot water and took them along with a tray of the yogurt and fruit cups to the upstairs lounge. None of the guests were awake yet, so I took the opportunity to set seven place settings and arrange packets of assorted teas and sugar and cream on the table.

Then I returned to the kitchen to assemble the French toast. I started by whipping eggs, a dash of salt, vanilla, brown sugar, and a cup of our dark chocolate stout. I whisked them together until the mixture was light and frothy. Next I cut hearty slices of the brioche and dredged them in the egg and beer mixture. I layered the bread in a baking dish and set it aside. For the filling, I mixed cream cheese, butter, powdered sugar, and more stout. Once it was smooth, I spread it generously over the eggy bread, sprinkled on frozen blueberries, and then added another layer of dipped brioche. I finished the French toast with a dusting of cinnamon and more blueberries. Then I slid it into a hot oven to bake for thirty minutes. While it baked, I poured maple, blueberry, and raspberry syrups into ceramic dishes and took them upstairs.

Ali and Brad were seated at one end of the table drinking coffee, wearing matching plush robes and slippers.

"Morning. I hope I didn't wake you," I said, placing the syrups in the middle of the table.

"No, we were roused by the smell of this delicious coffee." Ali warmed her hands with the ceramic earthenware mug.

"Excellent. Breakfast should be ready in about twenty minutes." I left to finish prep. By the time I returned with the bubbling stout French toast and a platter of bacon, Kevin, Jenny, Mel, and Swagger had joined the table. The only person missing was Liv.

"How did everyone sleep?" I asked as I dished up servings of my beer-infused breakfast.

Jenny batted her fake eyelashes at Kevin. "I don't remember sleeping much."

He ignored the insinuation. "Do you have anything stronger? I thought since we were staying at a brewery, we'd get a real beer for breakfast." He looked like he'd had a rough night. His eyes were bloodshot and his cheeks puffy.

I pointed to the grandfather clock. "Unfortunately, we don't serve beer this early. The tasting room opens at eleven. You're welcome to come down for a pint then."

"I thought this was breakfast with beer." Kev looked to his friends for a reaction.

"Yes, all of our breakfasts are made with our signature beers." I went on to explain that I had made the French toast and creamy filling with our stout.

He wasn't impressed. "That's not going to get my morning buzz on."

"Probably not," I agreed.

I went downstairs to refill the coffee and tea carafes. On my way, I considered stopping to knock on Liv's door. I didn't want her to miss out on breakfast, but I figured she was likely trying to avoid the other breakfast guests. If she was hungry when she woke up, I could make a fruit and yogurt cup and some toast for her. I felt bad that she was skipping the morning meal, but I couldn't blame her for wanting to avoid any drama and I could save her a plate to warm up later.

Aside from Kevin, everyone else was complimentary

about breakfast. By the time I had finished cleaning up, Kat and Garrett had both made their way into the kitchen.

"Man, Sloan, I don't know about this whole breakfast thing," Garrett said, pouring himself a cup of coffee.

"Why?"

"I sat in my room smelling those delicious aromas. I kept wondering how bad it would be if I went and swiped one of the guests' plates."

"Me too," Kat agreed. She opted for a cup of hot chocolate. I appreciated that she wore a pair of flannel pajama pants, UGGs, and a Nitro hoodie. No one could claim that our style at the brewery was anything other than laid-back.

"Don't worry. I saved us some." I pulled out a second small dish of French toast and bacon.

"I'm giving you a raise." Garrett pressed his hands together in thanks. He wore yet another beer T-shirt. This one read BEER MAKES ME HOPPY.

I would have loved to steal a glance at Garrett's closet, as his collection of terrible T-shirts with beer puns appeared to be limitless.

"You don't have any money to give me a raise. I do your finances," I bantered back.

"Fine, but when the money starts pouring in, you get a raise." He helped himself to a plate of the gooey French toast.

We went over the schedule for the day while polishing off breakfast. Kat would be responsible for touching up the guest rooms. Simple tasks like making the beds and restocking towels. I needed to make our daily soup and assemble snack trays for the pub. Garrett would open the bar and check on the kegs.

With a clear plan for the beginning of the day, we parted ways. Knowing that we would likely have a large skiing crowd in later, I decided on a beef stew with carrots, potatoes, onions, garlic, and a secret ingredient—stout. The stew should satisfy even the hungriest of appetites. Then I would assemble meat, veggie, and cheese trays, load up the pub with pretzels and chips, and make a batch of my famous beer brownies for dessert.

The morning passed quickly. Shortly before noon, Kat came into the kitchen with a worried look on her face. She had showered and changed into a pair of skinny jeans and a T-shirt. "The guest rooms are all cleaned, but I think we have a problem."

My heart rate spiked. "What kind of a problem?"

"Who was the woman who was staying alone? Liv or Liz?"

"Liv."

"Right, Liv. Her room is a mess. Like, total disaster. It looks like someone had a party up there. Her clothes and toiletries are all over the floor. I don't know, maybe she's super messy, but I've never seen anything like it. And the really strange thing is that the bed is made. It doesn't look like it was even slept in."

"What?" I placed the lid on top of my stew. "Did you see her after I left last night?"

"No, but it slowed way down after about nine, so Garrett told me I could go out. I went and met some friends for a movie."

"Okay. You sit tight. I'll go check with Garrett and then head upstairs." I hurried to the bar to find a small lunch crowd already gathered in the tasting room.

"Sloan, good timing. We have two orders for meat and cheese trays." Garrett expertly topped off the head of a foamy pint.

"No problem. I'll grab them in a sec, but first, you haven't seen Liv by chance?"

He shook his head. "No, not since last night. Why?"

"She didn't come to breakfast, and Kat said that her room is a mess but that her bed wasn't slept in."

"Weird."

"Did you see her last night?"

He thought about it for a minute. "I thought I saw her go upstairs, but I think you were still here. Wasn't that when Brad and Ali came down? I never saw her after that."

"That's when I remember seeing her too. She left without her coat, which I assumed meant she wasn't going far, but I never saw her return."

"Are you worried?" Garrett frowned. He glanced around the tasting room, as if hopeful she might be at one of the tables.

"I don't know. She might have gone out for a morning walk. I'll grab those trays for you and then go take a closer look at her room."

I did just that.

A cold chill ran up my arms as I stepped into the room. It felt weird to invade someone's personal space, but if Kat was right and Liv hadn't come back last night, we would probably need to let Chief Meyers know. One glance around the room confirmed Kat's suspicion. Something weird had gone on here. As Kat had mentioned, Liv's bed was made, but everything else had been strewn about the room. Her suitcase was open, and her clothes were scattered throughout the room. Her purse hung on a hook by the door, but its contents had been dumped on the floor—the tube of lip gloss I had seen her applying last night had been smashed. A wave of fear washed over me. Something wasn't right. Either Liv had freaked out and dumped out all of her things, or someone else had been in her room.

CHAPTER
FIVE

I RACED DOWNSTAIRS. KAT WAS pulling pints at the bar. Garrett stood at the far end of the long wood counter, filling bowls with chips and peanuts. "Kat, can you hold down the fort for a couple minutes? I want to talk to Garrett. You were right about Liv's room. I'm going to call Chief Meyers. Something about it feels really wrong."

Her eyes widened. "Yeah, of course. Do you think she's okay?"

I could hear the breathless quality of my voice. "Honestly, I don't know, but it's definitely time to involve the police."

Garrett caught my eye. I motioned for him to follow me into the brewery. "What's the word?"

"She didn't sleep here for sure. Her purse and jacket are up there, but everything's been dumped on the floor, like someone was going through her stuff. I have a bad feeling about this. I think I should call Chief Meyers. If she had gone for a walk, wouldn't she have taken her coat and even her purse? And given her demeanor last night, I can't imagine that she would have tossed everything around the room. I think someone's been in there. She could be in danger. What do you think?"

"Absolutely. We should call the chief." He ran his fingers through his hair. "I hope she's okay."

"Me too." I thought to last night and Liv's strange reaction to seeing Brad and Ali, and her argument with Kevin. Maybe there was a simple explanation, like she found somewhere else to stay in an attempt to avoid a breakfast confrontation. But if that were the case, why wouldn't she have come back for her things?

I put in a call to the police station. Chief Meyers wasn't in, but the officer I spoke with took extensive notes and promised he would have her come to the pub as soon as she returned. There was nothing to do but wait, so I went to the bar.

Ali and Brad had pushed their stools so close together they were practically sitting on each other's laps. Yet again, they were dressed in matching outfits. This time in jeans and hoodies that read HIS and HERS, with arrows pointing toward each other.

I motioned to the nearly empty tasting tray in front of them. "Did you have a favorite? Can I pour you a pint of something?"

Brad held up a taster of our winter ale, aptly named the Winter Warmer. "This is my top choice. I'll take a pint. How about you, hon?" He massaged Ali's shoulder. I thought I noticed a flash of irritation on her face, but she smiled broadly. "I liked that one best, too."

"Excellent, two pints of our Winter Warmer, coming up."

I brought them their full-bodied copper ales. This beer was one of the best we had brewed, with a malty sweetness, smooth bitterness, and a hit of bright hops on the finish. "You're not skiing today?" I asked.

Ali gave Brad a strange look. He jumped in. "We were going to, but it ended up being a later night than we expected. Your beers are too good—we had one pint too many, as they say, so decided to do lunch and have a couple pints now and maybe get in a few late-afternoon runs. The lifts stay open late, right?"

In my experience most skiers saved lunch and pints for *after* a day on the slopes.

"Did you help close the pub down last night?" I asked, placing a bowl of Doritos in front of them.

Again, Ali's face tensed.

Brad responded for her. "It was pretty fun last night. We got to talking to another couple in town from Seattle. Ended up staying until Garrett kicked us all out, right, honey?"

"Right." Ali's teeth clenched.

"You didn't happen to see the woman who was sitting over there yesterday evening, did you?" I pointed to a barstool two chairs down. "Her name is Liv. She's staying here too."

"Nope. Didn't see her." Brad responded so quickly he didn't even have a chance to look in the direction I had pointed.

Ali simply didn't respond.

I dropped it and went to check on the other guests in the tasting room. Chief Meyers ambled in not long after. She wore her standard khaki police uniform along with a wool scarf and a cable-knit hat.

"Afternoon, Sloan. I hear there's trouble?" She had a notepad at the ready. I had known Chief Meyers for almost twenty years and appreciated her direct approach and the fact that she didn't rattle easily.

"To be honest, I'm not sure." I proceeded to tell her about Liv.

She scratched a few notes and listened intently. When I finished, she flipped the notebook shut. "Let's take a look upstairs."

I took her to Liv's room.

Chief Meyers tugged a pair of blue latex gloves on before examining the contents of Liv's purse.

"I already looked through that," I said pointing to my bare hands. "I never thought of fingerprints."

"It's fine. Call it a precaution. If this turns into a missing persons case, we'll sweep the room. I'll anticipate finding prints from you and anyone on staff."

"Right." I watched as Meyers sorted through Liv's things. Next she checked the bathroom cabinet and bed-side tables.

"Do you have a photo of the missing guest?" she asked after making a few notes.

"No." I shook my head.

"Any other information? Can you give me a description? Her credit card info? Residence? How did she book the room?"

"She did pay with a credit card." I tried to recall what Liv had been wearing last night. "She's about five six, with honey-blond shoulder-length hair and dark eyes. Her hair is definitely dyed. It doesn't match her skin tone."

47

Chief Meyers noted my description. "Is there anything else? How'd she get to Leavenworth? Did she drive?"

"Yes." I felt relieved to be able to at least provide the chief with some tangible information. "I know she drove because she didn't want to have to drive back to Spokane last night. I have her license plate on file downstairs. We keep plate numbers so that we can track parking in the back lot. Otherwise, you know how insane parking gets in the village. I can grab it for you."

"Good." The chief made another note. "Did she seem distressed? Had too much to drink?"

"Well, there were a couple strange things." I told her about Liv's reaction to Brad and Ali and her argument with Kevin. "I sort of wondered if she decided to stay at another hotel in town because she didn't want to face any of them at breakfast."

"Typically you'd take your bags and credit cards with you to a new hotel." Meyers's tone indicated that she thought the circumstances were suspicious, too. "Not to mention, why are her things scattered around the room? I don't know many people who unpack like this." To prove her point, she lifted a pair of Liv's tights with her pen. "Nope. I don't like the looks of this at all. Did you see anyone else come in or out of this room?"

I thought for a moment. "No. But, I'm not upstairs much. I set up breakfast this morning and noticed that Liv didn't join the others. Her door was shut, and I never bothered to knock. I thought she was sleeping in and avoiding Kevin."

Chief Meyers removed her gloves and tossed them in the garbage can.

"What do you do now?" We left the room and returned downstairs. I found the registration form Liv had filled out last night and gave the chief her license plate number, credit card, and address.

"I'll have my team canvass the village. We'll check the hospital, hotels, train station. We'll look for her car. I'll be in touch. If you think of anything else, or if Liv returns, call me ASAP."

"Thanks, Chief." I walked her to the door. Tiny flakes fell from the sky, dusting the sidewalk. I hoped that the police would find Liv soon. It was a cold day to be outside without a coat or gloves.

"What's the word?" Garrett asked when I scooted around to the back of the bar.

"Chief Meyers is going to look for her. She said she'll check the hospital and ask around the village."

"I didn't even think about the hospital." Garrett wiped a tap handle with a cotton dish towel.

"Neither did I. I guess we could have started there."

"It's probably better to leave it to the police." He cleaned the next handle. Brewing is as much about cleanliness as anything else. Not only did we keep the fermenting tanks in the brewery spotless, but the bar was always wiped down and glistening.

I was relieved that Kevin, Jenny, and their friends weren't anywhere around. They must have ventured out to ski or explore the village. Brad and Ali lingered over a tasting tray. I circulated the room, picking up empty pint glasses and taking lunch orders.

"Hi, Sloan." Taylor, the local mechanic, greeted me with

a grin. His denim coveralls were splatted with grease. I appreciated the fact that Nitro was the kind of space where people from all walks of life gathered. From working locals to tourists, we were a spot where you could relax over an afternoon pint and a hot-from-the-oven pretzel with gooey cheese.

"Are you working on a Saturday?"

"Ski bus broke down again." He sneezed into his arm, leaving a grease stain on his nose. "I keep telling the guys it's time to upgrade. The thing is a piece of junk, but hey, it keeps me in the black, so I won't complain."

"Fair enough." I smiled and handed him a coaster. "Can I get you a beer? Lunch?"

"I'll take a pint of your stout and whatever your soup is today."

"Do you want to hear about the soup?"

"No, Nitro makes the best soups in the village, everyone knows that."

"Thanks." His compliment made me smile wider.

"Was that Chief Meyers I saw leaving?" Taylor tapped the coaster on the tabletop.

"Yeah. She was just here." I glanced toward the front window, which was thick with steam.

"Having a beer?"

"No. We have a guest who we're worried about, so she came by to help."

He puffed up his chest. "Is a guest giving you trouble? I'll defend you, Sloan."

"It's nothing like that. Thank you, but a guest has gone missing." I tried to smile, but I was distracted by the thought of Liv.

50

Taylor flipped the coaster over. "Missing?"

"We're not entirely sure. She was here last night. You saw her. She was sitting at the bar alone when you ordered drinks. She didn't show up for breakfast, and it didn't look like her bed had been slept in. We're probably being overly cautious, but you never know."

"Where would she go?"

"I don't know. That's why I called Chief Meyers."

"Oh, *you* called the chief."

Taylor seemed oddly intrigued with Chief Meyers's presence at the pub.

"You're talking about that bottle blonde who was here drinking late last night, yeah?"

"That's right. Did you see her after I left?" I leaned closer.

"I saw her here at the pub last night. She was pretty sauced. Stumbling all over the place. Knocked over someone's drink."

"When was this?" Liv had been slurring her words, but she hadn't seemed out of control. Garrett would have said something if he had cut her off.

Taylor tried to wipe the grease spot on his nose but only managed to smear it onto his cheek. "Late. I don't know. Closing time. She got into it with some guy and his wife. Then she knocked over the drink and stumbled outside."

"You're sure?"

"Pretty sure. She was hard to miss. Stumbling, slurring insults on her way outside. I didn't know she was staying here."

"But, do you know a specific time?" Now I was intrigued. Taylor may have been the last person to see Liv.

"Late. Maybe close to midnight. I came to get a pint after my

51

shift and ended up running into some buddies. We stayed for a while. She made the rounds. She was tipsy from the start, but at closing she looked wasted."

I couldn't believe Garrett hadn't noticed Liv. And I found it hard to believe he would have continued to serve her past her limit.

"I think I saw her walking toward Blackbird Island when I left. I saw somebody down that way. It could have been someone else, I guess. It was dark."

"Thanks for the info. I'll go get your beer and soup." I stopped in midstride. "You don't know her, by chance, do you?"

Taylor coughed twice and thumped his chest. "Sorry. Swallowed wrong. No. Don't know her. Never seen her. Why do you ask?"

"I thought you said something about her looking familiar."

He cleared his throat. "Oh yeah, true. She did kind of look familiar, but I don't know her."

I went to put in a call to Chief Meyers before getting Taylor's lunch. She answered right away. "Any news, Sloan?"

"Maybe a lead." I told her what Taylor had just reported.

"I'm on it. We'll add Blackbird Island to our search perimeter. No one named Liv was admitted to the hospital, and no Jane Does either."

"I guess that's good news."

Chief Meyers was silent. "My team has asked every hotel in town, and no one had availability last night. If Liv did end up at another hotel, she slept in a broom closet."

I glanced at the clock. It was almost two. Liv had been missing for over twelve hours now.

"There's more," she continued. "We found the car. It's been vandalized. It's splattered with paint. Some choice words written on it."

"What?"

"Yep. It looks like someone dumped a bucket of paint on it. We're heading to Blackbird now. I'll be in touch." Chief Meyers hung up.

Who would have vandalized Liv's car? Did that mean it was more likely that she was in trouble? I wasn't sure what to think. Was it a good sign that Liv hadn't been found yet, or as time churned on, were the odds of finding her getting worse?

By the time Taylor had finished his soup and a pint of our thick, decadent stout, the sound of sirens erupted outside. I cleaned up his dishes and went to the front windows for a better look. A police car with its lights flashing zoomed past Nitro and headed for Blackbird Island. Had they found Liv? And was she okay?

MY ANSWER CAME WHEN CHIEF Meyers entered the bar thirty minutes later. Her face was long, and the slight shake of her head told me the news wasn't going to be good. I braced myself on the counter.

"Sloan, Garrett, a word—in private." She nodded toward the shiny, stainless steel fermenting tanks behind us.

Garrett placed his hand on my arm. "This doesn't sound good."

"I know," I whispered, following him and the police chief to the brewery.

Once we were out of earshot of anyone in the tasting room, she frowned. "We found a body in the river."

"What?" I felt sick. Garrett steadied me with a firm grip on my waist.

"Liv?" he asked.

Chief Meyers nodded. "We think so. We're going to need

54

to identify the body. Do you feel comfortable taking a look at a couple of pictures?"

Garrett released his grasp on me and stepped forward. I appreciated the gesture. Meyers showed him a few pictures on her phone. "That's her," he said, looking away.

"Can one of you come down and officially make an ID?" She put her phone back in her pocket and turned down the volume on the walkie-talkie clipped to her belt.

"I'll do it," Garrett volunteered.

The room felt as if it had shifted. Liv was dead. I had just seen her last night, and now her body had been found in the river?

"How?" I managed to ask.

"We're not at liberty to divulge details at this point, but I will tell you it wasn't an accident."

Not an accident? The gray cement floors of the brewery suddenly looked wavy.

"We're going to need access to her room and to shut it off from the public. We'll be notifying next of kin." Chief Meyers continued to speak, but her words were a blur. "I'll be taking statements from anyone who interacted with her or saw her yesterday."

"Of course." Garrett reached for his keys. "I can go unlock the room for you right now."

"It wasn't locked." My voice sounded off.

Chief Meyers surveyed me. "You good, Sloan?"

"Yeah, yeah. I'll be fine." I tried to keep my emotions in check. "The room wasn't locked when I went up there."

"You're sure?" The chief asked.

"Positive. You can check with Kat. Maybe she left it unlocked, but it wasn't locked when I went up there."

"So the victim had her key. Yet we didn't find a key on her person. Interesting." She tapped her index finger to her chin. "We'll add a room key to the search list."

I swallowed a lump forming in my throat. "Why would someone have wanted to hurt her?"

"That's my job to figure out." She tipped her head to me and went upstairs.

I took a moment to compose myself. If Chief Meyers believed that Liv's death was no accident, what did that mean for us? Last night's odd interactions and blowups took on a different meaning in light of this news. Could one of our guests have killed Liv, or was it a random act of violence?

Leavenworth was known for our alpenglow and safe streets. Kids biked and walked to school. Neighbors left pies for one another on their front porches. The only "thefts" we worried about were black bears lumbering down from the mountainside to swipe a pawful of boysenberry pie. I couldn't fathom the idea that someone in the village could have killed Liv. But if it wasn't one of us, who could have killed her?

There was one person who immediately came to mind—Kevin. She had insulted him in front of his friends. He wasn't the kind of guy to take that lightly. He was the kind of guy who was used to bullying people around. Could he have followed Liv last night? What if he went after her to confront her—or put her in her place—for shooting him down? Maybe things got heated. Could it have been a crime of passion? In the moment, he snapped, killed her, and tossed her body in the river?

A chill ran up my spine at the thought.

What about Jenny? I had overheard her threatening to do something drastic. Murder was certainly drastic. Still, I couldn't imagine her having the strength to kill Liv. However, she could have vandalized Liv's car. Maybe they were in on it together. Jenny trashed the car, while Kevin killed her.

I also couldn't rule out Brad. I was sure that he and Liv had recognized each other. They had pretended not to—why? For Ali's sake? Were they former lovers?

What had brought Liv to town? Who was she? If I could figure that out, there was a chance that might lead to whoever had killed her. She had certainly seemed distraught last night. If only I'd had an opportunity to speak with her longer. She had been on the verge of opening up. What was she going to tell me? She had said that whatever she wanted to get off her chest might make me think less of her. Could she have been involved in something dangerous? But what? Leavenworth was hardly known as a hub for big crime.

Most visitors traveled to Leavenworth for recreation and adventure—the holiday lights, Oktoberfest, a ski weekend getaway—Liv hadn't come for any of those things. I had a sinking feeling that her reason for coming to the village was connected to her death.

I inhaled slowly through my nose, allowing the calming effect of a deep breath to help center me. "You have work to do, Sloan." I tugged on the strings of my gray hoodie sweatshirt with our Nitro logo—a hop in the shape of an atom and the slogan DRINK BEER FROM HERE. It was a new marketing message we had been testing out. There had been a national trend of smaller breweries getting bought out by big corporate chains. We wanted our customers to know that when they bought a pint at Nitro, they were supporting locally brewed beers, sourced with ingredients from the region. Everything we used in each batch of our signature beers was grown in Leavenworth or the nearby Yakima Valley.

The tasting room was packed with the Saturday lunch and après ski crowd. The size of the line at the bar could also be due to the fact that news flowed faster than any keg in our tiny village. I spotted April Ablin pushing her way through to the front of the line.

Great. Just what I needed.

In an attempt to avoid April, I darted behind the bar and began taking orders. "Sorry, Kat, I didn't realize you were slammed."

Kat's round face was flushed with color from running back and forth from the bar. She flexed her toned arms as she lifted a tray of full pint glasses. "We weren't, and then I looked up and suddenly—boom."

"You take those out, I'll start working the line." I jumped in to relieve Kat, ignoring April, who waved both hands in the air trying to get my attention. She could wait in line like everyone else. By the time she inched her way to the front of the bar, I had poured at least a dozen pints. "Hey, April, what's your poison?"

"Sloan, please." She smoothed the ruffles on her green-and-white-checkered skirt. "Beer is loaded with carbs. One moment on these lips, and it would be straight to my hips. I have to keep my girlish figure intact."

I rolled my eyes.

She elbowed a guy trying to put in an order. "I'm not here for your beer. I'm here to talk about the . . ." She paused and looked around her. Then she mouthed the word "murder."

How had she already heard?

"April, I can't talk right now. If you want to order something, go for it. Otherwise, step aside."

Her face scrunched into a scowl. "Sloan Krause, you're not getting rid of me that fast. I have it on good authority that the woman they found in the river was staying here, and I want details. I need details. It is my responsibility to keep the village informed. I saw the police towing away a car that looked like a preschool art class had used it as a canvas. There's something big going down in the village, and it is absolutely imperative that I have all of the details to keep everyone calm and reassured."

More like to spread the gossip.

I motioned for the guy behind her to step forward. "What can I get you?"

"A pint of the stout."

April waited for me to pour his drink. She folded her arms across her chest. "Look, Sloan, I'm not budging. You owe me. I thought we were supposed to be friends, and here you are withholding important information from me."

If anyone was owed, it was me. I had recently helped April out of a tight spot. I didn't owe her anything, but I also knew that if I didn't give her something, she would never leave. I tucked the tip that the guy had given me into a stein on the counter and leaned closer to April.

"Chief Meyers is upstairs right now going through her things. That's as much as we know. She was here last night and had intended to stay, but never showed up for breakfast. That's when we called the chief."

"What's her name? Where was she from? Why was she in town?" April's makeup made me wonder if she'd applied it in the dark. Her maroon lipstick clashed with her red hair. Her blush had been swept in round circles on both cheeks, and her bright green eyeliner squiggled in uneven lines beneath her eyes.

"Her name was Liv, and I don't know the rest of your questions. She mentioned driving from Spokane, but Chief Meyers is looking into all of that."

April clapped twice. "Excellent. I'll head upstairs and have a one-on-one with her right now. She likes to keep me in the loop. She knows that I'm the village source. It would be a travesty if people came to their most trusted source only to discover that I wasn't in the know."

"Go for it." I motioned to the back, knowing that there was no way that Chief Meyers would let April anywhere near Liv's room.

April curtseyed and hurried off.

Good luck with that, I thought as I opened the tap handle to pour another pint. Garrett's deep voice made me spill the foamy head of the beer.

"All set upstairs. Meyers said to tell you she's going to

want your official statement next." He mopped the beer. "I told her everything I could remember."

"Yeah, about that." I asked him about what Taylor had said earlier. "Was Liv stumbling drunk last night?"

Garrett expertly filled tasting flights with samples of our entire line. "No. What?"

"He said that she was slurring her words and then stumbled out of here, making a big scene."

"Not on my watch." He labeled each beer on a small slip of paper and tucked it behind each of the tasting glasses. "She went upstairs when you left. I never saw her again. Ask Kat, maybe I missed something. I started brewing and when Kat came back she helped clean and close, but I came up a couple times to check on things, and I never saw Liv."

"Weird."

Jenny and Mel appeared at the bar. "What's with the police cars outside?" They both had windburned cheeks and lift tags attached to their parkas.

"There's been an accident at the river." I didn't elaborate, nor did I mention anything about a murder. I wanted to gauge their reactions. "Looks like you got up to the ski hill."

"Yeah. We're thinking of going back for night skiing later. The powder was amazing. So fresh." Jenny adjusted her ski cap. "What's the accident?"

"The police found a body in the river."

Mel threw her hand over her mouth. "A body?"

"Unfortunately, yes. A woman's body was recovered from the river earlier. The police have Blackbird Island closed at the moment and are here investigating as we speak."

Jenny tugged on her lift ticket. "Here? Why are they here?"

"The woman was a guest. She was staying here. I think you met her last night. Liv."

Her response was immediate. She yanked the lift ticket and ripped it from her zipper. "Oh my God. Oh my God. Liv, that witch who dissed Kev last night?"

I nodded.

Jenny's eyes darted from me to her friend, then back again. "She's dead. Oh my God, I gotta go." With that, she turned and ran upstairs.

I looked to Mel. "I'm not sure we've officially met. I'm Sloan."

"Mel." She appeared distraught as she watched Jenny flee.

"Is everything okay?"

Mel removed the red fluffy ski hat. Her hair was flat on the top from being smashed under the knit hat. "Can I talk to you?"

"Absolutely." I checked around us. The line had died down. "Do you want to talk here, or we can go to my office?"

"Your office would be great."

I showed her into the brewery and unlocked the office door.

I moved a stack of brewing magazines and supply catalogues to make room for her to sit.

"What's going on?"

Mel twisted uncomfortably in her chair. "I don't want to betray my friendship with Jenny or anything, but I'm super worried that she did something drastic."

"How so?"

62

"She was really upset last night. I think you were there when that woman—Liv?"

I nodded.

"Yeah, when Liv shot Kevin down. I was laughing internally about it. Kevin can be such an ass. I don't know what Jenny sees in him. He treats her like dirt, but she keeps coming back for more. I've tried to talk to her about it, but she has total blinders when it comes to Kevin."

I wasn't sure why Mel was telling me this, but I stayed quiet and let her speak.

"Jenny was upset. I think she thought that if she defended Kevin, he would somehow see that as a sign of her loyalty and start paying more attention to her." She gave a half laugh. "Right. Like that was going to happen. Kevin knows exactly what he's doing with Jenny. He toys with her emotions to keep her on a short leash. It's hard to watch."

"I understand."

"I've tried to be a good friend and support her while still encouraging her to move on, but I think she may have taken things too far. You're saying that woman—Liv—is dead?"

"Yeah."

"Jenny went after her last night. She said she was going to teach her a lesson and prove to Kevin that she would do anything for him. I thought she was tipsy and just spouting off, but now I'm not so sure."

"What do you mean, she went after Liv?"

"Liv left the bar. It was late. I don't remember how late, but Jenny took off after her. She was gone for a few hours. I saw her sneaking back to her room late last night. I couldn't sleep and went to the little library alcove to borrow a book."

"What do you think Jenny might have done?"

Mel held her head in her hands. "I don't know." Her voice was thick with emotion. I thought she might cry. "I don't want to believe that she would hurt someone, but she was pretty buzzed, and she's obsessed with Kevin. Swagger, my boyfriend, and I have been trying to intervene. He knows even more than I do that Kevin is not into her. It's a one-way relationship. Kevin only asks her out when everyone else turns him down. Jenny's a smart girl, but she's oblivious when it comes to Kevin. What if Jenny accidentally hurt Liv? I know she wouldn't do anything on purpose, but she might have . . ." Mel trailed off. I assumed she didn't want to say out loud what she was thinking internally—that Jenny might have killed Liv.

The same thought had crossed my mind.

"I don't know what to do. Should I talk to the police? I don't want to get Jenny in trouble, but if she had anything to do with this, I can't stay silent."

I reached out to pat her knee. "You're doing the right thing, and yes, you should tell the police what you know. It is probably nothing, but a woman is dead, so any information that you have to share is critical to their case."

She started to sniffle. "I never should have come this weekend. You know when you have a bad gut feeling about something?"

I smiled. "Yes, I do."

"I had that about this weekend. Kevin is such a jerk, but Jenny wanted moral support, and I thought I could go do my own thing and ski. Now I feel like I'm in some kind of nightmare."

"If it would make you feel any better, I'm happy to introduce you to our police chief. She is professional and extremely reasonable."

Mel rubbed her eyes. "Okay."

I took her upstairs to meet Chief Meyers. Was Mel right? Could her friend have killed Liv in a fit of rage?

CHAPTER

SEVEN

CHIEF MEYERS LISTENED TO MEL'S story with her usual stoicism. She took a few notes and offered a curt nod every now and then, but otherwise her face was devoid of emotion. "Where is Ms. Jenny Ankeny now? I presume still upstairs?"

"Uh, she was in the taproom a while ago." Mel gnawed on a hangnail. "I don't know where she is now."

"Thank you for your statement. It goes without saying that none of you are free to leave Leavenworth without checking with me. Understood?" Chief Meyers's tone conveyed the seriousness of the situation.

"I get it." Mel winced in pain as she chewed the edge of her nail. "Can we go night skiing, or do we need to literally stay here in the pub?"

"Skiing is fine as long as you return here for the evening. You're not cleared to leave the village permanently until I tell you otherwise."

"Okay. Okay. I won't leave, and I'll do my best to make sure everyone else stays." She didn't sound convinced.

Meyers gave her a piercing look. "Not your responsibility. If they attempt to leave, I'll arrest them."

Mel looked to me. "What do I do if they try to leave? Kevin won't listen to me. He doesn't really even listen to much of what Swagger tells him, and they're best friends."

I walked her downstairs. "Like Chief Meyers said, you're not in control of your friends." That was a life lesson I hoped I had imparted to Alex. One thing I learned from the foster care system is personal responsibility. We are the only people in charge of our own destiny.

"But I know Kev. He's going to try and leave. I promise you he won't listen to me."

"I know Chief Meyers. She'll ensure he doesn't leave. She's not kidding about arresting him, so maybe you can tell him that."

Mel's face went pale. "I can't believe that I'm mixed up in this. I thought this was going to be a fun ski weekend."

We parted ways at the bar, and I went to talk to Garrett, who was explaining the best way to sample our tasting trays to a group of tourists gathered at a high-top table. There is an art to sampling craft beer. We recommend starting with the lightest beer styles like pilsners and pales, working up to hoppy reds and IPAs, and finishing with the darkest stouts.

When he saw me, he excused himself from the conversation and came to the opposite side of the bar. "Well, don't leave me hanging." He leaned his elbow on the wood countertop. Nitro had a casual vibe, with a large chalkboard menu behind the bar, a small tasting room with an assortment of high-top tables and booths left over from when Garrett's great-aunt Tess ran the space as a diner, and a small outdoor patio that was closed for the winter. Garrett was a minimalist by nature. I appreciated that, especially since Mac had more packrat-like tendencies. But when it had come to furnishing the pub, the blank white walls, cavernous ceiling, and open-concept brewing operation left it feeling cold and unwelcoming. A few small touches, like Edison string lights, a wall of black-and-white photos, and hanging wreaths of hops and greenery had made a world of difference. Of course, if April Ablin had her druthers, we would have decked the space out with as much German kitsch as possible. Her idea of impeccable taste involved plastering every wall, ceiling, nook, and cranny with mass-produced cheap German flags, cuckoo clocks, garden gnomes, and pewter beer steins.

I lowered my voice and leaned closer. "I was upstairs with Mel and Chief Meyers. She actually thinks that Jenny might have killed Liv."

"Who?" Garrett looked confused. "Chief Meyers or Mel?"

"Mel." I told him about my conversation. "It's possible, isn't it? If Jenny went after Liv last night. They could have gotten into a fight. Maybe it wasn't intentional. Or maybe Jenny had other plans. Could she have been the person who dumped paint on Liv's car?" As I thought aloud, I wished that I had asked Chief Meyers about the cause of death. Had Liv drowned, or was she killed first and then tossed in the river? The thought made my stomach queasy. I steadied myself on the edge of the distressed wood bar.

"At the moment, I would guess that all theories are on the table. Unless Chief Meyers knows more than she's telling us." Garrett knocked on the bar twice. "I haven't had a ton of interaction with Jenny, but she doesn't present as being very stable. Either is possible. Maybe Liv caught her vandalizing her car and they got in a fight. Then things could have escalated from there."

"Exactly." I wanted to talk to Jenny, but I was going to have to get in line because Meyers was ready to make her exit and waved me over.

"Sloan, Garrett, you know the drill." She gave us a two-fingered salute as she left.

"Now what?" Garrett asked.

"I guess we wait. They have to notify Liv's family, and Meyers explicitly told Mel that no one is allowed to leave. We might be in for a long night."

Garrett massaged a tap handle. "At least there's beer."

"That could be a slogan for one of your shirts."

"What, you don't like this one?" He pretended to be hurt. April never failed to be chagrined by his collection of beer pun T-shirts. She wanted us to subscribe to the "Leavenworth way of life," which, in her warped interpretation, meant dressing in dirndls and lederhosen. I hated to break it to her that it was never going to happen.

He pointed to his intentionally faded red T-shirt. "You're dissing on hoppiness? Come on, Sloan, this is a classic."

"It's bad." I raised an eyebrow.

"Exactly. That's the point. The punnier the better."

I didn't try to argue with him. Brewers were constantly trying to outdo their competitors with clever beer names. As the craft brew craze had gained national and international notoriety, it had become harder and harder to create punny names for our pints. Many of the bigger brewing operations had trademarked hundreds of potential beer puns, most of which weren't even in use but being held in a virtual vault so no one else could come in and scoop them up. It was a point of contention within the brewing community and rightfully so. The big guys not only reserved the best beer names, but they also bought out the trendiest hop varieties for decades. Nanobreweries like us had to bargain with hop farmers for a tiny slice of the pie.

Kevin barged into our conversation, slapping a hundred-dollar bill on the bar. "Can I get a beer or what?" His face was as red as a pint of our amber. "I've been sitting there trying to get your attention for a half hour."

That was an exaggeration. I'd only been behind the bar for a few minutes.

Garrett came to my rescue. "You may have noticed that there's more going on this afternoon than just pouring beer."

I appreciated the gesture, but I didn't need his help.

Kevin glared at us. "That's your business plan? You're going to stop serving because there are police around." His sarcastic, condescending tone made me want to slap him. "Brilliant, brilliant idea. Why would you want to make money? You're doing this for the love of craft, am I right?"

"We're not stopping service, but I would hope that you'd employ more patience knowing that the police are investigating the death of one of our guests." I kept my face neutral. Kevin wanted a reaction from us. I wasn't about to give it to him. "What would you like?" I forced a smile.

"I'll take four of those IPAs." He pointed a short finger at the taps. "What's the big deal, anyway? Didn't that woman jump into the river? Not a wise move in the middle of winter, but she didn't seem like the sharpest tool in the shed."

His reaction to Liv's death was disturbing. "No, the police think that she was murdered." I stared at him.

He physically took a step away from the bar, as if my words had struck him. "Murdered? Who said that?"

"The police," I repeated, placing the first pint in front of him.

"They think she was murdered?" He had lost some of his arrogance.

"Yep." I handed him another pint.

"Are they coming here?" He shot his head from side to side as if Chief Meyers was about to sneak up behind him and cuff him.

"They are. The police chief will be taking statements and interviewing everyone who was here last night. They'll be retracing Liv's steps, and they've told everyone to stay in town until they've cleared you." I shot him another meaningful look.

He reached for his vape pen and flipped it in his fingers. "You mean, like, they're going to want to talk to me?"

Garrett caught my eye across the bar.

I stood firm. "Like I said, everyone who was here last night will be questioned."

"But I didn't even know her." He blinked rapidly.

"That doesn't matter. This is a murder investigation. The police are trying to piece together every movement Liv made before her death." I felt an internal satisfaction watching Kevin try to regain control of his emotions. Maybe I was stooping to his level, but at the moment, I didn't care.

He grabbed one of the beers. "Well, I don't even think I have to talk to them, and they can't keep me here. It's a free country, you know."

"I don't think that's the way the legal system works."

"Whatever." He took two of the pints to their table near the front windows, then returned for the second set of beers. "Do you know the police chief? Is he some kind of backwoods guy?"

"*She* is not."

"She? Your police chief is a woman. Great. That should be a joke."

It was everything I could do to contain the urge to reach over the bar and smack him. Who was this guy? Mel was right to be concerned about Jenny's well-being. I hated to admit it, but Kevin made Mac look like a knight in shining armor.

I watched him tell Mel and the rest of the group about how ridiculous it was that the police were going to question them. I couldn't help but wonder if he was reacting so strongly because he had something to hide. Why would it matter, otherwise?

Jenny appeared in the doorway. Where had she been?

She went over to the table, whispered something to her friends, and then came up to the bar. "Mel said I should talk to you about getting some extra towels?" Her hands trembled as she spoke.

"You need extra towels for your room?" I had stocked every guest room with stacks of fluffy towels yesterday.

"Yeah. Can I get a couple now?" Her voice sounded as shaky as her hands.

"Sure, come this way." I led her upstairs, where I unlocked the supply closet. "Are you okay? You seem a little jittery."

She looked to her hands, which quaked. Was she cold or going into shock?

"Why don't we go into the lounge, and I'll get you a cup of hot tea?"

Her only response was a half nod. I grabbed two folded towels, locked the closet, and guided her into the lounge. The teakettle had gone cold. I flipped it on. "Do you like lemon?"

"Sure." She rubbed her feet back and forth on the carpet.

While the water warmed, I sat next to her. "Is there anything I can help with?"

She shuddered. "I don't know. I think I'm in real trouble."

"Real trouble how?" Was she going to confess to murdering Liv?

"You know that woman who was at the bar last night?"

"Liv," I offered.

"Yeah, yeah. Liv. The police think that I killed her. They think that I killed a woman. I can't believe it. I don't know what to do. I called my parents. They're in Seattle. My dad is finding a lawyer and told me not to say anything to the police until I have a lawyer. I think I might be in real trouble."

Had Chief Meyers already interrogated Jenny? Because if she was walking around the village, the chief obviously hadn't made an arrest.

"I'm such an idiot. I never should have followed her last night."

The teakettle whistled. I got up to pour our cups. "You followed Liv?"

73

She kicked off her boots and continued to rub her feet on the carpet. I was worried that she was going to leave marks in the floor with the force she was using. "Yeah, but not to kill her. I just wanted to mess with her. She was so rude to Kev. I couldn't let her get away with that."

I plunged lemon-ginger tea bags into the piping hot water. "When was this?" My original theory that Jenny had been responsible for vandalizing Liv's car was seeming more likely.

"Late. I'm not sure. It's all kind of fuzzy. I was pretty buzzed. I think it was after midnight. Liv took off, and I told Kev and the rest of my friends that I was going to go have it out with her. That's it, I swear. I followed her down to the park. It was kind of creepy. It was dark and cold. She was practically running. I couldn't keep up with her. Once I got down to the bridge, I lost sight of her. There are all those trails that go off in multiple directions, and it was too hard to see, so I turned around and came back."

I handed her a cup of tea. "Did you explain that to Chief Meyers?"

"Yes." Jenny sounded unsure.

"But?" I sat next to her on the couch, careful not to spill my tea.

"Like I said, I had had a few pints. I wasn't thinking as clearly as I should have been. I didn't want to come back to the bar and not have anything to show for my efforts, so I decided to try and sneak into her room. I didn't even know what I was going to do when I got in there. Maybe, like, break something and have her get blamed. I didn't have a plan, but her door was unlocked when I came up here."

I couldn't believe Jenny was telling me this. "Then what happened?"

"Nothing. Someone had already gone through her stuff. The place was trashed. Her clothes were everywhere. The contents of her purse had been dumped on the bed. It freaked me out. I wasn't sure if she had gone nuts or if someone else had been in there."

Jenny questioning Liv's mental stability was the textbook definition of irony.

"What did you do?" I asked.

She sipped the tea. "I took off. I went to my room and went to bed. I must have passed out, because the next thing I remember was Mel knocking on our door and telling us that we should get up for breakfast."

"And you're sure that's all that happened?" I gave her my best mom look.

"Yeah, what do you mean?"

"Did you do something to her car?"

Jenny's top lip curled. "Her car? No. I didn't touch her car."

I wasn't sure that I believed her. Her skittish behavior made me wonder if she was lying. "What did Chief Meyers say?"

Jenny released her grasp on the teacup and held out her left hand. "She took me in for fingerprinting. I know that she's going to arrest me. They're going to find my prints on Liv's doorknob and in her room. I've seen enough movies to know that finding my fingerprints in a dead woman's room is bad. Like, so, so bad. That's why my dad told me not to meet with the police until he and my mom get a lawyer. But what do I do? What if they come back and want to talk to me again, or worse, arrest me?"

"I don't think you need to worry about that." I tried to console her. "Chief Meyers isn't likely to jump to conclusions without evidence and proof."

"But that's the problem. She's going to have proof. I'm telling you my fingerprints are all over Liv's room."

I wondered how truthful Jenny was being. Why would her prints be all over the room if she had simply walked in, realized that someone else had rifled through Liv's things, and left again?

"What about her car?" I asked again, pausing for effect.

Jenny's face flamed with color. "I swear I don't know what you're talking about."

It didn't take an expert to see that she was lying. "Liv's car was damaged last night. Someone poured paint all over it."

She let out an audible gasp, but didn't admit to anything. "They're going to arrest me. Am I going to go to jail? I can't go to jail! I'm a Kappa Gamma. What will my sorority sisters think?"

Worrying what her friends would think summed up Jenny's vapid personality. Maybe she and Kevin deserved each other after all. "I don't know. I don't know enough about the investigation."

"You have to believe me. I didn't kill her. I didn't even talk to her. I was jealous. That's all. Kev was totally hitting on her, and she shot him down. I guess it just got under my skin, you know? I've been into him for three years now. He could care less, but he sees her for five minutes and is ready to take her out. It's so unfair. I know it wasn't her fault. I know he's a jerk. Mel tells me all the time, but I can't stop loving him. How do you do that?"

"If I had the answer to that question, I would be a wise woman." I felt sorry for her. Over the years, I had developed an ability to read most people, and Jenny seemed sincere. Obsessed with the wrong guy, but not a killer.

"The worst part is Kev doesn't know any of this. I'm going to end up in jail for him, and why? Because I followed that woman down to the park? I peeked into her room? I'm stupid, but I didn't kill her."

"And that's all you did?" I pressed.

She hesitated. "Uh, yeah."

"Maybe you should go try and relax for a little while. Take a nap or a bath. I'm sure that Chief Meyers will be reasonable, and it sounds like your family is offering lots of support."

She cradled her tea. "Yeah, that's why I wanted the towels. We didn't have any in our room, and I thought if I took a bath, I might be able to calm down."

"You didn't have any towels?"

"No. Not a single one. Kev looked for some too, but he couldn't find any."

That was odd. I knew for a fact that I had stocked their room with plenty of towels.

Jenny set her tea on the table. "Thanks for the tea and towels and for listening to me. I know I sound like I'm unstable, but I'm not. I can't go to jail, though. I just got my first real job as a buyer for one of the highest-end department stores in Seattle. What am I going to tell my boss? They'll probably fire me, won't they?"

She was starting to spin out of control. I placed my hand on her knee. "Go take a bath. Try and focus on your breathing. There's no need to worry about anything at this stage."

"Okay." She took the towels and left.

There was a chance that I was reading her wrong, but I didn't think she had killed Liv. She sounded sincere and, more than anything, scared. She had also given me another clue to go on. Someone else had been in Liv's room before Jenny. Who? And could whoever had rummaged through Liv's things have been looking for something important? Something worth killing for?

CHAPTER

EIGHT

CONCENTRATING ON OUR CUSTOMERS HELPED slow the spinning spiral of thoughts in my head. That was until Mac showed up. He and I had been trying to find a new way of operating in the world, or better yet, in our small village, but we hadn't reached an equilibrium yet. Mainly, my strategy had been trying to avoid him.

Mac strolled into Nitro like he owned the place, pausing at high-top tables to chat up our customers. Mac had a natural charisma that was hard to deny. My friends used to call him the "golden one" because of his light blond locks and his ability to turn almost anything he touched into gold. Of course behind his charm, there was a different side. A side I had gotten to know well during our years together. Mac was prone to jealousy and had a constant need to be the center of attention. Living with him had been exhausting at times, especially when he'd call on a whim to tell me we were hosting an impromptu party for two dozen of his "closest" friends.

"Hey, Sloan." He flashed me a flirty grin and sat at an empty barstool, placing a satchel on the stool next to him.

His playful smile evaporated the minute he saw Garrett. "Oh, hey."

Garrett greeted him like any other guest, smiling and tossing him one of our signature coasters.

"I thought you were getting Alex?" I asked, lifting the sleeve of my hoodie to check the time.

"He got a better offer. A bunch of his friends invited him up to the ski hill."

"Ah." I noticed that Mac had trimmed down since our breakup. In recent years, he had put on a few extra pounds due to sampling too much of Der Keller's product line, but now his waist looked trim. "I'll get you a pint of the stout."

He reached into his satchel and grabbed a stack of paperwork.

So he intended to stay for a while. Great.

"What's up with Chief Meyers?" he asked, taking the chocolate-toned beer from me. "She's got half the block closed off."

"A woman was found in the river."

"That's horrible." Mac locked his baby blues on me. His gaze used to make me feel dizzy. It didn't anymore.

I gave him the condensed version of the morning's events.

"Damn, Sloan. I'm sorry. That sucks for you guys."

I knew that Mac was sincere, but I didn't want his sympathy.

He changed the subject. "Have you talked to my mom lately?"

My breath caught in my throat. Ursula had been the mother I had always dreamed of. When I met her and Otto, it was love at first sight. They welcomed me into their family, taught me their craft, and enveloped me in the German heritage. Ursula had been kind and loving without being overbearing. She had given Mac and me our own space, while at the same time making herself available to help care for Alex when he was young or dropping off a pot of goulash for dinner on busy work nights. Ever since Sally's phone call, I had been going out of my way to make sure that I had little to no interaction with Otto and Ursula. Being a product of the foster care system meant that trust had never come easily to me, but Sally was the exception to the rule. As my case worker, it had been her responsibility to ensure my well-being. She had done that and more. Even as a child, I knew that Sally's care and concern for me went beyond her professional duties. When she had come to see me in Leavenworth a few months ago, that had been confirmed. She had explained that she had tried to adopt me, only to be denied. Her supervisor had claimed that she was too old and too single to adopt. What was even worse, though, was that someone above her went out of their way to try and erode my trust in Sally. Not long after Sally placed the adoption request, she began getting transfer notices for me. Every few months, she was forced to move me.

Recently Sally had learned that my case files had gone

missing—all of them. Years' worth of documented court-ordered visits entirely erased from the records. She was convinced that there was a connection with the Krauses. I kept hoping that she was wrong, but the more time that passed, the more likely it seemed that Otto and Ursula were lying. Ursula had confirmed that herself. She had told me that she knew my mother and decided to keep that information from me for my entire adult life. Why? I wanted to believe that she had a good reason, but it was becoming more challenging to accept.

Sally was due to arrive tomorrow. I had waited this long to find answers about my parents; another few hours shouldn't matter, but I had a feeling I wasn't going to be able to sleep until then.

Worry flooded my body as Mac waited for my response. Did he know? Had Ursula said something to him?

"No, I haven't talked to her for a while. Things have been slammed here, trying to get everything brewed for the Ice-Fest and launching our guest rooms. Why?"

"No reason. It's probably nothing. She's been quiet lately. That's all." Mac was horrible at hiding his emotions. His eyes betrayed him. They held a deep concern. He was obviously worried about Ursula.

Hopefully, Sally would have some answers for me. I couldn't go on avoiding the entire Krause family, especially since Otto and Ursula had generously gifted me a large percentage of ownership in Der Keller. Hans, Mac, and I were long overdue for a meeting to discuss next steps. Der Keller was about to undertake its largest expansion in the past decade. After much deliberation, we had decided to switch from bottles to cans for distributing Der Keller's award-winning German beers. There were a number of reasons for the switch, but the top of the list was the reduced environmental impact. Cans are lighter than bottles, meaning that their carbon footprint is also lighter. They require much less packaging material and are made of more recycled materials than bottles. Not to mention that the design options for cans offered endless creative possibilities.

Mac must have read my mind. "Hans stopped by the brewery this morning and wants to know when you're free for dinner. We need to decide about some new hires and the swap to cans. It's going to be a major undertaking, and since you and my brother have both deserted me, we're going to have to hire more help."

Like many other large breweries, Der Keller had traditionally bottled its beer for distribution. Otto and Ursula's humble brewing roots had evolved into a major operation. Der Keller employed dozens of locals in its restaurant, pub, brewery, bottling plant, and distribution center. Prior to our split, Mac had enjoyed being the face of Der Keller. He would usually saunter into the brewery sometime late in the morning and make his rounds, which involved flirting with the barmaids and high-fiving the bartenders. It used to drive me crazy. Mac's work ethic rivaled that of a sloth. His idea of a strenuous workday was schmoozing with vendors over a long beer-fueled lunch and keeping office hours for employees to come air any complaints. Not that anyone ever took him up on his offer. Otto and Ursula treated their employees well, providing them with generous benefit packages, free food and beer, and plenty of extra perks—like

Der Keller merch, trips to brewfests throughout the country, and employee picnics, rafting adventures, and ski weekends.

For many years, it had been me and Otto in the brewery early every morning. I had loved the ritual of starting each day with my father-in-law, who imparted his wisdom on the craft and life in general while cleaning the brite tanks or walking me through how to restart the filtration system.

Those days are behind you, I reminded myself as I focused on Mac. The one thing I could say about my soon-to-be ex was that in the past few months, he had been more engaged in brewery operations than in the entire time I had known him. It was evident in everything, including his attire. Gone were the Der Keller T-shirts and lederhosen. They had been replaced with black slacks and black button-up shirts with the Der Keller crest embroidered on the pocket.

"When do you want to meet?" I asked.

"Tonight?" Mac looked hopeful.

"I can't." I motioned to the busy tasting room. "Chief Meyers has us on semi-lockdown."

"We can come here." He tapped the file folder. "I have a ton of spreadsheets to review, on top of finalizing the candidates."

Spreadsheets? Did Mac even know what a spreadsheet was?

His offer caught me off guard. "Uh. I guess."

"Okay. Tonight. How about seven?"

"But what about Alex? Tonight is your night with him." I tugged on the strings of my hoodie. If I could hold Mac off until after Sally's visit, I would feel much better.

84

Mac waved me off. "He told me not to wait on him for dinner. They're going to ski until the lifts close and then grab pizza. This is our future, you realize. His friends have more sway than us now."

So much for using our son as an excuse.

"Sloan, I know what you're doing. You've been avoiding me for weeks, but it's not going to work. I know I screwed up. I ruined everything." His voice turned husky. "I'll apologize to you until my dying day if that's what it takes, but we have to call a truce and put whatever is between us aside and focus on the business. Der Keller is floundering, and I don't want that on my shoulders, too."

I was surprised by his candor and his maturity. Usually I had to rein Mac in, especially when it came to spending. Had he taken a serious look at his life? Maybe our split was better for him than I had imagined. The man sitting in front of me was a shadow of the man who had cheated on me with the beer wench a few months ago.

"Okay. That's fine. Tonight will work. I'll see you and Hans here at seven." I left him to take a drink order. It was probably good that he was forcing my hand. Otherwise I could live in denial, cutting off my connection with the Krauses, for a long time.

Mac nursed his dark chocolate stout at the end of the bar while I circulated through the tasting room. The vibe was subdued. Most likely because the reflection of the police lights outside danced on the windows and cement floor. I wondered how long Chief Meyers would have the park shut down. They had been on the scene for hours now. She had

85

said that she intended to interview everyone who had been at Nitro last night, but I wasn't sure if she meant that she would hold court here at the pub or bring each witness to the small police office on the edge of the village.

The other unknown was what to do with Liv's things. Would her family come to pick them up? Was that our job, or would Chief Meyers have one of her officers take care of that? The thought of packing up a dead woman's clothes made my throat tighten and my eyes begin to well.

Poor Liv. What did I know about the young woman? She was in her late twenties. She had said that she had come to Leavenworth for the weekend. But why? Was she on business? Pleasure? She hadn't brought any ski or winter gear. The lights were certainly a draw, but were they enough to bring a single woman to town for the weekend? If only we had had a chance to finish our conversation last night. What had she wanted to confess? It couldn't be a coincidence that she had said she needed to get something terrible off of her chest only to end up dead the next morning, could it?

I wanted to talk to Brad. His reaction to seeing Liv at the bar had been visceral. The challenge was going to be getting him alone, without Ali. I didn't think he would be likely to open up about why he had recoiled at the sight of Liv with his wife sitting nearby.

I was in the brewery measuring the gravity of our latest work in progress—a hoppy pale ale that we intended to debut in early spring. Garrett and I used his old home brewing equipment to test smaller batches of our experimental brews. This creation had been fermenting in a five-gallon carboy for the last week. It would yield us about forty pints of beer. Once this pale had reached final gravity, we'd serve it on our special rotating tap and get feedback from locals before repeating the brewing process on a greater scale. I enjoyed the process of brewing smaller batches. It allowed us to stretch our creativity and try unique flavor combinations that we might not be as willing to test when brewing for the masses, and it involved our customers. I loved collecting their tasting notes at the end of an evening to see their feedback on our works in progress.

"Sloan!" I heard Garrett call from the side door that led to the back alleyway. "Can you come out here?"

I dried my hands on a dish towel and went to see what Garrett needed. We mainly used the side door for deliveries and to take out the recycling and trash.

Garrett stood next to the recycling bins holding a bundle of paint-covered towels.

"Where did you find those?" I yanked my hood over my head to shield myself from the cold.

"There." Garrett pointed to a blue and yellow splotch on the snow near the garbage cans.

"Someone must have used our guest towels to clean up after they dumped paint on Liv's car," I theorized.

"Exactly." Garrett set the towels back where he'd found them. "Do you recognize these colors?"

"It's our paint, too, isn't it?" I did recognize the yellow and blue hues that we had used in the water and hops guest rooms. My thoughts immediately went to Jenny. She had just asked for more towels. She had to be lying about vandalizing Liv's car.

"I'm going to find the chief," Garrett said, his hands dripping with soggy paint. "Let's make sure this door stays locked."

"Will do." I returned to the brewery, where I took a sample using a beer thief and poured the straw-colored liquid into a tasting glass. The beer thief, or sample thief, as they were sometimes called, was a long plastic device with a gravity valve on the base. It was used to swipe samples from the fermenter.

I heard a crash.

Was someone in the brewery? Garrett and I had put up very clear signage prohibiting customers from entering the back area. We offered guided tours of our brewing operation whenever someone asked or during busy festival weekends, but we didn't want people wandering around the industrial fermenting tanks or tripping over heavy bags of grain. The brewery could be a dangerous place.

I rested the beer thief on the stainless steel workstation and moved toward the sound of voices.

Ali and Brad were in the brewery, standing right next to a sign that read NO ENTRANCE. The long distressed bar was the only thing that separated the front area from the converted warehouse where our brewing operations were housed. Shortly after opening Nitro, we realized that we needed signage to keep people from wandering into the back to examine the clarifying tanks and pegboard wall where dozens of hoses, fittings, and brushes were arranged in a specific and orderly fashion. (That was one of the great things about working with a scientist turned brewer. I could always count on Garrett to have the brewing equipment organized and tidy.) We allowed guests into the brewery during tours, but otherwise it was clearly marked as off-limits.

I was surprised to see Brad and Ali had disregarded our signage.

Unlike yesterday, when they hadn't been able to contain their PDA, Ali's body language exuded negativity. She had her arms crossed against her chest. Her face was strained with anger.

"Why was she here, Brad?" She practically spit as she spoke.

"I have no idea. You have to believe me, Al," Brad pleaded. "We've been over this, like, a thousand times. I was as surprised as you to see her at the bar last night."

"Yeah, right," Ali huffed. "I'm so tired of your lies. To think I was going to have a baby with you and now we're right back where we started. You can't be trusted, Brad. Every time, I think, *This is it—you're really going to change.* But you never do. You never do."

Brad tried to touch her.

She recoiled, almost knocking over a bucket of hoses soaking in sanitizing solution. "Don't. I'm done. I can't live like this."

"What are you saying?"

I couldn't see Brad's face but was all too familiar with his desperate tone.

"You know exactly what I'm saying, Brad. We're done. This time it's for good. I'm not going to take any more of your lies. Look at me. I'm a wreck. I've lost fifteen pounds that I didn't have to lose this year."

"Ali, I know. I know I screwed up in the past, but you have to trust me. I didn't know she was going to be here."

"So you're telling me that we just happened to bump into her in Leavenworth, Washington? Come on!" Ali's high-pitched screams reverberated throughout the converted warehouse. "This is hardly LA or New York. We're in the middle of the mountains. I'm not an idiot, Brad. That's the worst part. You're staring at me with those ridiculous puppy eyes like I'm going to believe that. No one would believe that."

Ali ducked under the NO ENTRANCE sign and started toward the stairs.

"Where are you going? You can't leave like this. Let's talk. Let's work this out."

She shot him a look of utter disgust. "There's nothing to work out. I'm done. Do what you want, but I'm done."

Brad buried his face in his hands as she stomped away.

I gave him a minute and then came up to him. "Is everything okay?"

He startled. "Sorry. I didn't hear you."

I pointed behind us. "I was working in the back. I wasn't trying to listen in to your conversation, but it was kind of hard not to."

"We probably shouldn't be in here, should we?" He glanced at the rope that partitioned the brewery. "Sorry."

"No problem. It sounded like you and Ali were upset."

He stared after Ali, who was long gone. "Yeah. That's an understatement."

"I couldn't help but overhear some of your argument. Is there anything I can do? Bartenders are known for our listening ears."

He faked a smile. "I could actually use a listening ear. Yeah."

"Why don't you come into the brewery with me? I have to test a few things. We'll have more privacy back here."

"Okay."

One trick that I had learned to get Alex talking was distraction. Our deepest conversations occurred when we were both busy making pancakes in the kitchen or driving through the winding countryside. Hopefully the same would be true for Brad.

"Can you hand me that tester?" I asked, nodding to the beer thief. I explained the process of checking the beer's gravity and why it mattered.

"I had no idea that so much work went into brewing." Brad ran his fingers along the cold surface of the tank.

"Do you want to taste it? The beer at this stage is young, but you should be able to pull out the nuance of flavors that are going to continue to develop as it ferments. This is a pale with notes of pineapple and bananas. You might even get a touch of citrus from the subtle hops. We're hoping this beer will finish at about forty-five IBUs. Enough of a hop profile to please Pacific Northwesterners, but not in-your-face hops like some of the IPAs we brew."

Brad tasted the beer. "It's nice. I don't know if I'm tasting pineapple and bananas because you told me to or if they're there, but I like it."

"That's half the battle when it comes to tasting. One of the things I always encourage people to do when I'm giving brewery tours is talk with their friends during a beer tasting. Often if you pull out a specific flavor, like pineapple, for example, your friend will be able to pick that note out as well."

"The problem is I don't have any friends at the moment." Brad stared at the epoxy floor.

I couldn't have asked for a better segue. Getting Brad to focus on beer had had the effect I was hoping for.

"What's going on with you and Ali? You seem like such a solid couple."

Brad drummed his fingers on the stainless steel tank. "We were. Well, I thought we were. We've had some problems, but we've been working through them, and last night we came downstairs, and I spotted Liv at the bar, it was like I was living a waking nightmare."

"You know her?" I didn't let on that I already suspected as much.

"Yeah. We both know her." He kept his gaze focused on the tank and didn't elaborate.

Maybe getting information from him was going to be more challenging than I had counted on. I walked to the next tank. "Do you want to try this? It's another batch of winter ale. This beer is almost ready to tap. As soon as the kegs run out up front, we'll be kegging this, and then we'll move on to brewing more of our spring line."

Brad nodded. "Sure."

"Ali knew Liv too?" I asked, siphoning a sample of the pine-infused winter ale.

"Yeah." He looked around the deserted brewery. "This is between us, right?"

"Of course." However, if he told me anything related to Liv's murder, I wouldn't hesitate to break his trust and tell Chief Meyers.

"Ali's been through a lot. She's seen way too much loss

for someone our age, and to compound that, she learned that she couldn't have kids a few years ago. It's been rough on us. More so on her, but it put a strain on our marriage."

"I'm sorry to hear that," I replied with genuine empathy, but I was also surprised, since Ali had mentioned she wanted to have a baby with him. Maybe she hadn't wanted to go into detail about their personal life.

"It's okay. We got through it. The infertility was only part of the issue . . . I cheated on her. I'm not proud of my choices, and I've worked hard to try and restore Ali's trust in me. I love her. I don't know what I would do without her."

Brad sounded remarkably like Mac.

"I'm not condoning my mistakes. But Ali was obsessed. She went to dozens of fertility specialists. She dragged me along, too. It was so emasculating. I told her I didn't care, and I didn't. I would have been fine if it was just the two of us, or I told her we could adopt, but she had tunnel vision. She was so depressed, too. I think it brought up old grief. She lost her sister young. She would cry all day. Hallmark commercials, shopping at IKEA, everything we did, there were babies around us. Then our friends started getting pregnant. It was torture on her."

I felt terrible for Ali. A few of my friends had struggled with fertility, and I knew what a painful experience it had been for them.

Brad stared at one of Garrett's chemistry charts as he continued. "I didn't set out to cheat on Ali. It happened unexpectedly. I was traveling for work, and I guess I was just looking for comfort and connection. I met a woman at the hotel bar, and one thing led to another. I felt so terrible the

93

next morning, I came home and confessed everything to Ali."

"Let me guess—the woman was Liv?"

Brad scowled. "No. I don't even know the woman's name. It was a one-night stand, which I've been trying to prove to Ali ever since."

"Recovering from that kind of mistrust is hard on any marriage."

"I know, but Ali and I have been working on it. We've been in counseling together and separately. It's made a huge difference. We've both learned a lot about each other, and up until last night, I thought we were closer than ever. That's what this trip was for, a romantic weekend to reconfirm our commitment."

If Brad hadn't cheated with Liv, why the strange reaction?

"We decided we were ready to have a baby. This time going into it, we knew it wouldn't be the traditional route, so we've been exploring adoption and surrogacy. We thought we had found the perfect surrogate, but it didn't work out, which was another setback. It feels like we can't catch a break."

"Why didn't it work?" I plunged the taster into a bucket of cleaning solution—a staple in the brewery.

"The surrogate backed out at the last minute. We were both upset. I hated seeing Ali's hopes soar only to have them smashed again. We were so close. The paperwork had been signed. The *T*'s crossed, the *I*'s dotted. Our lawyer had reviewed everything. We were due to have our final appointment with the OB-GYN to set a date for insemination, and then our surrogate bailed. Took the nonrefundable deposit

we had given her. Weeks and months of appointments, vi-
tamin supplements, coffee dates, were gone. Just like that—
poof. It was a huge blow to Ali. She had been buying baby
furniture and making plans to transform our guest room
into a nursery. She sunk back into a dark depression. I wasn't
sure she was going to find her way to the surface this time."

Brad's voice was heavy as he spoke. I didn't like the fact
that he had cheated on his wife, but it was clear that he
cared for her deeply. It wasn't my responsibility to judge his
choices.

"I took matters into my own hands. I told Ali I would do
whatever it took to find a replacement. I didn't want her to
worry or to have to be involved in the process. That's when
I found Liv."

"Liv was going to be your surrogate?" I could feel my
eyes widen.

"That was the plan, but I swear the universe is conspiring
against us. I met with Liv a few times without Ali. I wanted
to be sure it was going to work. I couldn't stand the thought
of her getting her dreams of having a baby crushed again.
Liv wasn't with an agency. I found her on a posting online.
Ali spotted us having coffee one afternoon and flipped out.
I tried to explain that the only reason I was meeting Liv was
for her, but she was sure it was another affair."

"Was it?" I interjected.

Brad shook his head. "No. It was strictly business. I showed
Ali the paperwork I'd had our lawyer write up. That made
her feel better. We arranged a meeting with Liv. Everything
was legit, but the paperwork must have spooked Liv. She
said she was trying to run away from drama, not run into it,

so she bailed. It was bizarre. Liv seemed solid. I thought she was going to be the perfect fit, but the minute she saw Ali, she freaked out and bolted. I didn't hear a word from her after that. She totally ghosted me. It sent Ali into a tailspin. Things have been rocky between us ever since. Seeing Liv here feels like a cruel joke. I mean, Ali's not wrong. I think it's a very strange coincidence too, but how am I going to prove that to her?"

I WAS QUIET FOR A moment, processing what Brad had said. He had tried to hire Liv to be a surrogate, but Ali assumed that they were having an affair. Could one of them have killed her? Brad's motive seemed less concrete, unless he was so desperate to save his marriage that the mere sight of Liv in Leavenworth made him panic. Could he have followed her to the river last night to ask her to leave town? What if she refused? Maybe he begged her to give him and Ali some privacy. If she said no, would that have been cause for him to kill her? Unlikely.

But what about Ali? I knew the desperation that came with feeling betrayed. Did seeing Liv trigger memories of Brad's indiscretion? If this weekend had really been about reconnecting and rebuilding their marriage, I could imagine that Ali might have done something drastic. What if she had left the bar last night to confront Liv?

Brad's voice interrupted my thought process. "I should go

check on Ali. I feel terrible. I have to find a way to convince her that I'm telling the truth. I had no idea that Liv would be here, and I had no interest in Liv."

"Sure." I nodded. "Let me know if you need anything."

"Know of any good marriage counselors around? I might need an emergency appointment." Brad sounded like he was only half kidding.

I cleaned my testing equipment and returned to the pub. Snow had picked up outside. It drifted down in fat, wet flakes outside Nitro's steamy front windows. Hopefully Alex and his friends were staying warm up on the slopes.

Kat was refilling bowls of Doritos. "We're going through snacks like crazy today. It must be the snow. People are sticking around for longer. Maybe they're hoping it will let up."

Or maybe they're hoping to catch the gossip on Liv's murder.

"The good news is that our food and beer orders are both up." Kat ripped open a second bag of chips. "We might have to go on a Doritos run, though. This is the last bag."

She wasn't kidding about people devouring our bar snacks. "I'll go. I could use some fresh air anyway."

Kat stared at the window. "I don't know about fresh air. It looks more like a blizzard out there."

"I'm used to it." I went to get my parka, scarf, hat, and gloves. Winters in Leavenworth mean perfecting the art of layering. I swapped my tennis shoes for my fur-lined boots and trekked outside. A new storm had brought in gusty winds and flakes the size of small snowballs. They splattered at my feet, exploding on the sidewalk in a burst of white. Given our elevation and location in the Northern Cascades, the village typically received close to one hundred inches of snow every winter. Those of us who had been here for years were used to the snowfall, which usually started not long after Halloween and lasted until spring. I was often taken aback when customers would ask if the snow bothered me. Why would I live in the mountains if it bothered me?

Snow never got old. I welcomed the calm of a thick blanket of white powder on the cobblestone streets and the way the streetlamps and lights on the trees dotted the fresh snow with sparkly color.

I tightened the hood of my parka and took a sharp left turn on Front Street. The grocery store sat at the opposite end of the village. It too was designed to resemble a Bavarian cottage with a brocade façade, white stucco walls, and dark wood shutters. In addition to traditional staples, it stocked a variety of German imports—chocolates, pickles, spicy mustards, and sweet cakes. I loved lingering in the imported section and discovering new treasures.

Unfortunately, I didn't have time to wander, so I headed straight for the chip section and piled my basket with three kinds of Doritos and a few bags of pretzels. I took my place at the end of one of the checkout lines and felt a tap on my shoulder.

I turned to see Taylor standing behind me. "Long time no see."

He held out his basket, which was filled with microwave dinners. "Decided to stock up in case the storm gets worse."

"Is it supposed to?" I hadn't heard that we were due for anything major.

"No. But you know how it goes around here. They say we'll get two or three inches, and we end up with another foot."

I hoped not. I didn't want to get snowed in at Nitro.

"Are the police still hanging around the brewery?" Taylor asked as we stepped forward in the line. He dug a crumpled twenty-dollar bill from the pocket of his coveralls.

"No, although they are going to be conducting interviews at some point." I was surprised he didn't know that, since he'd seen Liv last night.

"Yeah. I'm supposed to be back by five for Chief Meyers to interview me. Figured I'd grab some groceries. When I unload them at my place, I'll get a growler to bring with me. If I have to spend the evening at the bar, I might as well get a growler filled while I'm there, right?"

"We are always happy to fill growlers." Apparently, Chief Meyers had decided to conduct interviews at Nitro after all. That was probably good. If my meeting with Mac and Hans got heated, I would be less likely to want to punch Mac in front of the chief.

"So what's the deal? Have you heard anything?"

"About growlers?" I joked.

"About the murder. Do they have any leads yet?"

I didn't remember mentioning anything about murder when Taylor and I spoke earlier. "They aren't saying much, but I'm sure that Chief Meyers is going to be very interested in what you have to offer. You might have been the last person to see her alive."

Taylor adjusted his coveralls. "What? I don't think so."

We moved forward in the line. "According to what you

told me earlier, I think you might be. You said you saw her down by Blackbird Island, right?"

"No, no. I don't know if that was her. I said I saw someone running down that way. It could have been her, but it could have been anyone. It was dark, and I'd had a few. I'm not really sure what I saw."

That didn't exactly match what he'd said to me earlier at Nitro. What did he mean by "had a few"? Could one pint too many have blurred his vision?

"Lily, if it was her, was too far away to see." He shifted his shopping basket into his other hand.

"Lily? Do you mean Liv?"

He scrunched his brow. "Huh?"

"The guest who was killed, her name was Liv."

"Oh, yeah, okay. I don't know. I only know what I've heard with rumors around. Liv, Lily, whatever."

It was my turn to check out. I said good-bye to Taylor and said I'd see him at Nitro later. His attitude about Liv had shifted since I had seen him right after her body was found. It wasn't fair to jump to conclusions, but why had he pushed back on the idea of being the last person to see her alive? I had only mentioned it because I thought he would be a help to the police.

You have to stop, Sloan. I ventured back outside to the snowy skies. Smoke spiraled from chimney tops. The IceFest banners hanging from a row of antique streetlamps along Front Street were fittingly dusted with fresh white powder. Icicles clung to sloping rooflines, threatening to release their grip and cascade down upon an unsuspecting passerby's head.

It's not your investigation to solve, Sloan, I told myself as I ducked to avoid a precarious icy dagger dangling from a hand-carved window box.

The problem was that I felt the burden of Liv's death weighing heavy on me. She had been one of our first guests, and I had taken an instant liking to her, with the way she stood her ground in the face of Kevin's obnoxious attempt to flirt. I wished I had had more time with her. What had she wanted to tell me? Could whatever she had wanted to get off her chest have gotten her killed? She didn't deserve to die. No one did, and especially not in our sleepy winter village.

I returned to Nitro and busied myself with restocking snacks, running a load of pint glasses, and prepping for the dinner crowd. We rarely varied our bar menu. It was easier to serve the same five to six items for lunch and dinner service. It kept food costs at a minimum and helped to streamline our workflow. Since there were only three of us to brew the actual beer, serve drinks, and prepare our small selection of bar bites, keeping the menu small ensured we weren't overloaded.

At the grocery store I had picked up the ingredients to make a special winter dessert. If we were going to be the site of Chief Meyers's interviews, I wanted to have a few extra items on hand, including something sweet.

Kat had the bar running smoothly, and Garrett was checking the kegs to see if it was time to swap them out.

"I'm going to do dinner prep," I said to Kat, taking a final load of pint glasses with me to the kitchen. "Yell if it gets busy, and I'll come help you pour."

"Will do." She gave me thumbs-up.

In the kitchen I ran the last load of pint glasses in our

industrial dishwasher. It cranked out the heat and steam-cleaned the glasses in minutes. Then, I started the soup that we would serve for dinner. Next, I whipped butter, sugar, flour, and a dash of sea salt in the electric mixer. I planned to make a Krause family favorite—Berlin Bars. Ursula had brought the recipe with them when they immigrated to the States. The layered bars started with a shortbread crust, followed by raspberry jam and a fluffy and chewy mixture of egg whites, ground almonds, and melted dark chocolate. They were finished by coating them with more melted dark chocolate and sprinkling toasted almonds on the top.

I pressed shortbread dough into jellyroll pans and slid them in the oven to bake for fifteen minutes. Then I whipped egg whites until they formed stiff peaks. I gently folded in ground almonds, and shiny melted semisweet chocolate. My thoughts veered from Liv's murder to Ursula and Otto. The smell of the baking buttery shortbread and the light-as-air egg white mixture brought back memories of hours spent in her warm and welcoming kitchen.

The Krauses were the people I had cared most for in the world. When Mac and I broke up, I knew that they had genuinely wanted me to have a share of Der Keller. Mac had always been envious of my nose for hops and relationship with his father. Otto had taken me under his wing early on and taught me the art of brewing—how to marry flavors and pull out the subtle nuances in each hop. Mac resented the fact that despite hundreds of dollars in training classes and trips to his motherland of Germany, he'd never been able to discern the difference between Cascade and Centennial hops. As Otto said, some people just had "the nose."

The Krauses' offer of maintaining a share in their brewing empire had felt like an extension of their authentic generosity at the time, but not any longer. The more I ruminated on the situation, the more convinced I was becoming that I needed to turn down my share of Der Keller and walk away. Could they be trusted? Did they have an ulterior motive?

I had put them on a pedestal for all these years. They had done more for me than anyone I'd ever known, but now that was in doubt. Why? Why had they reached out to me? Why had they made me a part of their family? Was it altruistic or was it because in keeping me close they could keep my birth parents' secret? I hated not trusting Otto and Ursula. Maybe I was blowing things out of proportion. But then again, why would they have kept something from me that was so important, so valuable to understanding who I am today and where I came from? None of it made sense.

My timer dinged. I removed the trays of golden crispy shortbread from the oven and immediately slathered them with jars of raspberry jam. Next, I carefully spread the whipped egg whites, chocolate, and ground almonds over the top and returned the trays to the oven to bake for another twenty minutes.

The thought that Ursula and Otto may have betrayed me was much worse than Mac's fling with the barmaid. It was impossible to find any reason to justify them withholding knowledge about my past. Their lies also meant that my relationship with Hans was on shaky ground, too. I wanted to believe that he was in the dark, but if he wasn't, I would be ruined. Hans was more than a brother-in-law to me. He had become a true brother, a trusted friend, and a close confidant. I could tell that he knew something was up.

He had asked repeatedly if I was upset with him or if he had done something wrong. I blew it off, telling him that I needed some space. That things were awkward with Mac. That I didn't want to jeopardize his relationship with his brother or put him in the middle. He dropped it, but I knew that it wouldn't be long until he broached the subject again. Hans was astute. He was one of the only people I'd ever known who could read my emotions. How could I tell him that his parents had been lying to me for decades?

And what should I do about Sally's warning? She had begged me not to say a word to anyone until she arrived. What did she know?

As I waited for the bars to bake, I reviewed the little I knew about my past thus far. My memories of my early childhood were hazy at best. The most solid memories I had were of my years in foster care. Jumping from house to house. Never feeling settled. Learning to rely on myself. Sally was the only constant in my life. My check-ins with her had been the one highlight in an otherwise lonely existence.

When we reconnected, she had shared that I never fit the stereotype of most children placed in care. She told me that I had been well-cared for, dressed in clean clothes, with braids in my hair, and a bright intelligence in my eyes, despite the fact that I was terrified and alone. Most of the children on her caseload had been severely neglected and had a variety of developmental delays. I used to dream of going into Sally's office and hearing her say, "Sloan, I want to adopt you."

It turned out that my dream wasn't so far off. Sally had attempted to adopt me, but was told that as a single, older woman she wasn't equipped to raise a child alone. As if having me bounce between foster homes provided any sense of normalcy or stability.

Sally and I lost contact after I graduated from high school. I credit her with everything I have today. Her efforts got me a scholarship to community college and grant money to pay for room and board. If it hadn't been for her, who knows where I would be now.

As fate would have it, Nitro was what brought us back together. When I was helping Garrett get the pub ready for opening night, I found a stack of old photos that his great-aunt Tess had stashed upstairs. One of the photos made me almost faint. It was of a woman and her young daughter. The woman bore an uncanny resemblance to me. I couldn't help but suspect that I had stumbled upon the only photo of me as a young girl. After months of prodding, Ursula finally confirmed my suspicions. She confessed that woman, Marianne, and her daughter had come to Leavenworth for a week with a man named Forest, who claimed to be Marianne's brother. Forest offered Otto and Ursula a generous amount of cash to buy Der Keller, which was in its early days. However, he never intended to actually buy them out. The contract he had drawn up was a fake—he had a habit of taking advantage of immigrants. So much so that the FBI was tracking him. Marianne left, and Ursula never saw her again. That is, until she met me at a farmers' market.

I worked at the market booth part time while bartending and going to school. The booth owner allowed me to bake a variety of treats to share with customers. Otto and Ursula quickly became regulars at my booth. I thought that they had taken me under their wing because they'd fallen in love with my German chocolate cupcakes, but her revelation changed everything. For nearly two decades, they had lied to me. They knew that I was Marianne's daughter and had not once uttered a word about my past. In fact, when I talked about trying to search for my birth parents, Ursula had insisted it was a bad idea. "Sloan, ziz search for your parents, it is not a good idea. Ze past, it should stay in ze past, *ja*. We are your family. We love you. What more could you need?"

I hated knowing that Ursula had lied to me. The question was why? What reason could the Krauses have for keeping my past a secret? Was Sally right? Could the sweet couple who had served as my surrogate parents for all these years have a sinister secret of their own?

The scent of the baking bars pulled me back into reality. I checked them to see if they were ready for the final step. They were, so I removed them from the oven to give them a minute to cool while I melted more semisweet chocolate and poured it over a cup of butter. The act of swirling the chocolate into the butter until it had a luscious sheen made me feel more grounded. I drizzled the liquid chocolate across the bars and used a flat-edge spatula to smooth it out. For an added touch, I sprinkled toasted sliced almonds over the chocolate and set the trays in the refrigerator for the chocolate to set.

Garrett came into the kitchen to grab a load of clean pint

glasses as the first batch of my bars finished cooling. "What smells so good, Sloan? I was making a few notes in the office, and the scent of whatever you're baking kept wafting in. It's distracting."

"Sorry." I smiled.

"Don't apologize, just give me a taste of your delicious creation."

I opened the fridge to reveal the trays of Berlin Bars.

"What are those?" Garrett stood behind me, ready to swipe a taste.

"Berlin Bars. They're Ursula's special recipe." I tapped the top of the cooled chocolate. "I think they're ready to slice." I removed a tray and proceeded to cut the bars into four-inch square pieces.

Garrett took the glasses to the bar and returned quickly. "I didn't want to leave you waiting for someone to sample your dessert creation. It seemed unfair."

"Absolutely." I chuckled and handed him a slice. "What did Chief Meyers say about the paint towels?"

"She came by while you were at the store and took them. She had her team take pictures of the area and said to keep the door locked. Other than that, she didn't say much. You know the chief, she's a woman of few words, but with extraordinary resolve." He closed his eyes as he bit into the bar. A symphony of sounds originated from his mouth as he savored each bite. "My God, Sloan, these should come with a warning label."

"Oh no, you don't like them?"

"Like them? I love them. If you don't hold me back, I might eat that entire platter. I think these might be the most addicting thing I've ever tasted. That middle layer, it's crunchy and light and yet dense with chocolate flavor. Then you get the tang of the raspberry and the buttery crust. These should be illegal."

"That might make them hard to sell."

"Sell? You can't sell these. Let me hoard them." He pretended to gather up the platter that I had arranged the bars on.

"It's your bottom line." I winked.

"Fine. I guess we can sell a few, but let's save some for later, deal?"

"Deal." I followed him to the front with the platter of Berlin Bars. I placed them in the center of the long bar with a handwritten note that read *Dessert special: Berlin Bars. Pair with a pint of chocolate stout.*

We sold five bars with pints of our stout within minutes of putting them on display. I'd found that many of our regulars liked our rotating dessert specials. Often, we'd get groups of doctors and nurses from the hospital or people coming in after work for a pint. They liked to linger with something sweet to share as they used our inviting bar to unwind after a long day.

"See? It's a good thing I saved a stash," Garrett noted, placing ten dollars in the till.

Chief Meyers and two of her police officers arrived as I delivered a plate of Berlin Bars to a ski crowd who had taken over two tables near the windows. "Sloan, I hope you don't mind us conducting interviews here. Garrett mentioned that it would be okay." She used her index finger to press on her Fitbit. "I'm getting my steps in with this investigation. I have a feeling it's going to be a lot of back and forth."

"Of course, anything to help." I showed them to a round four-person table in the far corner of the bar that we had reserved for them. "Any updates?"

The chief clicked off her walkie-talkie and placed a stack of papers on the table. "Nothing solid, but we're confident that we'll be able to make an arrest."

That was good news.

"I meant to ask earlier, how did Liv die? Did she drown?"

"No." She shook her head. "The medical examiner noted trauma to the head. The perp killed her first and then dumped the body in the river."

I was sorry I had asked. The image I conjured in my head made me queasy. "That's terrible."

"Yep." Chief Meyers took a seat. "I'm going to need to keep the victim's room preserved at least for another day or two. Is that going to be a problem?"

"Not at all."

"Good." She laughed. "Even if you'd said yes, I would have told you too bad."

Taylor opened the front door, stepped inside, and looked around. His eyes landed on the chief, and he headed in our direction.

"It looks like your first witness is here. Can I get you anything? I made a batch of Ursula's famous Berlin Bars."

"If I could trouble you for a cup of tea." Chief Meyers looked to her colleagues. They both nodded. "And I wouldn't turn down a Berlin Bar."

"You got it." I left to get them tea and dessert while they began interviewing Taylor. I wished I could listen in. I was curious about his responses, especially after our conversation at the grocery store.

When I brought tea and Berlin Bars to the chief, Taylor was talking animatedly. "I don't know why you're asking me the same question over and over. I don't know if it was Lily I saw down by Blackbird Island. It was a woman, but I don't know if it was her."

The chief made a note. I handed out cups of steaming lemon lavender tea and placed a plate of Berlin Bars in the center of the table. She didn't appear fazed that I was still nearby as she continued her questioning. "I'm asking you again, because we have another witness who has identified you. They've placed you at the scene of the crime, so you might want to take a second and think through your response before you answer."

Taylor's cheeks turned as light as our pale ale. "Who?"

Chief Meyers reached for a bar. "A credible witness, son. Does that change what you want to tell me?"

He gulped. "Maybe."

CHAPTER

TEN

I DIDN'T DARE MOVE. I wanted to hear Taylor's response. I tried to make myself look busy by repositioning coasters at a nearby high-top table.

He twisted off the cap of his empty growler and spun it between his thumb and finger.

"So, is there more you want to tell us?" Chief Meyers waited with her pen at the ready.

"I did see her at Blackbird Island," Taylor confessed. "I saw her leave the bar, and I felt bad for her. She wasn't in great shape, and it was cold outside, so I followed after her. I was trying to be a gentleman, like my mother taught me."

"Mmmm-hmmm." Meyers waited for him to continue.

"She was on a mission. I could barely keep up with her. I followed her over the bridge and then I lost sight of her." He flipped the cap into his other hand. "I gave up. I decided it wasn't my problem. It's not like I knew Lily or anything."

"Liv," Chief Meyers corrected him.

"Yeah, right. Liv. I didn't know her. I was trying to be a good guy. I didn't have a plan or anything either. I figured if I caught up to her, I would offer to give her my coat and to walk her back to her hotel."

"Then what happened?"

He tapped the cap on the top of the table. "Nothing. I went home. Like I said, it was late and I was cold."

Meyers gave him a hard stare. "Any reason you failed to mention this the first three times I asked?"

Taylor hung his head. "I felt guilty, I guess. I should have made more of an effort. I could tell she was upset, and I shouldn't have let her head out into the woods alone at night in the snow. If I had wanted to, I probably could have caught up with her. Or I could have called you. I mean, not you, but the police."

Chief Meyers made a note. I got the sense she was letting the silence linger in hopes that Taylor would say even more. He didn't.

"What time did you return to your apartment?"

He shrugged. "I don't know. Maybe twelve thirty or one."

"Did you see anyone else? Did anyone see you?"

"No. I don't think so."

She made another note. "What did you do upon your return?"

He coughed. "I went to bed. Why?"

"We need to establish whereabouts for anyone who had contact with the victim last night."

"I didn't have contact, though. I just saw her. I don't know her." He pointed to the chief's notes. "I already told you that."

"Yes, and you've already admitted to withholding information from me."

Taylor twisted the cap onto the growler so tightly I thought the thick glass might shatter. "Am I a suspect or something? I don't know the woman, why would I kill her?"

Chief Meyers took a long, slow sip of her tea. Her lack of response said it all.

Taylor shifted in his seat. "You think I'm a suspect?"

"I think that anyone in town who came into contact with or witnessed the victim before her death is imperative to this investigation."

"Okay, is there anything else?" Taylor sounded annoyed.

"Not for the moment, but we'll be in touch if we have further questions."

Taylor stood and tucked the growler under his arm. I made myself busy, stepping to a nearby table to clear pint glasses. The chief huddled with her team. I waited until they were done talking and Taylor was out of earshot before venturing over.

"I take it you heard that, Sloan?" She didn't look up from her notes.

"Sorry. I didn't mean to eavesdrop."

"I would have asked you to leave if I cared."

That I believed. Chief Meyers was nothing if not direct.

"Anything you want to add?" she asked.

I told her about my initial conversation with Taylor and then how his story had changed when I bumped into him at the store. "He referred to Liv as Lily then, too."

"Noted." She scribbled something. "Taylor seems to have a habit of changing his story."

I agreed, but why? Unless he and Liv had had an argument that no one else had seen, what would his motive be for killing her?

"Sloan, I'd appreciate it if you'd continue to keep an ear open and let me know right away if you hear anything out of the ordinary."

"Will do." I left the chief and went to check on the rest of the bar. It was humming with the weekend happy hour crowd. Skis and boots were propped up near the front doors. The pulsing beat of Depeche Mode played on the speakers overhead. The windows had begun to steam, and the taps flowed freely.

I spotted Ali sitting by herself with her head buried in a book.

"How's it going?" I asked.

She looked up at me. Her eyes were red and puffy, and her cheeks streaked from tears. "Do you want the truth? Or should I just say I'm fine?"

"It's up to you." I gave her an empathetic smile. "In my experience, I've learned that the truth usually finds a way out regardless. I'm happy to pour you a pint and leave it at that, but if you need to vent, I'm also happy to listen."

She swept a finger beneath her eye and nodded to the empty chair across from her. "Do you want to sit?"

"Can I get you a drink first?"

"No thanks. I'm fine with water for the moment."

I sat down.

"It feels weird talking to a stranger. I've spent so much time hiding my problems from my friends and family." She dog-eared a page in the book and closed it. I cringed internally. It's a huge pet peeve and a source of irritation between me and Mac. He wasn't much of a reader, but on the rare occasion he would pick up a book, it would end up looking like it had weathered a blustery winter storm. Mac would return books to their shelves with cracked spines, crumpled pages, and beer stains.

My response to Ali was immediate and honest. "I know something about that."

"You do?" A sad smile tugged at her cheeks. "Maybe it's better to confess our issues to someone we don't know well. It takes the pressure off, you know?"

I nodded.

"It's Brad." She stared toward the stairwell. "He cheated on me."

"I'm sorry to hear that." I could tell that she needed someone to talk to, and I didn't want to let on that Brad had already given me background on their relationship.

"Part of that is my fault."

I raised my eyebrow. "How?"

"I was pretty horrible to him." She ran her fingers along the pages of the book, allowing them to fan out. "It wasn't intentional. We had been going through infertility treatments, and it was stressful, demoralizing, and sent me into a bad place."

"A couple of my friends struggled with fertility issues, and I know the process can be a roller coaster."

Ali nodded rapidly. "Roller coaster, yeah, but what's even worse? One of those rides that takes you up fifty stories and lets the bottom drop. That's what it's been like. When Brad and I got married, we were so happy. He saved me.

I had gone through a really dark time before I met him. He brought me back to life. We traveled, we skied, hiked, you name it. Everything changed when we started trying to have a baby." She sniffed. Then she reached into her purse and swapped the book for a package of tissues. She dabbed her nose before she spoke. "I probably should have asked for help, but I didn't want anyone to know. It was embarrassing. All of my girlfriends were pregnant. Everywhere I looked there were babies. I felt so alone."

"That's understandable."

"Maybe. It didn't feel understandable. It felt unfair. Why could everyone else have babies and not me and Brad? A few of our friends weren't even that excited about having kids. That was the worst part." She folded the tissue. "Things got pretty bad between us. We were fighting all the time. At first Brad was super supportive. He tried to help. He went to tons of doctors, naturopaths, specialists, but it was obvious that nothing was going to work. Then I started pushing him away. I guess at some strange level, I felt like if I could hurt him, it would make my own pain feel better. When I say that now, I know how messed up that sounds, but at my core I knew that he loved me. He was the only person I could push away, because he was the only person going through it with me."

"That's a lot to carry on your own."

She nodded. The strain on her face showed in the tightness of her jawline and the tiny blue veins bulging on her temples. "Brad wanted to go to counseling. He thought I should see someone on my own too. He wanted me to look into taking an antidepressant. I freaked out. He claimed that he was only saying that to 'get me over the hump,' but it was like I had hit rock bottom. If Brad thought I needed medication to function, then I must have been a total mess. It brought up so many issues that I thought I had dealt with. Have you ever lost someone you loved?" Ali's voice cracked.

"Yes," I answered truthfully, thinking of being abandoned by my mom. I wasn't sure which was worse: death or being orphaned.

"Then you understand. Grief finds a way in." She twisted her fingers together and cracked them.

"Did you try counseling?" I asked.

"Yeah. I went to a therapist every week for three months. I was working really hard to try and feel normal again. That's when Brad cheated on me."

"I'm so sorry." I reached for her arm.

She met my eyes. I recognized the expanse of despair on her face. "It was such a blow. I had slowly started to come out of the fog. I was eating again. I had started walking—at first just a couple blocks, and then all around our neighborhood. I was feeling stronger. Feeling more in control. I was even starting to think about other paths to motherhood— adoption, surrogacy, foster parenting."

"How did you find out?" I considered telling her about Mac, but the timing didn't feel right.

"He told me. Can you believe that?" She shook her head and clutched her hands into fists. "Why? He said he couldn't live with the guilt. I told him that was selfish. I would rather have never known. He could have taken that secret to his grave, for all I cared."

Her response surprised me. I'm not sure I felt the same, but our situations were very different.

"He claimed it was a one-night stand and that it would never happen again. How could I ever trust him after that? It ripped open my old wounds. It sent me spiraling again. I hated him for telling me. I wanted to kill him." Her eyes narrowed as she spoke. Her voice was laced with anger.

"But you both seemed so happy when you arrived yesterday, and you're here celebrating your anniversary." If I sounded confused, it was because I was confused.

Ali sighed. "I know. We were. I was pissed at Brad for months, but I kept going to see my therapist because it was the only way I was able to maintain any sense of normalcy. She helped me understand my role in the relationship and how distant I'd been. Eventually, Brad came to sessions with me, and we were able to work things out. In some ways it felt like we were closer than we had ever been before. We had to unpack a lot of baggage and show each other our worst parts."

"What happened to change that?"

"Liv." Ali's voice cut like a dagger. "I caught them together. Liv and Brad. He swore that he was meeting her about potentially being a surrogate. He even showed me the contract he'd had our lawyer write up. It was a trigger for me. I believed him, but not one hundred percent. When I spotted them in our favorite coffee shop, they looked pretty cozy. Brad had his arm around the back of her chair, and they were sitting super close. It didn't look like a business transaction to me. It looked like they were into each other."

Brad hadn't mentioned that to me. Had he left that part

out intentionally, or was Ali extra sensitive, given the fact that he had cheated on her?

"He called it off. We had been working with an agency but had a potential surrogate fall through, so he said he was only trying to help. I wanted to believe him. I worked hard to believe him and keep moving forward. That was one of the reasons we came for the weekend here. To try and have a purely romantic getaway and take our minds off everything. Our therapist told us to act like newlyweds. To hold hands and kiss and find nice things to say to each other. It was working until last night. When I saw Liv in the bar, I wanted to explode. Brad swears it was just a coincidence. But I'm not an idiot. Seeing that woman here proved that our marriage is over."

I thought she was finished talking, but she picked up the tissue she had so carefully folded and scrunched it in her hand. "I've been fuming ever since. I don't know when or if I've ever felt this much rage." Her knuckles turned white. "I'm actually scaring myself."

CHAPTER
ELEVEN

ALI WAS SCARING ME TOO, with her bulging eyes and clenched fists, but I remained calm in my response. I told her about Mac's infidelity and how I had walked in on him and the beer wench.

My story seemed to steady her. She loosened her fists.

"I remember feeling the same way," I told her in my gentlest tone. "Anger is a normal reaction."

She stuffed the crumpled tissue into her purse. "Thanks. That makes me feel better. I just don't trust myself right now. If I see Brad, I'm afraid I'm going to punch him in the face."

I nodded. "Yeah, I've been there."

A line had started to form at the bar. She gathered her things. "I'm sorry. I've taken way too much of your time. You probably need to get back to work, and I think I'll go walk around the village and try to move through some of this negative energy. I really appreciate you listening. It helped—a lot."

"Anytime." I gave her a half hug before she left. I felt a connection to Ali. Her pain was visible on every pore on her face, but she had also just admitted that she had gone into a rage—her word, not mine—at the sight of Liv. She'd been through a lot—infertility, depression, Brad's infidelity. Could she have snapped? I didn't want her to be Liv's killer, but I couldn't rule her out either. She definitely had motive, and she wasn't functioning at the most rational level at the moment.

I looked over to where Chief Meyers was holding her interviews. She was in the middle of a conversation with Kevin's friend Swagger. I didn't want to bother her but made a mental note to give her a quick recap of what Ali had just told me. At this rate, I was going to have to ask her to keep me on a retainer. Now, that would infuriate April. I chuckled to myself as I ducked between tables and returned to the bar.

"Check out the Berlin Bars," Kat said, pointing to the platter, where only four bars remained.

"We sold that many?" I was incredulous. It wasn't yet dinnertime. The happy hour crowd rarely went for dessert. I'd figured they would disappear later in the evening but not this early.

"Blame Garrett. He's been telling everyone they're the best thing he's ever tasted."

"That sounds like an exaggeration."

"I don't know. People are loving them. I'm no expert, but I think you have a winner in that recipe." Kat bent down to adjust her UGGs. "Are there more in the kitchen?"

Fortunately, Ursula's recipe made six dozen bars. "Yeah, I'll go restock. How are we doing on food orders?"

"Fine. The soup's been a big hit, but mainly people are drinking and swapping ski stories." Kat's dimples pierced her cheeks when she made a sheepish face. "Well, that and some chatter about the murder. I think there are a few people hanging out in hopes of listening in on the police interviews."

"I'm sure you're right."

Swapping ski stories sounded more like the usual happy hour crowd. It was interesting to learn the rhythm of the pub. Our day typically started with a handful of regulars who ambled in and enjoyed a leisurely pint. They came for socialization more than the beer. We knew them by name and knew about their families, jobs, personal struggles. The modern craft brewery had become a community gathering space. People from every socioeconomic range and cultural background could find a place to connect or enjoy a brief respite from their day. As the lunch hour approached, a business crowd tended to spill into the pub (assuming we weren't in the height of festival season). These were predominantly locals who made valuable use of their lunch breaks to stop by for a bite. As the afternoon wore on, more tourists tended to come in, followed by the happy hour crowd, like we were experiencing now. Since we weren't a sit-down restaurant, dinner wasn't a huge draw, but we got a nice share of business from people wanting a quieter off-the-beaten-path place to share a small meal and from people who wanted to keep the evening going after having dinner somewhere else. Each window of time brought a different energy to Nitro. Garrett had asked me once if I had a favorite, and I couldn't pick one. I supposed it was because I liked that we were in constant flux, the rotation of new and old faces in and out of our doors, and serving up our carefully crafted beers and food with genuine appreciation that people had chosen to spend even a small part of their day with us.

I stacked more Berlin Bars on a plate and checked on the soup pots simmering on the stove.

Chief Meyers had finished her interview when I brought the plate with the strategically stacked dessert treats to the bar.

"Do you have a second?" I asked the chief, pausing to refill their teacups with hot water.

"What have you got for me?" She clicked her ballpoint pen.

I gave her a quick rundown of my chat with Ali. Like before, she made a few notes, but mostly nodded as I recounted Ali's frustration and deep suspicion that Brad and Liv were having an affair.

"It is an odd coincidence. Not impossible. But noteworthy." She stuffed her pen into the spiral circles of her notebook. "Thanks, Sloan. Anything else like that you can learn, bring it to me."

"Will do." It felt good to know that if nothing else, I was providing her with information. I just wished there was more I could do. At times like this, I regretted going into the beer business instead of something more tangible when it came to the public good—like criminology.

I didn't have time to ruminate on my role in the investigation or Ali as a potential killer because Mac and Hans arrived together.

Damn. I had almost forgotten that I had agreed to have our long-overdue "talk" tonight.

"Do you want to sit up here or go to my office?" I asked, meeting them at the door.

"Your office is the size of a coat closet, Sloan. We won't fit in there, unless you want to get cozy." Mac winked.

"Up here is fine." I pointed to a tall table with three bar-stools that was being vacated by a group of doctors I recognized. "Grab that one. I'll get us drinks." I didn't need to ask what they wanted. I knew that Hans would opt for something light like our honey wheat blonde, while Mac would definitely go for a stout—or three. Before I got our beers, I swung by the bathroom to appraise myself. A long day in the pub compounded by Liv's murder had left my face looking tired. I knotted my hair into a low bun and splashed water on my face. Then I massaged my cheeks with moisturizer and applied a shimmery lip gloss and a touch of matching eye shadow that brought out the gold and green flecks in my eyes. I would never describe myself as a great beauty, but I knew I wasn't unattractive, thanks to my Grecian features. Since Mac had cheated on me with the beer wench who wasn't much older than Alex, I had developed the annoying habit of noticing every tiny line on my forehead or hint of an age spot on my angular cheeks. I didn't like this unfamiliar insecurity.

"You've got this, Sloan." I gave myself a pep talk, feeling slightly more refreshed.

"Cheers," I said, setting their pint glasses on the table along with my water glass. We maintain a strict rule of no drinking while serving. When we're brewing, we tend to taste as we go and will often have a pint while we're working out new recipes or testing new hop varieties. I knew of some pubs where the beertenders would pour one pint for the customer and one for themselves. Not only was that a violation of liquor laws, but it set a bad precedent and tone. A bartender should be in charge and in a clear state of mind.

"You brought me a stout?" Mac scowled.

"You love stouts." I looked to Hans to back me up.

Mac flexed his arm muscles. "Not since I started weight lifting. It's only light beer for me now."

"But you ordered one earlier."

He pressed his hands on his stomach. "I'm working on a six-pack of abs. No more six-packs for me. One heavy beer for me a day. That's my limit."

"Okay. I'll have Garrett offer this as a comp and get you something else."

Hans stopped me. "Sit, Sloan. I'm sure you've been on your feet all day. I'll go get Mac another beer." Hans must have come directly from his workshop. He was dressed in his Carhartt pants and a fine layer of sawdust. The only thing missing was his tool belt. It was rare to see him without a hammer or screwdriver at the ready. I loved that Hans always smelled of cedar and sandalwood. I also loved that he always came to my defense, regardless of the fact that Mac was his flesh and blood, not to mention much older brother.

"Thanks." Although I would rather have had another couple minutes to get in the right headspace.

"My kid brother," Mac scoffed. "Always trying to show me up."

"How is he showing you up?" I watched Hans with his long stride as he easily chatted with Garrett at the bar. Mac and his brother couldn't be more opposite. Hans was tall and thin with blond hair, a scruffy beard, and a calm demeanor. Mac, was shorter, bulkier, with light blond hair, bright blue eyes, and a tendency to flip out over the small things.

"He's making me look bad in front of you. I was going to offer to go get a different beer, but he beat me to it."

I wasn't going to bite. Mac had a way of flipping most situations to make him look like a victim. I had heard variations on this theme for years, especially in terms of brewing. Hans didn't have much interest in following the family brewing legacy, but he had a natural talent when it came to pulling out flavors and building balanced beers. It drove Mac crazy.

Despite the fact that he and Hans were vastly different, they had found a way of staying connected as adults. I credited that to Otto and Ursula's parenting style. They had created a family that, no matter what came between them, always had each other's backs.

Or was I wrong? Had I imagined the Krause family as happy, healthy, and supportive because I had projected my own dreams onto them?

"One light beer for you, brother," Hans said, handing Mac a pale pint. "All right, should we get right to it? I don't want to keep you too long, Sloan."

"I appreciate that." I smiled.

Hans set a stack of papers on the table. "These are the résumés for a new manager for Der Keller. I went ahead and weeded through them. We received over thirty applications. These are my top ten picks."

We had agreed that now that the three of us were the majority shareholders in Der Keller and neither Hans nor I had any interest in taking on a management position, our first order of business was to hire a general manager. Mac had offered to take on the role, but Hans and I were in agreement that Mac at the helm, alone, could spell disaster. He had a tendency to spend at will and flirt outrageously. I could already picture a slew of lawsuits from the female members of Der Keller's staff if Mac was in charge.

Instead we had decided to make Mac head of brewing operations. He would be responsible for overseeing production and distribution, and would be involved in launching our new line of cans. The general manager would be responsible for staffing issues, managing the creative team and marketing department, and overseeing the front of the house—including the restaurant, pub, bar, and beer garden.

"Thanks for doing that, Hans." I opened the file folder and reached for the résumé on the top of the stack. "It must have taken a while."

He waved me off. "Nah, it wasn't that hard. Trust me. There were a number of applications that went straight into the trash."

"People who were unqualified?" I asked.

"People who didn't bother to answer any of the questions we asked in the job posting. If you can't answer six basic questions and follow our instructions, I don't think you're a candidate for an interview, and certainly not for managing a multimillion-dollar brewery."

"Good on you, bro." Mac clapped Hans on the back.

I noticed that Hans's forearm was wrapped in gauze. "What happened?"

He glanced at his arm. "It's nothing. I had a run-in with a saw."

"Ouch." I winced. Hans's wood shop was one of Alex's favorite spots to spend an afternoon. Hans had taught him how to make everything from birdhouses to chessboards over the years. Their latest project, with Otto, had been making hand-carved canoes.

"Don't worry. The saw took the brunt of the damage." Hans chuckled.

"You need to be way more careful," Mac snapped. "You could have sliced off your entire arm. I've been telling you that for years now. Your wood shop is a danger zone."

"Chill." Hans held out his hands to try and settle his brother. "I'm a professional. These things happen."

"These things better not happen when our son is working with you, am I right, Sloan?"

I sighed. I had a feeling that Mac's reaction had more to do with the low level of tension between them, or was because of me. I didn't want to fan the flames. "I know that Hans is extra cautious when Alex is around." I handed him the résumé I had been reading and picked up another. It was time to steer the conversation in a new direction. "So far these candidates look impressive."

Hans nodded. "I placed them in my preferred order. The top contenders are first in the stack. I thought maybe we could invite our top four or maybe five to interview. You never know how someone is going to come across in person versus paper. We want to make sure we find someone who is going to be a good match with the staff."

"Agreed." We took a while to read through each of the résumés and decide on which candidates we wanted to invite for interviews. Once we had agreed on our top five, the discussion shifted to progress on the canning project.

"Do you have an update to share, Mac?" Hans asked, giving me a brief look of solidarity. I appreciated that he was taking the initiative to move the conversation along.

Mac did something I had rarely seen. He produced his own file folder and proceeded to give us copies of nearly twenty pages of spreadsheets that mapped out the cost of transforming Der Keller's bottling operation to canning, sales projections, and the PR gains we would likely receive by changing to a more earth-friendly delivery method.

"Wow. This is great." Hans sounded as dumbfounded as I felt. Mac normally ran into company meetings late, with a coffee or a beer in hand, totally unprepared to field any question he might get asked.

"Amazing," I agreed.

The slightest tint of pink spread across his cheeks. "Thanks. As you can see from the first two pages, the upfront cost to update the bottling system is a pretty penny, but the long-term return on the investment makes it well worth the effort."

Mac couldn't proceed with the project until Hans and I signed off.

Hans asked a few questions about vendor quotes and whether our current marketing staff could create new label designs or if we would have to outsource creative work.

"I have a meeting tomorrow with the team to see their first round of design mock-ups," Mac answered. "I'll email everything to you guys, and we can go from there."

It was hard for me to add anything because I had prepped myself for this meeting to be rife with personal arguments and bitterness. Instead, we sounded like true brewing professionals. It was a refreshing change of pace that made me wonder if maybe I could stick it out. I hadn't broached the subject of selling my shares with either of them.

"Anything you want to add, Sloan?" Mac asked, staring at me for a moment too long.

"No. It sounds good to me. I can make myself available for interviews starting Monday. Really, anytime except weekends and maybe the latter half of the week, since we might start to see an uptick in business with people arriving in the village early for IceFest."

"Yeah, I'm with Sloan," Hans agreed. "If we could schedule interviews for Monday or Tuesday, we might be able to have someone hired before IceFest."

"And throw them in with the wolves," I teased.

They both laughed.

Mac made a note on his phone. "Okay. I'll email you interview times and the label designs for the new cans on Monday. Anything else?"

There were about a thousand issues that we were going to have to tackle at some point, but for the short term, I was thrilled with the tone of this evening's meeting and the fact that Mac seemed to be stepping into his new role with a level of responsibility I had never seen.

"I'm good," I replied.

"Me too," Hans said. "This has been productive, but before we split up, I have something else I want to ask you both about." His eyes narrowed and his tone turned serious.

Uh-oh. That didn't sound good.

"Have either of you talked to Mama lately?"

"I see them basically every day, why, are you worried about them, too?" Mac studied his brother's face.

Hans didn't answer immediately. He turned to me. "Sloan, what about you?" His golden brown eyes pierced me.

My heart flopped. I prided myself on my ability to keep my face passive. It was a skill set I had developed in foster care. But if anyone could see through my façade, it was Hans. He had an uncanny ability to read my emotions like no one else. "Not really. I've been busy here."

I could tell that he wanted to say more, but instead he nodded. "I don't know how to explain it, but I think something is wrong with her."

Mac sat up straight. "Right? I know. Something is up with her, for sure. Any idea of what's going on with her? Is it her hip? Do you think she could be sick?"

Hans shook his head. Then he brushed sawdust from his shirt. "I don't know. I can't exactly pinpoint what it is, but she hasn't been acting like herself for a while now. I've tried to ask her about it, and she says that she's fine, that it's her hip or being worried about Der Keller, but I think there's more to it. Maybe I'm imagining it, but it's almost like she's depressed."

I swallowed. Hans wasn't imagining anything. He was right. Ursula was probably depressed, and I knew the reason she had been down lately—me.

CHAPTER

TWELVE

"I'LL TALK TO HER TOMORROW. I hope she's not sick. Do you think it could be something serious? You know Mama, she wouldn't want to worry us." Mac's voice was thick with concern.

Hans shrugged. "I don't know. It's hard to put into words because it's nothing definitive, she's just not acting like herself."

I tried to buy myself a minute to think of an appropriate response, so I took a long drink of my water. "To be honest, I've sort of taken a step back from your family." I felt Mac's eyes on me. Sally's warning burned in my ears. I kept my gaze focused on Hans. "Maybe that's part of it."

He nodded, but didn't look convinced. "Could be."

"She's upset with me," Mac replied. A shade of deep crimson spread from his neck to his forehead. Mac's pale complexion made him flush after one pint, but I wondered if his cheeks were also reddening due to his guilt. "She won't say it, but she's still upset about what I did to Sloan and Alex."

I didn't want to have this conversation here.

Hans must have sensed that. "Honestly, Mac, I don't think that's it." He gathered the résumés. "I'll keep an eye on her and report back if I learn anything."

I left them to finish their beers. My body felt shaky, like I'd had too much caffeine. The meeting had gone better than expected, but Hans's mention of Ursula being depressed was a glaring reminder that her involvement in my past, or at least her lack of acknowledgment about who I was, was going to forever alter our relationship.

"Everything cool?" Garrett asked, his eyes traveling to where Mac and Hans sat.

"Cool. Yeah, better than I hoped, actually."

"That's good," Garrett said, but his raised eyebrows made me wonder if he could see through me, too.

I had been forthcoming with Garrett about my role at Der Keller. He had been a good sounding board, and his newness to Leavenworth meant that he wasn't entrenched in the past. It was refreshing to have a friend and business partner who didn't know every single detail of my life—from what items frequented my grocery cart to all the gory tidbits of Mac's romp with the beer wench. There were ample benefits of small-town life, but the one glaring con was lack of anonymity.

"You didn't sign away your shares, did you?" He studied my face.

"I didn't."

"Even better." He gave me a fist bump.

Garrett had cautioned me about giving up my shares in the profitable brewery. Most likely because he knew the amount of work and long hours that went into building a craft beer brand.

I compartmentalized any thoughts about Ursula and my past and focused my attention on Nitro. The rest of the evening was uneventful.

"You know, you can take off anytime, Sloan," Garrett said sometime after eight. "You've been here since breakfast, and it's slow."

"Okay. I was contemplating baking a breakfast casserole to bring in for the guests anyway."

"Or just go home and get some sleep." Garrett gave me a concerned stare. "You can't keep burning the candle at both ends. You'll end up burning out."

"Me? Never."

I took his advice and left. In truth, the thought of the empty, rambling farmhouse made me want to call April and put in an offer on the property up the street right now. Being alone outside of town felt especially isolating at the moment. It was something I was going to have to get used to. Not only because of sharing custody of Alex with Mac, but in a couple years, he would be away at college and I would be entirely on my own.

Instead of heading for my car, I found myself strolling through the village. It was no wonder that so many tourists opted to venture to our version of Bavaria each winter. I stopped to soak in the beauty of the illuminated trees and the shimmery rooflines. White, gold, and yellow lights pulsed from every tree. A trio of musicians serenaded everyone from the balcony of the nearby Hamburg Hostel. Packs of kids bundled in winter gear sledded down the snowy hill next to the gazebo, which looked like something straight from the pages of a German picture postcard, with colorful lights twisted around its cheery wooden columns. *This is where I need to be*, I thought to myself, as I drove past a handful of tourists strolling along Front Street holding hands and admiring the light display.

If I have to be on my own again, April is right. I need to be in the middle of activity and feel connected like this, with people around. If I stay in the farmhouse, I'm going to cave in even more. It's a skill set I'm familiar with. One that I spent years trying to release. I can't go back to that life again.

Without even thinking, I found myself steering the car into an open parking space in front of April's office.

This is nuts. She's probably long gone from her office by now, I thought, but it was like someone else was controlling my movements because I turned off the car, got out, and walked up to the porch. There was one light on inside her office.

I tried the door handle, but it was locked. So I knocked. "April, it's Sloan. Are you still here by chance?"

To my surprise, I heard her call, "*Ja*, be right there!"

"Well, well, look who we have here. Sloan Krause in the flesh. What can I do for you, my dearest?"

I almost ran back to the car.

April placed her hands on her waist, which had been made at least a half inch smaller by the tightly cinched German apron. "Well, are you going to stand out in the snow with your mouth hanging open, or are you going to come inside, and we'll write up that offer?"

"But, but ..." I sputtered. "I didn't say anything about writing up an offer."

"Sloan." April rolled her eyes. "This is my business. I can see by the way you're bouncing your left foot and wringing your hands that you're nervous. You are rarely nervous—at least not outwardly—which leads me to believe that you're here for one reason alone. To put in an offer on that fabulous little chalet. I approve. So let's go get it done."

She pointed in the direction of her office, which would be better described as a shrine. A shrine to all things German and to April herself. One wall was plastered with pictures of April posing in a variety of costumes and outfits. The remainder of the space was taken up with posters for every event Leavenworth had hosted in the past decade, from the fall leaf festival to Maifest. There were also awards and ribbons for April's service to our village, and a huge pair of ceremonial ribbon-cutting scissors.

"Sit, Sloan. Sit." April spoke as if she was commanding a puppy. "I know you're here about the cottage, so let's *hetzen*."

I had to admit that her deductive skills were impressive. Her German, not so much.

"What are you thinking you want to offer?" She started typing so fast that her fingers blurred together.

"Uh, I don't know. Maybe this is too rash. I should come back in the morning or something."

"NO." April raised her index finger. "Plant your butt in that chair. You want this house. You need this house, Sloan. It's not rash. You've been thinking about it for more than six weeks now. We've toured it three times, and the owner called me this morning. They want to officially put it on the market before IceFest. The house is meant for you. Are you really willing to stand up, walk away, and let it go to some Seattle socialite?"

Were there Seattle socialites?

April tapped her long fake nails on her desk. "Shall we?"

"Okay." I sat down and exhaled. I did want the house. It was a perfect cottage, with two bedrooms, a chef's kitchen, living room, dining room, stone fireplace, and wraparound deck on the back that overlooked the miniature golf course and had a peekaboo view of the Wenatchee River. The sooner I could move into the village, the better. The meeting with Mac and Hans tonight was proof that things had already changed. I needed to change with them.

April suggested putting in an offer just shy of the asking price but explained that since I'd be purchasing the property with cash, it would make closing fast and easy.

I signed the offer letter and an earnest money check. Instead of feeling nervous or like I was doing something rash, I felt a sense of relief.

"We should have a response by the end of the day tomorrow, if not sooner," April said, stacking the papers on her desk. "I'll email these over tonight. Assuming everything goes as expected, you should have your new keys within a few weeks. Congratulations—or as your in-laws would say—wishing you *das Unglück!*"

Did April know that her well wishes actually translated to "disaster or misfortune" in German? I doubted it, but I thanked her and headed for home. Or, my temporary home.

I wondered how Alex would react to the news. I had taken him along on two of the showings, and he was enthusiastic, at least outwardly. He said he had always wanted to live in town. Plus Mac had been looking at a condo near Blackbird Island. If he bought the condo, Alex could easily walk back and forth between our places. I liked that idea.

It wasn't Alex's fault that Mac and I had grown apart. He shouldn't have to bear the burden of our mistakes. At least if Mac and I both purchased new homes in the middle of the village, Alex would have the freedom to come and go as he pleased. When he was young, living out on the farm meant that he and his buddies could run wild. They used to play hide-and-seek amongst the hop vines and flashlight tag in the open fields at night. But now that Alex was grown, living in the village made much more sense. He could walk to the high school. It wasn't more than a half mile from Nitro. In the spring and summer, he could walk to the river or hike through Enchantment Park. Being in the village would put both of us in the middle of all the activity, and for the first time since Mac and I had broken up, I felt like I had a blurry vision of what the next stage of my life could look like.

CHAPTER

THIRTEEN

THE NEXT MORNING, I WOKE to an empty house and a nervous stomach. Sally was arriving tonight. She couldn't get here soon enough. My conversation with Mac and Hans had made it painfully clear that I was going to have to face my future at Der Keller sooner rather than later.

After my late night with April, I'd been too tired to bake, so I padded into the kitchen, made a strong pot of coffee, and gathered ingredients to make a breakfast casserole for the Nitro guests. I started by cracking a dozen eggs in a mixing bowl and whisking them until they were light and fluffy. I added heavy cream, salt, pepper, chopped fresh herbs, sausage, and sharp white cheddar cheese. I layered it into a casserole dish and placed it in the oven to bake for forty-five minutes. We had plenty of fruit left at Nitro, and on my way to work, I could stop at Strudel, the local German bakery, and pick up some pastries.

With the casserole baking, I took a long, steaming shower.

My thoughts returned to Liv's murder as the water doused my skin. I hated to admit it, but Ali seemed to have the most motive and a deep-seated rage from everything she'd been through. I wondered if Chief Meyers had uncovered any new information in her interviews last night. I would have to find time to check in with her today. In the meantime, I intended to keep a close watch on Ali.

Once my skin was sufficiently red and warm from the shower, I got out and layered for the day. With more snow in the forecast, I opted for a pair of thick wool tights, a black knee-length skirt, a maroon cable-knit sweater that brought out the natural olive tones in my skin, and my favorite lace-up fur boots. I kept a few pairs of knee-high brewing boots at Nitro, but we weren't brewing today so I dressed for work in the kitchen and tasting room instead.

To finish the look, I blew my hair dry and tied my long, dark hair into two braids. I dusted my cheeks with a touch of blush, added lip gloss, mascara, and a hint of cream eyeshadow. I couldn't wait to share my news with Garrett and Kat. I knew they would be thrilled for me. Not to mention, like Alex, once I moved into the new house, I could walk to work every day. I could even go home for lunch or drop by to meet Alex after school. The more I thought about it, the more excited I became.

My breakfast casserole had baked to a bubbly, cheesy goodness. I wrapped the base with a thick kitchen towel and took it to the car. Then I grabbed my parka and gloves, tugged on a gray hat—yet another that Ursula had knitted for me—and headed for the village.

Sunday mornings in Leavenworth are typically lazy, with

tourists venturing out for late brunches. I only saw a handful of people out and about on the snow-covered sidewalks as I left Strudel holding a box of assorted German pastries.

My arms were loaded with *Lebkuchen*, a gingerbread-like cookie; apple strudel; and *Zwetschgenkuchen*, a traditional plum cake. If my reaction time had been quicker, I would have ducked back inside the bakery, but instead I froze at the sight of Ursula, who was coming directly toward me. I recognized her gray striped wool shawl and her unsteady gait as she supported herself with a cane in order to step over a six-inch mound of snow pushed up against the curb.

"Sloan! *Guten Morgen*," she said, pressing her cane onto the sidewalk when she reached me.

I bent down to greet her with a kiss on each cheek. "Good morning."

Her hands shook slightly as she returned my greeting. I wasn't sure if it was because she was still recovering from hip replacement surgery or if she was nervous to see me, too.

"You look well, Sloan." She appraised me carefully. The lines etched across her forehead might have revealed her age, but her piercing blue eyes were as bright and astute as ever.

"Same to you." I nodded to the cane. "You're navigating the snowdrifts like a professional snowboarder."

Ursula laughed. Then her face shifted. "Sloan, ziz has been ze hardest zing for Otto and me. We miss you so much, my darling daughter, and we want you to know how sorry we are. I have been awake every night, zinking of our last conversation about your mother. I know it wasn't fair of me to keep what I knew from you, but I had my reasons. I don't expect you to believe ziz, but I was sure I was helping. I was sure of many zings, and now I don't know...." Her voice trailed off.

My back went rigid. I tightened my grip on the pastry box.

"I hope you can forgive me. I hope you will sit down with Otto and me, and we will tell you our side of ze story. It might not be enough, but we owe you zat and much, much more." She hung her head.

My natural instinct was to try and console her, but I resisted.

"Ursula, I'm just not ready yet." That was true. As was the fact that I had no intention of meeting with the Krauses until after Sally's visit.

"*Ja, ja,* I understand." She used her free hand to cinch her shawl tighter. "It is cold, *ja*? Zey say we will have plenty of fresh snow for ze IceFest, so zat is good."

I was about to respond, but before I could, April's nasal voice cut through the morning air. "*Guten Morgen*, ladies, *guten Morgen!*"

She was hard to miss in her head-to-toe yellow. Her garish outfit made her look like an oversized bumblebee.

April practically danced across Front Street. "The Krause ladies together—awwww, it makes my heart go pitter-patter." She thumped her chest. "Ursula, you are looking absolutely wunderschön." As always, April butchered her German pronunciation.

"Thank you." Ursula offered her a curt nod. "I'm feeling better day by day."

"No, no. Don't be so modest. The entire village has been absolutely flummoxed at the thought of our matriarch out

143

of commission. I have been beside myself with worry. I had heard mention that you weren't going to lead the IceFest parade this year. Now, I assure you, I would have taken on that responsibility willingly to help you, but I'm thrilled to see that you're up and moving about the village. This is the most wonderful news." April paused for a moment and looked thoughtful.

I wasn't sure what she was talking about. Ursula had been "up and moving about" the village the moment her doctors had given her the okay. She was definitely walking better as she grew stronger, but April made it sound as if Ursula had been on bed rest for months.

"Although," April continued, holding her index finger to her lips and staring at Ursula's cane, "if you think it's too much to navigate the icy street, I completely understand. Perhaps it makes the most sense for me to take over your parade duties, in the name of an abundance of caution for your personal well-being."

April wasn't fooling either of us.

"No, not at all." Ursula shot me a wink. "I am fine for ze parade. Otto and I will be zere bright and early, with bells on, as zey say."

"Oh, excellent." April tried to force a smile through clenched teeth. "I'm so happy to hear that. What a relief." She glanced behind me at the bakery. "Well, duty calls. It's an early start for me this morning. My stack of paperwork demands some delicious pastries. Sloan, I'll be in touch later."

I breathed a sigh of relief that April didn't mention anything about my offer. Not that Ursula wouldn't support my decision to move out of the farmhouse, but I wanted to make an escape as quickly as possible.

"We have a word for zat woman in German," Ursula said once April was safely inside Strudel.

"What is it?"

"*Schadenfroh*," she replied in her native tongue.

"I don't think I've ever heard that."

"It means taking pleasure at others' misfortune. Zat is April, *ja*?"

I chuckled. "*Ja*."

Ursula patted my hand. "Sloan, you take care of yourself. We will be waiting for you whenever you are ready to talk."

The air in my lungs felt like it was evaporating. "Okay, thanks." I left her with another kiss on the cheek and headed straight for Nitro.

Not surprisingly, there was no sound of movement from Garrett, Kat, or our guests upstairs when I unlocked the front door. I cranked up the heat and went to the kitchen. Maybe the scent of brewing coffee would stir everyone. I turned the oven to low to keep the casserole warm while I put the finishing touches on breakfast. The routine of preparing a meal helped keep my thoughts from drifting too much. Seeing Ursula had thrown me off. I'd been so careful, avoiding Der Keller during times of the day I knew that she and Otto were likely to be there, making sure Mac picked Alex up from their house after Sunday dinners, and sending Garrett to the monthly village business owners meetings. Of course I would have to bump into her at the pastry shop early in the morning. Come to think of it, why was she out this early? Der Keller wouldn't open for lunch service for another four hours, and Ursula usually arrived an hour or two before the lunch rush.

Was bumping into each other an accident, or had she intentionally tried to track me down?

Hopefully, Sally would have some answers and concrete information for me. I couldn't go on living like this and trying to avoid the most prominent and beloved couple in town for much longer. What did Ursula want to tell me?

Her words replayed in my head as I went through the motions of making the morning coffee. She had said that she and Otto had more to tell me. Why hadn't she told me everything the fateful night she'd come clean about knowing my mother?

None of it made sense.

They had intentionally lied to me about my past. No matter how much I loved and cared about them, I wasn't sure how I was going to forgive them.

What could their reason be?

Ursula made it sound like keeping my identity secret had been an attempt to help me. Help me what? Help me spend decades feeling lost and confused? Help me close myself off to emotions? To learn how to keep everyone at a distance?

No.

It wasn't fair.

She couldn't expect me to trust that lying to me for all of these years was absolvable because she was well-intentioned. Trust didn't come easy for me, and as of late it felt like the universe testing my resilience. First Mac, then his parents. What was next?

The smell of coffee wafting through the kitchen pulled me away from my thoughts.

Sloan, you have to focus. I pressed my fingers and thumbs together and inhaled slowly. There was nothing I could do until Sally arrived, so for the moment the only way I was going to stay sane was to wrap myself in as many sensory tasks as possible—like making breakfast.

Baking and cooking had been a form of self-help since my early years in the foster care system. It was probably one of the reasons I also enjoyed brewing. There was something about working with my hands while completely immersed in the sensory process of brewing coffee, baking bread, or steeping grains.

Once the coffee was ready, I took it upstairs along with clean plates and silverware and began setting our communal breakfast table.

Ali wandered out first. She rubbed sleepy dust from her eyes and tied her plush bathrobe tighter.

"Good morning, would you like coffee?" I asked.

"Yes. Thank you." She took the cup I poured for her and added cream and sugar. Then she took a seat at the end of the long walnut table. The room was snug yet comfortable, with a collection of vintage ski posters on the walls and bookcases with a multitude of reading options for guests. Alex had helped me stock our mini library. We had hit the annual library sale armed with empty hop boxes that we filled to the brim with a variety of sci-fi, romance, and historical fiction, along with plenty of mysteries, classic literature, and regional hiking guides.

"Are you feeling any better?" I set a tray of the pastries in the middle of the table and turned the teakettle on.

"A little." She cradled her earthenware coffee mug. "I'm wiped out. Brad and I were up until three in the morning trying to hash things out."

"Were you able to come to an understanding?"

"He keeps insisting that there was nothing between him and Liv. I don't know what to think. He sounds like he's telling the truth, but I just don't know if I can believe it. What are the chances that she would have picked the same weekend to be in Leavenworth and to stay at the same hotel?"

I placed a dish of tea packets on the table. "I don't know if this helps. I should have mentioned it yesterday, but I didn't think about it at the time. Liv wasn't planning to stay here. She came to the village without a hotel reservation, and once she got here, she tried every hotel in town. We were a last resort. In fact, I was the person who offered it up to her."

"Really?" Ali's face brightened.

"Yes, I felt sorry for her. She had nowhere to go. In fact, she even mentioned driving back to Spokane. That's when I offered her the extra guest room upstairs. We weren't technically ready to be fully booked with guests, but we didn't want her stuck without anywhere to sleep."

"Huh." Ali stared at her coffee. "I don't know. It's still a pretty huge coincidence that she was here in Leavenworth the same time as us."

"True." I couldn't argue with that.

Kevin, Jenny, and their friends emerged from their rooms.

I gave them coffee and went to get the casserole and fruit salad.

When I returned to dish up breakfast, I noted that Brad was absent. Had he intentionally stayed in his room to give Ali space?

"That crotchety police officer told us last night that none of us can leave," Kevin complained, helping himself to three pastries. "What are we supposed to do? Just stick around here? I have a very important meeting tomorrow that I need to be back for."

Mel and Swagger almost seemed like they were trying to distance themselves from Kevin. They had scooted their chairs to the far end of the table, near Ali. Mel sighed under her breath at Kevin's outburst.

Jenny gnawed her fingernails. "I know. I already sent my boss a text message, but I'm worried I'm going to be in trouble if I don't show up tomorrow. I mean, I don't understand why the police won't let us go home. They have our contact info."

Unless Chief Meyers is confident that one of you is the killer, I thought to myself.

"When is she coming by?" Kev asked me.

"I have no idea. What did she tell you last night?"

"Nothing. Not to leave town. That's total crap. I'm calling my lawyer. I'm not paying for another night here or getting charged late checkout fees because I'm forced to stay here. That's crap."

Unless Garrett had said something to the contrary last night, I didn't think we had any intention of charging late checkout fees. "We don't have any new guests checking in today," I said to the group. "You're welcome to stay past checkout, and if the police determine that you need to stay in the village longer, I'm sure we can work something out."

"I can't wait to get out of this stupid small town," Kevin muttered.

"In that case, ignore what my colleague just said." Garrett came up behind me. He gave me a knowing look.

I didn't bother to respond to Kevin's dismissive comment. Jenny nudged him. "Kev, don't be rude."

He snapped his head and shot her a look that made me flinch. "I'm not being rude. I'm calling things like I see them. You want to be stuck here for a week? This is total crap. They can't hold us like common criminals."

The way he stared at her with his eyes bulging as if he was about to have a brain hemorrhage sent my thoughts back to Liv. This brief flash of Kevin's temper highlighted the fact that he had a short fuse. If Liv had ignited Kevin's fiery streak by embarrassing him in front of his friends, it was plausible that in a moment of rage he had killed her.

I watched as Kevin shot Jenny another look of disgust and then started devouring the casserole. The sooner he checked out, the better.

Garrett and I went downstairs together.

"That guy scares me, Sloan."

I was surprised to hear Garrett admit as much. It wasn't as if Garrett had a meek personality. Nor did he have a slight stature. He was tall and trim, thanks to his daily runs through the cross-country trails on Blackbird Island.

"No, I'm not worried about him coming after me." Garrett

answered the question I hadn't asked. "I don't like the way he treats women. Did you see how he shot Jenny down? I'm not sure if the chief has any evidence pointing to him, but I'm going to be keeping close watch on him. I don't trust him at all."

"My thoughts exactly." I filled the coffee maker with water and more grounds to make a fresh pot.

"He has no respect for women," Garrett fumed. "What I don't understand is why women like Jenny tag along after him like puppy dogs. Can't she see the way he belittles her?"

"Unfortunately, I think that's part of the cycle. I'm not sure that Jenny has a lot of self-confidence, and guys like Kevin take advantage of that."

"It's hard to watch." Garrett broke an apple pastry in half. "How bad would it be if I punched him?"

"You'd get a standing ovation from me, but we might have a lawsuit on our hands." I helped myself to a cup of coffee.

Garrett bit into the flaky pastry. "Let's hope the chief lets them go soon. I'm not sure how much longer I can play nice with that guy."

As it turned out, we didn't have to wait long for Chief Meyers to appear. Not more than fifteen minutes later, the front door buzzed. Garrett went to answer it and returned with the chief. Her sandy hair with its natural curls was cut short around her apple-shaped face. She had a perpetual tan. I'm sure that was due to the fact that she spent the bulk of her days ambling up and down Front Street keeping the peace.

This morning her face looked drawn, and her eyes tired.

"Can I get you a cup of coffee? A pastry?" I pointed to the half dozen pastries I'd reserved for us.

The chief took a strudel. "Coffee, please. Black."

I poured her a cup.

Garrett topped off his coffee. "What's the latest? Please tell us that you're here to arrest Kevin."

"Nope. Not ready to make an arrest, but I do have some news I'd like to share." She leafed through some papers. "Check this out."

I picked up the top sheet, while Garrett stood behind me to look over my shoulder.

"Do you see the name?" Chief Meyers asked.

"Lily Palmer?" I replied, not sure that I was reading the paperwork correctly. "Who's Lily Palmer?"

"The deceased woman. Her name wasn't Liv Paxton. It was Lily Palmer." Meyers gave me a knowing look. "Ring any bells?"

"Taylor," I said.

Chief Meyers brushed crumbs from her bottom lip and gave me a nod of approval.

"I'm confused," Garrett interjected as I handed him the paperwork for a closer look.

"The other day in the bar, Taylor kept calling Liv Lily," I offered. "He has to have known her."

"That's right." Chief Meyers polished off the pastry. "He's out at the ski hill jump-starting a car, but when he's back in the village, he and I are going to have a nice long chat."

I thought back to my conversation with Taylor. He had mentioned that Liv—or Lily—looked familiar. Maybe there was a simple explanation. "What do you think it means? Why did she change her name?"

"No idea." She shrugged and stacked the papers. "People

do this sort of thing for many reasons. The good news is that we've tracked down and notified her family. I'm here to get her things and then you can have your guest room back. Don't want to hold up business for you two any longer than necessary."

"That's low on our priority list," Garrett said with sincerity.

"I appreciate it." She took a drink of her coffee.

"What about the other guests?" I asked. "Should we plan to have them another night?"

"I don't know if that will be necessary. I should have a better sense later this afternoon, but I wouldn't book any new reservations in the short term." She gulped down the rest of her coffee. "Duty calls. I'll head on upstairs if you don't mind."

"Of course." I took the fresh pot of coffee and showed her upstairs. Liv was really Lily, and Taylor knew her in some capacity. Could that mean he had a secret motive for killing her?

CHAPTER

FOURTEEN

APRIL SWEPT INTO THE TASTING room the minute we turned the sign on the door to OPEN. "Sloan, I have news!" She swung the contract we had signed last night between her gaudy fake nails. "Your offer has been accepted! *Wir freuen uns sehr!*"

In German, that meant "We're very happy for you." I wasn't sure what she meant by using the plural. Were the owners also happy for me?

"Offer?" Garrett tossed a bar towel over his shoulder.

April pounced. "Sloan didn't tell you? Oh, shame, shame." She shook her index finger at me. "We put in a very generous offer on that adorable cottage at the top of Front Street. I'm sure you must know that cottage I'm talking about. It's simply the sweetest little property, with a lovely deck on the back that looks down over the miniature golf course and Waterfront Park."

"You're buying a house in the village?" Garrett sounded stunned.

"I was planning to tell you and Kat this morning, but we got so busy with Chief Meyers."

"Chief Meyers? Chief Meyers was here?" April forgot about the contract and practically lunged at us. "Why? Is there news on the—" She glanced around to make sure no one was listening, despite the fact that there was no one else in the tasting room. Or with April, it was more likely that she was actually hoping someone would overhear her as she loudly whispered, "*Murder?*"

Garrett tried to stifle a laugh. It was hard to take April seriously as she stood in front of us in a black and yellow barmaid dress with knee-high black socks, bright yellow snow boots, and a matching hat. I often wondered how much April's elaborate fake German wardrobe cost her. I rarely, if ever, saw her in the same outfit twice.

"They don't know," I answered, reaching for the contract. I wanted to hold it in my hands to make it feel real. "She was here to clean out the guest room."

"Oohhh, this is a new development. I must go find Chief Meyers. I'm surprised she didn't come to me first, but then again, I wasn't in my office. As your real estate agent, I take pride in reviewing every offer—line by line. That's the level of service I provide, even at the expense of my duties to our community. Look this over, Sloan. Call me with questions. I'll get the inspection lined up for this week, and it should be smooth sailing from there." She spun in a full circle. "Now, before I make my departure, can we please

155

discuss the monstrosity you have going on in here? IceFest is in less than a week, and this space looks like a clean lab. Where are the IceFest posters I delivered? Where's that box of Bavarian thermometers I had sent over? We need every business in the village on board with decking the halls for IceFest, *verstanden*?"

Neither of us responded.

April clapped. "Chop, chop. Get decorating. I want you to *der*-bling this place! The next time I'm here, I want it to look like winter threw up all over." With that she gave us a curtsy and danced to the front door.

"Whew." Garrett mopped his brow with the towel. "Der-bling? What just happened?"

"April Ablin happened," I joked. I had stashed the box of thermometers that April wanted us to display. They were plastic miniature log houses designed to resemble German cottages with baby fawns, window boxes, and a thermometer for a front door. The houses were some of dozens of kitschy items that April was constantly trying to get us to display at Nitro. Thus far she'd been unsuccessful in her attempts to force us to "Germanize" (her word) the brewery, and I hated to break it to her that there was no chance of that changing anytime soon.

He tapped the contract that April had left on the bar. "I can't believe you bought a new house, Sloan. That's awesome. You're going to be so close. A real villager, as they say. Plus, that means you can walk home." His gaze turned serious for a moment. "I'm glad. I worry about you driving those winding country roads in the dark, especially this time of year."

I thumbed through the signed contracts to avoid his eyes.

"Thanks. I know those roads well, but yeah, I think being in the village is going to be a nice change."

Garrett hesitated for a minute. "What are you going to do about your farmhouse?"

"You want to know the truth?" I tugged on one of my braids.

"Of course." He arranged a stack of IceFest flyers on the bar.

"I have no idea," I admitted. "Putting in an offer on the cottage is the most spontaneous decision I've ever made. I hope I don't regret it." What I didn't tell him was the only other rash decision I'd made in my life had been marrying Mac.

"No way. You won't regret it. I think living in the village would be . . ." He paused, trying to find the right word. "A relief for you, I guess. I've never been inside your farmhouse, but I've seen it from the highway, and it looks like a lot of work, not to mention that drive. I know that Leavenworth is a far cry from Seattle, but no part of me misses getting in the car every day. I love waking up and coming downstairs to start work."

"Thanks." I smiled. Garrett's enthusiasm made feel better about my decision.

"Does Alex know yet?"

"Know what?" Kat interrupted. She had been out getting supplies for the day. Her arms were loaded with grocery bags. Garrett went to help her.

"Sloan put in an offer on a cottage here in the village," he said, setting one of the grocery bags on the bar.

"No way. That's awesome," Kat squealed. She chomped on a piece of gum, and I had to remind myself that Kat wasn't that much older than Alex. "That's going to be so much better for you. I always feel bad every time you have to drive home late at night."

It was hardly like my commute was terrible. There were many staff at Der Keller and some of the other restaurants and shops in town that commuted from Wenatchee every day. My drive paled in comparison. The farmhouse sat just outside of town on a small plot of acreage that Mac and I had cultivated into a small hop field. My daily drive took me past cherry and apple orchards on a twisty but beautiful two-lane road. I wondered if I would miss the drive once I moved to the village. It had been part of my routine for almost twenty years.

"Alex is going to flip," Kat continued. "Or has he already? When I was talking with my parents the other night, I was saying how cool it would have been to grow up here. So much freedom. You can walk everywhere, and it's super safe."

Aside from the recent murder, I thought to myself.

"That's exactly what I've been thinking," I said to Kat. "Fingers crossed that the inspection goes well. Soon we could be having a housewarming party at my new place."

Kat used her free hand to wave. "Oooh, let me plan. Please?"

"Deal."

She and Garrett went to the kitchen to put the supplies away. I felt grateful to have Garrett and Kat's support. Their energy made me realize that I was already starting to operate in the world differently. I'd been so worried about slipping into old patterns and closing myself off since leaving Mac. I had made new friends—friends who were starting to feel like family.

That happy thought spurred me on to do a walk-through of the tasting room to make sure everything was in tip-top shape. When we opened a few hours later, a couple of regulars strolled in, followed shortly by Kevin and Jenny and Mel and Swagger, who, like this morning, were still trying to keep their distance from Kevin. They had opted for the only open two-person table, which happened to be next to Kevin and Jenny. Had they finally had enough?

I plastered on my best server face as I waited on him.

"Might as well bring us a bunch of pitchers," Kevin commanded. "We saw that small-town cop upstairs, and she said we aren't going to be able to leave until tonight at the earliest."

"We don't serve pitchers." I didn't add that multiple pitchers would be way too many beers for the two of them.

"Who doesn't sell pitchers? Isn't this a brewery?" Kevin made his point by speaking at a volume typically reserved for football stadiums. Everyone in the tasting room turned to stare. "If we're stuck here, we might has well have some beer, am I right?" He looked to Jenny for confirmation.

"I'm happy to get you each a pint or a tasting tray, but we don't serve pitchers." I considered giving him a brief lesson in the art of serving a craft beer. Pitchers hold four pints and go flat and warm quickly. We had perfected our technique for pouring lovely layered pints at Nitro. The "pitcher culture" was dead in my opinion. In the '80s and '90s, many pizzerias and pubs would serve pitchers of mass-produced beer for a group of friends to share, but it was a rarity to see microbreweries serving their ales in pitchers.

"Fine, we'll each take two pints, right, babe?" He slung his arm around Jenny's shoulder.

She beamed. "Right."

"I can't serve you more than one pint at a time." Was he trying to be difficult?

"This place is such a hellhole." Kevin pounded his fist on the table.

"You're welcome to go find another spot," I offered. I wasn't going to put up with his drama, and he was starting to cause a scene, and Kevin was going to be out of luck. All of the other tables had filled in.

"Kev, chill. We'll get some beers and hang out." Jenny tried to mollify him.

Mel and Swagger shared a look of embarrassment, but they didn't say a word.

"Fine, just get us some beers," he sneered.

I had reached my limit. I narrowed my eyes at him. "I'm not going to 'just go get you beers.' We've gone out of our way to accommodate you and your friends, and I won't stand to be treated like this, nor am I going to allow you to disrupt our other customers. If you want to place an order politely, feel free. Otherwise, there's the door." I pointed to the front.

Kevin must not have been used to people pushing back. He hung his head. "Sorry. Can we have a round, please?"

His tone was less than sincere. I'd take his lackluster apology as a small miracle.

Mel gave me a soft clap from their nearby table, and Swagger sniggered. "Can I get you anything?" I turned my attention to them.

"A pint of IPA and one of stout would be lovely. Thank you so much." Mel's tone was thick with kindness. I wanted to believe it was sincere, but I suspected the show was as much for Kevin as it was for me.

As I headed for the bar, Jenny followed and tugged on the sleeve of my sweater. "Hey, I'm sorry about him. He's stressed about work, that's all. It's not fair to take it out on you, or any of us, but I know he's freaking that he's going to miss tomorrow's meeting."

I stopped before we reached the bar, and held her wrist. "Listen, you seem like a nice young woman. I'd like to offer you some advice. Kevin is who he is at his core. He's not going to change. You're not going to change him."

She sputtered. "I'm not trying to change him."

"You're not?" I raised my eyebrows.

"Well, I mean, I just think he has much more potential than he shows. He can be really sweet when we're alone. I think he needs me to soften him up, you know?"

I did know. She was a lost cause. "It might be hard to see this now, but trust me, you deserve better."

"You can't see what I see in him."

"Look, I barely know any of you, but I've worked in a position of service my entire life, and in my experience, the Kevins of the world don't change. I'm sorry."

She fought back tears. "You think he did it, too, don't you?"

"Did what?" I knew exactly what she was referencing, but I wanted to hear it from her.

"Killed Liv. Everyone thinks he did it." She fiddled with the fake cubic zirconia ring on her index finger. Her manicured nails were chipped and cracked. I wondered if biting her nails was a bad habit or if it was due to stress.

"Everyone?"

"Yeah." She traced a circle with her boot on the cement floor. "It's my fault. I shouldn't have ever said anything about Kev sneaking out that night."

"What?"

She was distracted by her emotions. I could tell that she needed to say this aloud, versus actually being heard. "Kev was stressed and needed to vape. It calms him down, you know. But he snuck outside to do it. That's one of the ways he's thoughtful. He was worried about my health. He knows vaping irritates my throat, so in such a super thoughtful way, he went outside in the cold to vape instead of vaping in our room."

"Uh-huh." Real thoughtful. Also, we have very clear signage throughout the pub, brewery, and guest rooms that smoking of any kind is strictly prohibited.

"He was gone for a long time, though. I waited up because I thought he'd have a quick vape."

"When was this?"

My question seemed to tug her into the present. She gave her head a slight shake. "I don't know. Maybe one or one thirty. I must have fallen asleep, because the next thing I remember, I heard him come back into our room. He was cold from being outside in the snow and jumped into the shower. That's all. The next morning, when she was dead, he asked me not to say anything. He knew it would look bad that he'd been outside. I agreed. But then I accidentally said something to Mel and Swagger. They both lost it. Even Swag, Kev's best friend. They're not even talking to him today. They said I have to tell the police."

"You do."

"But why? I don't want Kev to get into trouble because

of me. He's going to know it's me. I'm the only person who saw him that night. It wasn't a big deal. He was soaking wet from being outside in the snow, so I went to get him a bunch of fresh towels. I didn't want to wake anyone up. That's all. If I tell the police and they question Kev, it will be the end of our relationship."

"Maybe it's time to evaluate that relationship," I said as gently as I could. "If your relationship can't weather you informing the police about an important detail in a murder case, what kind of relationship do you have to begin with?"

She sighed. Tears dripped from her eyes. "I know, I know. That's true. If only this was a few weeks from now. This weekend has been so good for me and Kev. We've been closer than ever, and I think he's finally starting to realize that we belong together. I don't want to betray his trust."

"Here's the thing, Jenny. If he really has nothing to hide, if the reason he wasn't in his room the night that Liv was killed was because he stepped outside to vape, then he won't have any reason to be upset with you."

"I guess." She kicked the floor.

"You should go talk to Chief Meyers now. If Mel or Swagger talks to her first, you might be putting yourself into jeopardy. She could think that you're helping Kevin cover up his whereabouts. Providing a false alibi. This is serious. A woman is dead. Are you prepared to go to jail for him?"

"I never thought about that."

"There's something else you should consider, Jenny. He could be lying to you. What if going outside to vape was a cover for killing Liv? You could be in danger. You need to go talk to the police right now."

"Okay." She didn't move.

My thoughts flashed to Liv's damaged car. Again, I wondered what Jenny might have done to impress Kevin. "Is there more you're not saying?"

"No, no, why?" Her voice cracked.

"The car. You're sure you weren't involved in vandalizing the car? The police found the paint and dirty towels in our back alleyway."

She tugged her fake ring on and off her finger. "They did?"

"Yes." I studied her reaction. "If you know more and you're not saying anything to protect Kevin, you could be making things very bad for yourself. It's imperative that you tell Chief Meyers everything you know."

"Okay."

"Good. Let me point you in the right direction." I ducked behind the bar to give Garrett Kevin's drink order. "I'm taking Jenny to the police station. Be back shortly."

He gave me a serious nod.

I pushed Jenny out the door before she had a change of heart or before Kevin spotted us. Fortunately his face was glowing from the blue light of his phone as we left. Not only did I want Jenny to tell the chief everything she'd told me, but I wanted her as far away from Kevin as possible. If he was the killer, what would stop him from doing it again?

CHAPTER

FIFTEEN

I ESCORTED JENNY TO CHIEF Meyers's office. The wooden hand-carved POLIZEI sign had an inch of snow resting on the top, making it resemble a movie set. While the entrance to the village police station might have been charming, the façade immediately fell away once we stepped inside. An old oak countertop, circa 1980, served as a greeting station. There were a handful of desks and a small holding area. A police officer typed away on a computer attached to a bulky monitor that could have been the same age as the desk.

"Can I help you?"

"Is Chief Meyers around?" I asked, peering over the officer to see into the open area behind him.

"She stepped out for a minute. She should be back in five. Can I help you, or do you want to wait?" He nodded to a threadbare green couch.

"It's about the murder investigation, so we'll wait." I pulled

Jenny over to the couch and poured her a cup of water from the water cooler.

"I think this is a sign. The chief isn't here. I should go." She chomped on her pinky finger like it was a juicy brat. "I should go back to Kev before he figures out what I'm doing."

"Why would he figure out what you're doing?" I tried to exude calmness for her.

"Probably someone will tell him, or he'll suspect it." Her voice had a whiny tone. "I told him I was going to help you with the beers and then I just disappeared. He's not an idiot."

I begged to differ with her on that assessment, but I kept my mouth shut.

"Jenny, this is the right thing to do. You know that, at your core." I placed my hand on her knee.

She squished the paper cup and splashed water on her jeans.

Chief Meyers burst through the door. Her fur-lined hood was coated in snow. She stomped her boots on the mat before tromping inside.

Thank goodness. I wasn't sure I could have convinced Jenny to hang out much longer.

"Sloan." The chief acknowledged me with a two-finger salute.

I stood up. "Jenny shared some information that might be pertinent to your investigation, so we thought it would be best to come find you right away."

"Excellent. Follow me." The chief waved Jenny toward the back.

Jenny didn't budge from the couch.

"Do you want to tell me right here?" Chief Meyers shook snow from her coat and folded her arms across her chest.

"No." Jenny peered out the window. "Kev might come by and see me talking to you."

"All the more reason to talk in private." The chief lifted the hinge on the countertop and waited for Jenny to follow her. Jenny gave me a look of trepidation.

"I'll wait." I sat down again and leafed through a tourist brochure that touted the abundance of winter offerings from cross-country skiing on Nordic trails to downhill skiing and snowboarding at Stevens Pass and Mission Ridge, sleigh rides, dogsledding, and moonlit snowshoeing tours. There was never a reason to stay cooped up inside during the colder months. That was only scratching the surface; indoor options abounded as well, including a rotation of live music almost every night of the week at a variety of restaurants and pubs in town, a nutcracker hunt, wine tasting, theater performances, and art shows.

Was I putting Jenny in danger by encouraging her to talk to the police? I thought about it for a moment. Chief Meyers was astute. If Kevin was a suspect in Lily's murder, and if this information led to his arrest or another round of questioning, the chief would take Jenny's safety into account. I also wasn't convinced that Jenny hadn't been involved in vandalizing Lily's car. Every time I had mentioned the damage, her response had been less than convincing. Jenny knew more than she was saying, that much I was sure of.

She emerged about a half hour later. Her cheeks were streaked with tears. Her skin ashen.

"How did it go?" I asked.

"Fine." Jenny brushed her wrist under her nose and sniffled.

Chief Meyers hadn't come up front with her. "Are you free to go? Did the chief say anything about Kevin?"

Jenny sniffed again. "No. She said not to say anything. They're going to question him again, but she told me to act normal." She yanked the glittery ring off her finger and clutched it in one hand.

"Can you do that?" I trusted the chief's tactics, but Jenny was a mess.

She chewed her pinky. "I think so."

"Sloan," Chief Meyers called from her desk. "Can I have a quick word?" Her coat was propped on the back of a faded rust-colored chair. Melting snow pooled on the floor.

"I'm going to head back to the pub," Jenny said with a false sense of confidence. "I'll tell Kev that I wasn't feeling well and needed a quick walk. He knew that I was a little hungover this morning, I think he'll believe me."

"Okay. Be careful," I cautioned.

She wiped her nose and left. I walked to the back of the dated police station. There were three scratched oak desks, each with an ancient computer on it. Fluorescent lights hummed overhead. The main police headquarters were located outside of the village. This office was mainly used as a holding spot for tourists who imbibed too much during one of the many festivals.

"Well, what do you think?" I asked Chief Meyers, who was finishing typing notes into her computer.

"It's troubling." She didn't elaborate.

"Is it safe for Jenny to be around him right now?"

She scowled. "Sloan, give me more credit than that. I wouldn't feed her to the wolves."

"I know."

"I could use your help, though." Watching her type was painful. She used her two index fingers to bang out each word. I wanted to jump in and offer my transcription services.

"You bet. Name it."

"Could you tell Mel and Swagger—who in their right mind names their kid Swagger?" She made a grunting sound.

I shrugged. "Not me."

"Anyway, could you ask them both to stop by this afternoon? I don't want to raise suspicion around Kevin. I'd like him to feel comfortable, if you know what I mean." Her lip turned up.

Did that mean she considered him the top suspect?

"If you can casually ask them to come over to the station, one at a time, then I don't need to stir things up at the bar or send one of my officers over."

"Will do."

"Excellent. And keep an eye on Kevin, would you?" She dismissed me by returning to pounding on the keyboard.

"Sure." I left the station feeling more confused. Obviously, Meyers had to have Kevin on her suspect list, but she couldn't be convinced if she was letting him walk around the village free. Or maybe she didn't have enough evidence to arrest him yet. Either way, the thought of keeping an eye on a potential murderer was less than appealing.

At Nitro the vibe was subdued. Sunday afternoons often

had a lazy quality. Guests sipped pints slowly, staving off the return of the workweek with a golden amber or hazy IPA. Kevin and Jenny were both on their phones. There was no outward indication that Kevin thought anything was amiss. I stopped at Mel and Swagger's table.

"How is everything this afternoon?" I noted their empty beer glasses. "Can I get you a refresher?"

"No thanks," Mel replied. "We are going to close our tab and walk around the village. I need a break." She glared at Kevin and Jenny.

I leaned over to pick up their glasses. "On that note, Chief Meyers asked me to have you both stop by the police station. She has a couple follow-up questions for you."

"Oh, really." Mel kept her gaze on Kevin. "No problem. We'll do that right now, won't we, Swag?"

"Yeah, okay." Swagger reached into his wallet and handed me a platinum credit card.

"I'll go get your bill settled," I said stacking their glasses. They weren't making any attempts to mask their disgust with Kevin. The situation was becoming more bizarre by the moment. I took the glasses to the bar and ran Swagger's credit card. Did they know more that they weren't saying?

"You're all set." I returned with Swagger's receipt. Part of me wanted to press them on why they'd had such a change of heart about Kevin, but I knew that Chief Meyers wanted to talk to them ASAP. If whatever they told her would lead us closer to Kevin's arrest, that would be fine by me.

As they stood up to leave, Taylor came over to the table. "Is this free?"

Mel put on her coat. "Yeah, go for it."

"Let me wipe it down for you," I said to Taylor. "Can I get you a beer while I'm at it?"

"How about a pint of your red?"

"You got it." I grabbed a wet towel and asked Kat to pour a pint of red.

Taylor waited for me to clean the table before he sat down. He shrugged off his parka and thick work gloves. Kat delivered his frothy pint. "Need anything else?"

"This is fine." He looked around the tasting room. "No police action today?"

"Nope." Had Chief Meyers talked to him about Liv's true identity? I wanted to ask him, yet didn't want to overstep my role. I would feel terrible if I interfered with the investigation.

"Did you hear about Lily?" He ran a finger along the rim of the pint glass. His fingernails were black with grease.

Since he brought it up, I figured it was fair game to see what he might have to say. "No, what?" I wasn't sure if the slip of the name was intentional or not.

"That's her real name," Taylor continued. "Remember that first night when I said that she looked familiar?"

I nodded. He hadn't mentioned anything to me about recognizing Lily until later. But if memory served me correctly, he had definitely mentioned that she looked like someone he knew.

"That's why. I went to high school with her. I found my old yearbook in a plastic tub in the garage. She looked totally different then. Her hair, her style, her name, but her face was the same. I wish I had realized it before she was killed."

Another odd coincidence.

"Did you know her in high school?"

"Nah, not really. We hung out a few times, but we had different groups of friends. You know how that goes." His fingers left grease marks on the rim of the glass. Motor oil would definitely throw off the flavor profile of our hoppy red ale.

"Do you think she recognized you?"

He took a big drink of the beer. "I don't know. Why do you ask?"

"She was acting so strange the night she was killed. She kept saying very cryptic things."

"Like what?"

I wasn't going to share everything Lily had said to me, especially now that he was admitting he had known her. "I don't remember the specifics. It's more that she seemed scared."

"What's there to be scared of in Leavenworth? Lederhosen?" He smirked and gulped the beer. "Did she say something about me?"

Was it my imagination, or were the veins in his forehead bulging?

"If she said something about me, I deserve to know." He swirled his pint glass like it was a fine wine. "Whatever she said was a lie. That's what I remember about her—she lied."

CHAPTER

SIXTEEN

"WHAT DID LILY LIE ABOUT?" I asked Taylor.

"Never mind. Forget I said anything." He chugged the rest of his beer, reached for his well-worn leather wallet, and slapped a ten-dollar bill on the table. "I'm late. Thanks for the pint."

With that, he took off. The subject of Lily had hit a nerve. He was the one who had brought up the topic, though.

I felt defeated. Every new detail that surfaced sent me in a different direction.

"Why the long face?" Garrett asked.

"I'm starting to feel like I'm crazy," I admitted, filling him on the latest developments.

"You should go take a break. Or better yet, take the rest of the day off. It's slow. It's Sunday. You've been working all weekend, and you were up late writing the offer with April, and your friend Sally is coming from Seattle tonight, right? Why don't you take off?"

"Thanks." I wasn't sure that spending the rest of the afternoon by myself would be helpful. Alex wouldn't be home again. Mac had asked last night if it was okay to take Alex to dinner at his parents' house and spend the night with him. I couldn't refuse. Alex adored Otto and Ursula, and they him. I hadn't uttered a word about the strain between us right now. I didn't want to tear him away from his grandparents. Not unless there ended up being a reason to sever ties. Plus, if I was being honest, it was going to be much easier to talk to Sally without anyone else around.

"That really means no thanks, doesn't it?" Garrett scowled. "As in emphasis on the *no*."

I tried to laugh. "And to think I pride myself on my poker face."

"Poker face, you wish." Garrett winked.

"Hey, I've worked for years on this." I relaxed my jaw and allowed my eyes to focus on a photo on the far wall in an attempt to make my face as stoic as possible.

"Not bad." Garrett clapped. "I still think you should take a break."

"I feel like taking breaks is the only thing I've done for the past few days. Taking breaks to ask questions and follow up on hunches. I'm obsessed, aren't I?" I fought back a wave of emotion.

"No. Everyone is distracted by the investigation. As we should be." His face reflected his concern. "If we weren't upset by the fact that one of our guests was brutally murdered, I would be worried. Really worried."

"Fair point, but honestly sitting around by myself is only going to make things worse."

"Then go for it."

"Go for what?"

"Dive into the investigation. You said that Taylor told you he went to high school with Lily. Why don't you go to the library and do some research? As you know, the internet is spotty in here. Plus it will be good for you to get away from the pub for a while. You can probably find out a ton of information. They're so young that their entire yearbook might be online."

"That's a good idea."

He brushed off his shoulders. "I've been known to have a good idea every now and then."

"You're sure you don't mind?"

"Sloan, not only do I not mind, but if you don't get out of here, I'm going to fire you."

"That sounds like an empty threat."

"True. But I'm serious. Go. Take the rest of the afternoon. And I don't want to see your face around here tomorrow, either."

"Sally's only here until early afternoon anyway. You know how crazy the train schedule is." Leavenworth had one daily arrival from Seattle and one daily departure to Seattle. The fact that we had train service at all made locals happy.

"Okay, I'll see you tomorrow afternoon, emphasis on *afternoon*. Or maybe even not at all. Kat and I will cover breakfast. I'm thinking cold cereal and bagels, which means I don't want to see you here before the crack of dawn. Got it?" Garrett pursed his lips and pointed to the door.

The library was less than a quarter-mile walk from Nitro, just across Highway 2. White stucco with a pink and gold

175

German mural and carved archway formed the first floor. The second story was constructed from slatted wood, stained chocolate brown with multiple balconies. Icicle lights hung from the sloped roofline. The library and city hall shared the building. The entrance to city hall was to the left so I turned right to enter the library and made my way to a bank of public computers near the circulation desk.

Before I started my search, I jotted down everything I knew about Lily. Her name, her approximate age, the fact that she had lived in Spokane, and that I learned from Taylor that they went to high school together. I intended to plug his information in as well. I opened a browser and typed in *Lily Palmer*.

The first results returned were for Lily Palmers on the East Coast. I had to scroll for a while before I found a Lily Palmer in Washington State. It was worth the effort. I couldn't believe the number of articles that popped up from ten years ago.

The headline read TRAGEDY AT FISH LAKE, CHENEY, WASHINGTON.

I read on:

> The body of high school senior Chloe Downey was recovered from Fish Lake yesterday morning, putting an end to the weeklong search. Downey's friend, Lily Palmer, reported her missing on April 5. Police and volunteers have been searching Spokane neighborhoods and nearby outdoor sites without any leads. Toxicology reports show Downey's blood-alcohol level at .08%. Foul play is not suspected. The family asks for privacy at this time and for donations to be made to Sacred Heart Children's Hospital.

I exhaled and leaned away from the computer. How horrifically sad. My thoughts immediately went to Alex. I couldn't fathom what I would do if something happened to him, or imagine him losing a friend so young.

Poor Lily. I wondered if she and Chloe had been close. And had Taylor known Chloe, too? From the tone of the first article, it sounded as if her death had impacted the entire town. Much like it would here in the village if something like that occurred.

I read on and found a number of articles about Chloe's drowning. There were even a few videos. One was filmed at the high school on the day after the police recovered her body. Guidance counselors were on hand to support students in their grief, and one of the students they interviewed was a sobbing Lily.

I recognized her immediately, despite her change in appearance. She had the same doe-like eyes and almost skittish look.

"How are you and your classmates taking the news?" a reporter asked her, shoving a microphone in her face.

Lily tried to speak through her tears but couldn't get any words out.

A young man came up behind her. "Chloe and Lily were best friends. Leave her alone. She doesn't want to talk right now."

I squinted and scooted my chair closer to the screen. Unless my eyes were tricking me, the guy who rescued Lily was none other than Taylor.

I clicked PAUSE on the video. The library was empty aside from a mom reading to her two children in the nook with floor pillows and Legos tucked between the shelves of books for young readers. I was grateful for the solitude. This felt important.

Taylor had lied. He definitely knew Lily, and he must have known her well in high school to have jumped in and saved her from the press. He had made it sound like he could barely remember who she was. This video was proof otherwise.

Sure, I knew that for many people (myself included), high school was nothing more than a blip on the radar. I doubted I would be able to recognize the majority of my classmates today, but the situation with Taylor was different. He couldn't have graduated from high school more than ten years ago, so his memories would likely be much fresher, and there was the glaring issue of a classmate's death. You didn't forget memories like that. Maybe you forgot the name of the captain of the football team or your biology teacher, but you didn't forget a tragic death.

Impossible.

Those early memories of our own mortality become etched in our memory. The question was what was his motivation for lying?

Could it have to do with Lily's murder, or had seeing her triggered painful memories? Maybe it had been too much for him. Maybe he had tried to bury memories of the past and Lily brought them to the surface again.

I read through a few more articles before printing three of the most thorough and logging off the library computer.

Before I went to pick Sally up at the train station, I wanted to swing by the police station and let Chief Meyers know about Chloe's death. My guess was that she was already aware. Her team of officers was likely already looking into the connection, but I wouldn't be able to sleep until I off-loaded the information to the professionals.

CHAPTER

SEVENTEEN

179

CHAPTER

SEVENTEEN

AT THE POLICE STATION, I left a note for Chief Meyers. The officer on desk duty told me that she had gone to Spokane to follow a lead.

"Does it have anything to do with the death of a high school girl about ten years ago?" I asked.

"I'm not at liberty to disclose any details related to the investigation." The officer's canned response didn't surprise me. Nor did I blame him.

"I understand. Can you pass this along to the chief when she returns?"

"With pleasure." He placed the articles I had printed in the chief's in-box.

Nervous energy pulsed through my body, making my fingertips tingle and my throat scratchy as I drove to Icicle Station. I could hear the train's distant whistle before it appeared on the snowy tracks. My heart thumped as I hurried to wait for Sally to disembark. The station is actually just a long platform with a couple of benches and a row of antique streetlamps. A small cedar cabin served as a heated waiting area for passengers until the shuttle to town arrived. The station is located on the outskirts of the village. It's about a mile walk to the shops, which makes for a nice stroll in the summer when the weather is warm and the light lingers, but in the winter the train station feels quite remote.

April had been instrumental in convincing Amtrak to make the trek from Seattle to our village once a day. In the early 2000s, she'd been part of the mayor's campaign to bring rail service to Leavenworth in an attempt to bolster tourism. The daily train had been a huge success. It ran at full capacity during busy festival weekends, and many travelers took the train for a visually stunning day trip through the Cascade Mountains and Snoqualmie Pass.

Since it was the start of the week, the train wasn't crowded. I spotted Sally before she saw me. She stepped down from the train wearing a practical knee-length slate gray jacket, jeans, and sturdy boots. Her thick-framed black glasses were propped at the edge of her nose as she surveyed the platform.

"Sally!" I called, waving to her.

Her face broke into a wide smile. We greeted each other with a long embrace.

"How was the ride?" I asked, reaching to carry her suitcase.

"Absolutely gorgeous." Her wiry gray curls were cut short, accentuating her heart-shaped face. "Talk about scenery. I had a window seat and spent the entire ride drinking in the lush mountain landscapes. I counted at least a dozen frozen waterfalls and even saw a herd of winter elk, which I know is rare."

"How wonderful." I made way for a group of skiers unloading their skis, poles, and gear. "Are you hungry? We can go get a bite to eat or just head to my house."

"I ate on the train." Sally sounded almost sheepish. "It was such a luxurious experience. I ordered a glass of wine and a surprisingly good plate of chicken piccata. Talk about dinner with a view."

"That sounds divine." I lifted her suitcase and headed for the car. "I hope you saved room for dessert. I made my famous German chocolate cake."

"Lucky me." She squeezed my hand. "We have little time and much to discuss. A slice of your cake sounds like heaven. Especially in light of the situation."

The fifteen-minute drive to the farmhouse felt like an eternity as we kept the conversation to other topics. I filled her in on what happened to Lily and lamented about our first foray into guests at Nitro. I knew that there was no point in diving into what Sally had to tell me about Otto and Ursula until we were home and settled, but it took every ounce of control not to press the gas pedal to the floor.

When we finally arrived, I carried Sally's bag inside, got her situated in the guest room, and lit a fire in the kitchen. Soon the woody scent of crackling logs filled the space. While Sally unpacked, I steeped cinnamon tea and cut generous slices of the German chocolate cake I had made earlier.

"Sloan, this is so cozy," Sally said, returning to the kitchen. She held a stack of file folders in her arms. I couldn't take my eyes off of them. It was like I was staring at a bomb. Whatever was inside those files would likely alter the course of my life.

I motioned for her to sit and pulled up a chair next to her.

She pushed her glasses up to the bridge of her nose. "It's just us tonight?"

"Yeah." I nodded. "Alex is staying at Mac's tonight."

Sally sighed. "Excellent." She reached for my hand and pressed a packet of tissues into it. "Tools of the trade." She winked, but her eyes held a deep sadness.

I remembered Sally's office from my childhood visits. Despite its sterile white walls, Sally had tried to make it as warm and welcoming as possible, with bookcases packed with books and art supplies, a plush rug with a collection of stuffed animals, and a tranquil desktop water fountain. There had always been classical music playing and boxes of tissues strategically positioned throughout her office. I used to pride myself on the fact that I never needed tissues. From a very early age, I had mastered the art of stuffing my feelings deep down inside myself. If I had allowed the tears to flow, they may have drowned me.

Sally patted my hand. "To be honest with you, the more I uncover, the more confused I've become." She paused to take a sip of her tea. "I think it will be best if we start where we left off."

"Okay." I stabbed my cake, but didn't take a bite.

"As you know, once I started looking into your files, I realized that my intuition had been correct all along. I'm still kicking myself every day. I should have listened to my gut feeling. I followed up with every foster family when move requests came through, and none of them initiated a move, Sloan. Not one. They all reported that you were polite and respectful. Quiet, sure. Withdrawn, yes, but easy and considerate. None of them asked for you to be placed in different care."

"Sally, we've been over this. It wasn't your fault." I felt terrible that Sally was beating herself up for something that she'd had no control over. It wasn't until we reopened my case files that she learned that her supervisors had initiated my many moves from foster home to foster home. She believed they had done it intentionally to try and erode my trust in her. I had no idea why I'd been moved so many times, but I certainly didn't blame her.

She sighed. "Thank you, Sloan. I appreciate your kindness, but I was the adult. I was responsible for your care and well-being. This long lens into the past isn't looking kindly on some of my choices. I wish I had been more assertive. I could have done more. I could have stood up to them. I could have said, 'No, you are not moving her again.'"

"Don't do this." I placed my hand over hers. "It's okay, and it's in the past. I'm so grateful for everything you did for me. And, I'm even more grateful that you're here with me now. Let's focus on moving forward."

She squeezed my hand and blinked back tears. "Okay."

A log slipped from the stack, causing us both to startle. I used the poker to shift the log back into place and returned to the table.

"Obviously someone higher up doesn't want us to access your information." She folded her hands together. A gesture that I was familiar with. It made me wonder if she was trying to summon the strength to continue. "When I discovered that my notes and your files were missing, you know how paranoid I became. I haven't known who to trust, because I have no idea who within the agency was responsible for this. And then there's the issue of time. So much time has passed that my colleagues have scattered. There are only a few people left. After our last meeting, I started working underground. I've met with five of my former colleagues and until recently kept hitting dead ends."

My heart flopped.

"Then I tracked down an old friend. His name is Jim. He remembered your case. For the most part, we kept our case-loads separate. Sometimes we would consult with one another on difficult placements or kids we had flagged as high risk for involvement with the juvenile justice system. I had spoken to Jim about you a number of times. He had been a sounding board for me. It's taken me this long to find him. He retired three years ago and moved to Florida."

"How did you find him?"

She took a small bite of the cake. "A friend of a friend. I didn't want to go through the agency, because I don't want anyone to know that we're looking into your past." She ate another bite. "This is delicious, by the way."

"Thanks." I tried to smile.

Sally moved the cake plate to the side. "Jim and I had a long phone call about a week ago. His memories are as fuzzy as mine, but he has a good friend who works in Oregon. His friend has been advocating for updating interagency sharing methods between states. There's a big push federally for better sharing tools."

"Okay." I wondered where she was going with this.

"Jim's friend saved examples of case file sharing. Our old interface was archaic. If a case worker in another state needed information on a child on our caseload, we would have to print and fax documents. You get the drift."

"Right." I picked up my tea. It had begun to cool, so I set it down again.

"Here's where it gets interesting. Jim's friend had been gathering examples to showcase how desperately the system needs modernization. When Jim reached out to him, he went through his archives and found photocopies of some of your old files."

Thank goodness I had set my tea down. If it were still in my hand, I would have spilled it all over the floor.

"There's not a lot of information here." Sally strummed her fingers on the file folders. "Everything else has been deleted from the system. This happens to be notes from when Jim asked one of our counterparts in Oregon for help. I had completely forgotten about it, but when I went to Jim with concerns about how many times I was being asked to move you, he told me that he would send your notes over to a friend in Oregon and see if there was precedent for the multiple moves. Nothing ever came of it. These notes have probably been sitting in a dusty box for years. If it wasn't for the fact that Jim's friend is involved in this project to update the system, they likely would have sat for another twenty years or have been shredded."

I wanted to reach over and yank the files from Sally's hands.

"Most of what's in here are my intake notes, reports from

our sessions, in-home visits, et cetera. It's a condensed version, but it's something."

She handed me the first file folder. "Go ahead and take a look through."

"But what about Ursula and Otto?" I asked.

"Read through that first." She pressed her hand on the second file folder. "We'll get to them next."

I leafed through the old photocopies of Sally's notes. Her cursive handwriting was meticulous. The notes had been written professionally, yet I picked up her love and attachment to me through her descriptions of my behavior and some of the leading questions she asked a variety of my foster parents.

Sally nibbled on her cake while I read the fading pages. As she mentioned, there were only ten pages of notes, and most of the information she had already shared with me.

"It seems straightforward," I said, closing the file folder.

"Agreed." She dabbed her chin with a napkin. "It's not earth-shattering, but it is nice to have tangible proof of my memories and a record that you did indeed exist in the eyes of the state."

I hadn't even thought of that point.

She let out a long sigh. "But Jim's friend found more. He found this." Again she pressed her hand firmly on the folder. "This was not anything I had ever seen in your case files. I don't know where it came from or why I wouldn't have been looped in on this information, since I was your social worker. This must have come in before I was assigned to you." She slid the folder to me. "Take a look."

I swallowed hard. "I'm nervous, Sally."

"I know." She didn't try to save me from my emotions. Instead she held a firm, calming stance and waited for me to proceed.

I lifted the top of the folder. Otto and Ursula's photos reflected back at me with the word DANGEROUS stamped in red.

CHAPTER

EIGHTEEN

I WANTED TO FLIP THE file closed. "What is this?" I asked Sally, not able to contain the panic in my voice.

"Read on."

The cheery farmhouse kitchen felt like it was closing in on me. The normally pleasant scent of the wood-burning fire made my throat constrict as if the smoke were sucking the air from my lungs.

"No, this can't be. Not the Krauses."

Sally's glasses had slipped down her nose. "I know this is difficult, Sloan." She sat with perfect posture, holding the space for me.

"I can't believe the Krauses are dangerous."

"Are you ready to read on?" She nodded to the file.

I took three deep breaths and nodded. On the first page in the folder were grainy pictures of Otto and Ursula. I would have to guess that the pictures were taken in the early seventies. They looked to be in their late thirties or maybe just pushing forty. I paused to look at the word DANGEROUS stamped across their faces before I turned the page.

The next page had smaller headshots of both of them. Only not with the names that I had known them as. Under Otto's picture was the name Friedrich, and under Ursula's was the name Helga.

I thought I might throw up.

How could this be?

I wanted to run. I wanted drive to Mac's place, pick up Alex, and get as far away as possible from Leavenworth and the family I thought I had created.

"Sloan, are you okay?" Sally's gentle tone broke through the welling anxiety pulsing through my body.

"No." I clutched the file folder. "I can't believe this. It doesn't make sense."

"I know. If you're up for it, keep reading and then we'll work together to figure out what to do next."

"Okay." My fingers trembled as I read the text beneath the Krauses' photos. Most of the notes had been written in shorthand. I assumed they were meant for internal use amongst—who? The police? FBI? CIA?

> Friedrich and Helga vom Rath are suspected Nazi sympathizers. The couple, along with their two young sons, fled Germany after the attempted arrest of Friedrich's uncle Ernst vom Rath—wanted for Nazi war crimes. Ernst is personally responsible for the deaths of thousands of concentration camp prisoners. It's suspected that he is living in the US under a different alias and may try to communicate with Friedrich and Helga. Keep them on the watch list, as they are likely intending to harbor their family member as well as find ways

to funnel money to him. Federal warrant in place for wiretap. Agents will be monitoring activity.

"No. No way. Otto and Ursula Nazi sympathizers? Otto's uncle a full-fledged Nazi?" My voice sounded screechy. "I can't believe it, Sally. They are the sweetest people you'll ever meet. They've built such a community here in Leavenworth and are welcoming to everyone they meet. Everyone—every race, religion, sexual orientation—they can't be Nazis."

"I understand your confusion, Sloan." Her voice was steady and calm. "There's a bit more, keep reading."

I rubbed my forehead, wishing I could rub away what I had read. How could the Krauses have any affiliation with Nazis? They were the most loving and kind people I knew.

I turned to the next and final page. It was a document marked as classified. Most of the information on the page had been redacted. Between the sections that had been blacked out, there was a picture of me. An agent whose name was also unreadable had placed me in protection—protection in the form of state care. There were a few specific notes about making sure I wasn't in any home for more than twelve months and that the agent placing me in protective services would oversee my care.

"Sally, I don't understand." I dropped the file on the table.

"Neither do I, Sloan." Sally removed her glasses. "I have a theory, though. Would you like to hear it?"

I picked up my tea, which had gone completely cold. I took a big slug anyway. "Of course."

She appraised me for a minute. "You're sure you're okay, or should we sleep on this and start fresh in the morning?"

"No, I'm fine. I want to hear your thoughts. I refuse to believe that Otto and Ursula are Nazi sympathizers. It doesn't make sense. They would have been kids during the war. How can they be involved?"

"Family connections run deep. I've learned that over my years in social work. It's hard to break systemic family patterns. Yes, Otto and Ursula would have been children during the war, but not Ernst. If he fled to the US, they could have been helping him. That might have been what brought them here." Her lips turned down. "I'm not sure you're going to like my theory. It's sketchy and just a theory. I'm working on finding more proof. In fact, when I return to Seattle tomorrow, I have an appointment with an FBI agent. I'm hoping he can shed some additional light on this case, but here's what I've pieced together so far. Let's start from what Ursula told you. She claims that Marianne—who we're assuming is your mom—came to Leavenworth with Forest under the guise of trying to swindle the Krauses out of Der Keller. Do I have that right so far?"

I nodded.

"The Krauses realized that Forest's offer was fake, and the FBI got involved. Marianne was spooked and took off with her young daughter before the authorities arrived. According to Ursula, the FBI had been looking for Forest because he had been committing similar fraud for many years, correct?"

"Yep. That's exactly what Ursula told me." When Ursula had told me the story, she had been embarrassed that Forest had preyed upon them. That he'd taken advantage of the fact that they were foreigners and that English was their second language. She had confessed that when the FBI asked them not to speak about what had happened so they could continue to build their case against Forest, she had gladly agreed. She and Otto were mortified that they had been so gullible.

Sally scooted her chair closer. "What if that's not the reason Marianne was in Leavenworth?"

"What do you mean?" I glanced at the fireplace. The logs had smoldered into glowing red embers. How long had we been talking? It felt like minutes, but it must have been hours.

"What if Marianne is the agent whose name is redacted on those documents? It can't be a coincidence that someone in the agency placed you in protective care. I think that Otto and Ursula's story about Forest is fake. I think that Marianne and maybe Forest—although I'm not sure what his role is in all of this yet—were in Leavenworth to track Otto and Ursula. Maybe they got a lead that Ernst was going to make contact? Maybe they learned how the Krauses were getting him money. My guess is through Der Keller's distribution channels. Something must have gone wrong to blow their cover, and they fled. I'm guessing whatever went wrong must have put you in danger. That's why Marianne put you in custody. She wasn't abandoning you. She was protecting you."

I felt like I'd been punched in the stomach. "Maybe."

Sally met my eyes. "But you're not convinced?"

"I don't know. Your theory feels like it could be true, but you haven't met Otto and Ursula—or Friedrich and Helga—whatever their names really are. It's hard to explain, but you know how earlier you talked about your intuition and gut feeling about me? The same is true for me with the

Krauses. If you knew them, you would be conflicted, too. There's nothing about them that hints at such a horrendous past. Why would they come to Leavenworth? Why would they spend twenty years building such a beautiful community here?"

"But what if that's been their front?" Sally looked at me, then sighed. "I know. I can only imagine how difficult this must be for you. And you're right, I don't know them like you do, but in some ways Leavenworth is the perfect hiding spot if you want to escape your past. Think about it. You've said that they never talk about their past. That they never talk about their family. That no other family has ever come to visit. If you wanted to hide out, I would say that this is about as remote and as far from Germany as you can get."

She made a compelling argument. As strong as my relationship with Ursula and Otto had been, I knew very little about their past. They spoke of the "motherland" with love and affection, but only as it related to brewing and food. What else did I know about them? I racked my brain for any sliver of information they might have let slip. The only thing I'd ever heard them say was that they came to America to give their boys a better life. Could that mean a better life free of persecution due to their Nazi-sympathizing past or, worse, to help aid and abet a Nazi war criminal?

The thought made me nearly fall off my chair.

"There's one more thing that I've learned," Sally added. "It's about Ernst, Otto's uncle."

I wasn't sure how much more I could take. "What's that?"

"Jim did some searching for me, and according to what he found, it sounds like he might still be alive. According to authorities, he is on the FBI's most wanted list. He's one of the last known Nazis in the United States."

"How old would that make him?"

Sally cleared her throat. "That was my first question, too. I asked Jim the same thing. Apparently the FBI has a list of six of the most wanted Nazi war criminals still living, and his name is on the list. There aren't many left. All of them, including Ernst, are in their mid- to late nineties."

I massaged my temples.

"Sloan, you mentioned on the phone that the Krauses opted to gift you and their sons shares in Der Keller and pull back their involvement. That news is maybe the most unsettling of all. What if they're giving up their connection to the brewery because they're getting ready to run?"

"Run?" I sunk into my chair. "This feels like a bad dream."

"I know." Sally wrapped her hand over mine. "It's a lot to take in. Should we call it a night? I'm sure I said this to you dozens of times over the years, but if I've learned anything, it's that sleep and rest can do wonders for the soul. Why don't you try and get some sleep, and tomorrow we'll start fresh and decide where we go from here."

I wanted to protest, but my brain was on overload. There was no way I could think through next steps with so many questions pounding through my head. "Yeah, okay."

Sally stood. She kissed the top of my head. "Sloan, there's one important thing I want you to know, and that is that you don't have to face this alone. I'm here, and I'll do whatever it takes to support you. Whatever you need."

I fought tears. "Thanks, Sally. That means a lot."

She put our dishes in the sink, wrapped up my slice of

cake, and headed down the hallway. I sat and watched the fire burn itself out. I appreciated Sally's support more than I could ever express, but the truth was that with or without her here, this was something that ultimately I was going to have to face on my own.

In the morning we could make a plan, but I was already formulating my own. I knew what had to be done. It was time for me to face Otto and Ursula. I wanted to give my in-laws the benefit of the doubt. If they had been wrongly accused, I would work tirelessly to clear their name.

But if Sally's theory was correct, that changed everything. I had one responsibility—Alex. If his grandparents were indeed Nazi sympathizers, then I would work even harder to ensure they were brought to justice in whatever way possible. And I would do whatever I could to help the authorities track down Ernst and see that whatever limited time he had left on earth was spent behind bars.

I hoped that my intuition was right, because if it wasn't, the Krause family had no idea what was about to come. I might have lost my childhood because of them. I would not allow them to steal Alex's, too.

I hoped for their sake as much as mine that Sally was wrong, because if the Krauses were really wanted criminals who had been helping harbor a Nazi for these many years, they had no idea of the wrath they were about to unleash.

NINETEEN

SALLY WAS UP BEFORE ME and sipping coffee at the kitchen island when I padded down the hallway the next morning. "Did you sleep?" Her tone was gentle.

"I think so." I poured myself a cup and joined her.

She placed her hand over mine. It was warm from holding her steaming mug. "I didn't sleep much. Sloan, I'm regretting some of our conversation. Maybe I came on too strong. Like I said last night. These are just theories I'm working on. I don't know what the truth of the Krauses' situation is, but I do worry about you, and I promise I will not stop until we have answers."

I squeezed her hand. "It's okay. I can handle it, but the thing is I'm going to have to talk to Otto and Ursula. This is a small town. Alex is their grandson. Technically I'm still married to their son, and I own a piece of Der Keller. It's been terrible trying to avoid them. I can't keep this up. I need to hear their side of this."

"I know." Sally cradled her coffee mug. "I think that's our next play. I think you should talk to them. I just wanted to be sure that you had as much information as I could gather before you spoke to them. I knew that you would need to see the files. This isn't something that I could simply email to you. And if there's a chance that my theory has any truth, we could both be in real danger."

As could Alex, I thought to myself.

"It will be interesting to hear their side of the story. Maybe there's a reasonable explanation." Sally didn't sound convinced. I had the sense she was trying to appease me.

I swallowed hard. "You have no idea how much I'm hoping that's the case. The thought of having to tell Alex that his grandparents have Nazi ties makes me sick to my stomach. He adores them."

"There's no need to involve him yet. I suggest that you have a conversation with Otto and Ursula once you feel ready. I know that you're a master at masking your emotions, but keeping any sort of healthy detachment is going to be a challenge, to say the least."

I bit my bottom lip and nodded.

"It doesn't need to be today. In fact, it shouldn't be today. You need time to process everything we've discussed, but I do think it should be soon. Involving the FBI will likely mean that things will speed up. Jim is committed to helping, too. Do you remember when you were in junior high and dealing with that group of mean girls?"

"How could I forget?" Her words resurfaced memories of petite blond girls who all wore Guess jeans with a little triangle label on the back pocket and roamed around the school's hallways in packs, like wild wolves. Living in foster care meant that I rarely had any fancy clothes, let alone name-brand jeans. It didn't bother me, but there had been a group of popular kids who used to make snide comments in the locker room about my J. C. Penney jeans. When I had mentioned it in one of my sessions with Sally, she had been able to pull deeper issues out of me. It wasn't about the jeans. I didn't care about fashion, but they represented the lack of care and permanence that had been an ongoing theme in my childhood. "I've found that action and creating a plan helps balance the feelings of fear and insecurity that you're experiencing," Sally had advised. "If it's the jeans that matter, we can brainstorm a way to get them for you, whether that's through a donation or perhaps a part-time job. If it's more about the idea of feeling alone, then let's make a plan for that. You've shown a great interest in baking. What about taking an after-school class at the culinary school, or volunteering in the kitchen at the homeless shelter?"

It was Sally who had directed me toward a career in the restaurant business. Something I was forever indebted to her for.

"Let's use that same strategy and work out a plan. I'll meet with the FBI, I'll see what else—if anything—Jim has been able to learn, you sit down with Otto and Ursula, and we'll go from there."

"What about Marianne and Forest?" I asked. "How do we find them?"

"That's the next step." Sally stood to refresh her coffee. "I'm hoping that my new contact at the FBI will be able to guide us."

We polished off the pot of coffee, made another, and lingered over breakfast. Then I took Sally for a stroll through the property. The hop vines were dormant for the season, but the snowy fields and distant mountain ranges made for a scenic view. Before I knew it, it was time to take Sally to the train.

She handed me the files before we took her overnight bag out to the car. "These are for you. I made copies. Do with them what you will. I don't know if you want to use them in your meeting with the Krauses or if you want to show them to Hans or Mac. It's totally up to you."

The weight of the paperwork felt heavy in my hands. I hid the files under my mattress. There was no way I was going to risk Alex finding photos of his grandparents labeled as dangerous.

At the train station later, Sally gave me a giant hug. "Don't forget, we're in this together, Sloan. You're not alone."

"Thank you," I managed to say before tears began to spill. "Really, thank you for everything."

She kissed my cheek. "I'll call you as soon as I'm done with my meeting. You stay safe and go easy on yourself." With that, she walked to the train platform.

I drove to the village in a daze. *Now what?* I asked myself, pulling into a parking space about a block away from Nitro. The temp was starting to dip, and it wouldn't be long until the sun disappeared behind the mountains and the cold sunk in. I still had hours before Alex would be home. I could go into Nitro, but I wasn't ready. I needed a little time to think. Sally was right, having a plan was going to be a critical survival strategy. I was going to have to talk to Otto and Ursula soon, but in the meantime I needed to employ every tool I had learned in years of therapy. The mere thought of sitting across the table from them made my hands clammy.

Having free time on my hands wasn't something I was used to. My world revolved around Alex and brewing. Had that been a coping strategy, too? Had I filled every spare minute with tasks in order to avoid being alone with myself?

I wandered aimlessly until I found myself at Front Street Park, where I stopped and watched a group of young kids bundled up in puffy snowsuits lug bright yellow and red sleds up the snowy hill and screech with delight as they zoomed back down again.

I glanced across the street to the Der Keller compound. It was aglow with golden lights and the leaping flames on the outdoor fire tables. The brewery had been a haven for me. Every time I walked into the dining room with its German flags and banners, pewter beer steins lining the walls, and oompah music playing from speakers overhead, I had felt at home. The familiar scent of grains steeping in the brewery used to waft into the restaurant in the mornings. I loved starting my days surrounded by the warmth of Otto and Ursula's family heirlooms and the rich smells of sauerbraten simmering in Der Keller's massive kitchens. Had the Krause family deceived me? And how had I fallen under their charm?

I sucked in a cold burst of air and walked in the opposite direction. I couldn't stay here, and I wasn't about to go home now.

Keep it together, Sloan.

I willed my emotions to settle and walked toward the cottage. Maybe the sight of my new home would provide some relief.

The short walk led me past the bookstore, the Brat Haus, and the Rheinlander Hotel, where a trio of accordion players serenaded diners on the upstairs deck.

I couldn't believe after so many years I was finally going to live in the village. If I felt like staying late one night and brewing with Garrett, no problem. And if I ran out of milk or eggs, I could walk a block to the store instead of having to get in the car and drive into town.

The lights in the cottage were on as I walked by. The front porch was flanked by two large potted evergreen trees wrapped in wispy golden lights. A soft orange glow came from the antique lamp that hung above the front door. The eight-paned front windows were backlit from inside. I could see through to the opposite side of the house and the back windows that looked out over the miniature golf course.

I'm going to live here, I thought, rubbing my hands together in delight.

As I was about to continue on, a voice stopped me. "Sloan, is that you?"

I looked to my left to see the owner of the cottage standing at the front door. A hot blush burned my cheeks. I felt terrible for snooping.

"Terra, hi, sorry. I didn't mean to stand here like a creeper. I'm just so excited that you accepted my offer."

Since Leavenworth was such a small town, it was a rare occasion that business transactions, like home sales, occurred anonymously. But that didn't mean that I wanted to invade her privacy.

"No, no, we're equally thrilled. Won't you come inside and have a celebratory toast with us? Joe is opening a bottle of champagne as we speak."

"Oh, I couldn't."

"I insist." She waved me forward. "Please, come in."

"If you're sure." I hesitated.

"Positive."

Inside the cheery cottage, Terra's husband, Joe, raised a fluted champagne glass. "I knew Terra would convince you to join us." Joe was in his early seventies, with silver hair and kind eyes. He moved as if every muscle in his body was stiff. I knew his long career as a ski instructor had taken a toll on his knees.

"Thanks, Joe, I didn't mean to crash your party."

"Crash it? You're the reason for it." He shared a sweet look with Terra.

She clinked her glass to Joe's, then mine. "Absolutely. We can't even begin to tell you how thrilled we are that you are going to be the new owner of this labor of love. We'll have to break out our old photo albums. You wouldn't believe what the cottage was like when Joe and I bought it in the late seventies. Remember that terrible green shag carpet?"

Joe stuck out his tongue. "We were never sure if it was carpet or decades of mold."

"Yuck."

We all laughed.

"When we told April that we were ready to list the cottage and move to San Diego to be closer to our kids and grandkids, she mentioned that you might be interested, but Joe and I didn't want to get our hopes up," Terra said, staring at the tiny bubbles erupting in her crystal glass. "Like Joe said, we have renovated every square inch of this property, and we've loved our years here in the village. I guess I'm feeling nostalgic, but I hated the idea of selling the house to an investor who would turn it into a vacation rental. Knowing that you and Alex will be living here makes my heart so happy." She pressed her free hand over her heart in an easy show of emotion.

"I feel the same. You have done a spectacular job remodeling the cottage. I'm not changing a thing."

"Come sit, enjoy the view," Joe suggested, motioning to the living room, where two long couches were arranged in front of the fireplace. Large windows flanked each side of the stone fireplace, offering sweeping views of the snow-covered deck, the golf course, and the frozen river below.

We chatted for a while about their move. Joe gave me a rundown of the cottage quirks, like the fact that when he had installed new energy-efficient windows, it had made the house so airtight that whenever they lit a fire, they needed to crack a window slightly to allow the smoke to escape more easily up the chimney. As the evening wore on, they insisted that I stay for dinner. Terra served spicy bowls of her homemade chili along with thick slices of corn bread slathered with butter and honey.

The longer I spent in the cozy cottage, the more it felt like home. I could already envision placing a collection of family photos on the mantel above the fireplace and see Alex's soccer schedule stuck on the stainless steel fridge with one of my many beer magnets. The open-concept living room, dining room, and kitchen made the small cottage feel more inviting. Joe explained that they had debated about tearing down the wall that used to divide the living room and entryway but were very pleased with the result.

I concurred. I loved the dark hardwood floors and matching window trim. Skylights in the dining room and kitchen allowed extra light to flood the space, as did the wall of windows on the backside of the cottage. A hallway off the kitchen led to two bedrooms, a small den, bathroom, and laundry room. Cleaning would be a breeze. And it was hard to imagine not having acres of property to care for.

Joe cleared our dinner dishes, and Terra stoked the fire. I stood. "You've been so welcoming. Thanks for the history on the cottage and dinner. I should let you have the rest of your evening to yourselves."

"We can't wait to start packing," Joe called from the kitchen.

"It's true. We're going to miss the village, but the lure of living a few blocks away from our grandchildren is too compelling." Terra used a wrought-iron poker to move the coals. "Would you like us to leave you this? We won't need fire tools in sunny Southern California."

"Sure. That would be wonderful." Movement below caught my eye. I spotted Brad stumbling around the golf course with a flashlight in one hand and what looked like a growler in another. What was he doing? Was he drunk?

I said my good-byes to Joe and Terra, promising that I would come by with Alex in the next week or two, and then I hurried along the steep pathway that connected to the miniature golf course. Darkness had settled in, but fortunately the path was well-lit by streetlamps from above and a trail of in-ground lights. Perfectly manicured Christmas trees draped in purple, green, orange, and blue twinkle lights dotted the grounds. The course was only open seasonally, which meant that I had to trek through deep snow to reach Brad.

The greens were buried in snow, but the wooden bridges, miniature alpine chalets, and antique water wheels were aglow with hundreds of shimmering lights. It was a whimsical sight. Like something from a storybook.

"Brad, is that you?" I called as I followed deep footprints through the snow.

Brad swiveled his head in my direction. Although it was dark, the reflection of the lights landed on his face, revealing a look of what I could only describe as terror.

"Are you okay?" I stepped closer.

He swung the growler. "Stay away."

"Okay, okay." I moved back. He must be drunk. "Can I help?"

"Not unless you know a good lawyer." His words slurred together as he spoke.

"Why don't we go find a warm spot to sit down and talk?" I suggested, keeping my distance.

He tossed the growler on the ground. It landed in the snow with a thud. "What am I going to do? She did it. I know she did it, and it's my fault."

"Who did what?" I wanted to get out of the cold and go somewhere with more people around. Brad looked distraught. I wasn't worried about him harming me, but then again, there was no need to take any chances either. "Let's go around the corner to the Underground. We can have a coffee and talk."

He kicked the snow at his feet. "What am I going to do?"

"About what?"

"Ali!" he yelled, so loud that his wife's name echoed in the valley.

"What about Ali?"

His face blanched. It matched the opaque lights twinkling in the trees above us, with one major exception—there was no sign of joy in Brad's expression. "She did it," he repeated.

I moved closer to touch the sleeve of his puffy coat. "Did what?"

He met my gaze; his eyes were wild with fear. "She killed Liv. She killed her."

CHAPTER

TWENTY

"BRAD, WHAT ARE YOU TALKING about?" I asked, wishing I had the strength to drag him around the corner and into the Underground. My hands burned with cold. My toes started to tingle.

"My wife, Ali—she's a killer, and I'm the one to blame." He kicked the growler. It rolled down the slight hill on the slippery snow.

"Why do you say that?"

He shook his head. "Trust me. I know she did it."

"Let's go somewhere warm," I suggested again. "The Underground is right there." I pointed behind him. "We can get a hot cup of coffee, and I'll help in any way I can."

"Fine." He didn't sound thrilled, but he didn't resist either.

He followed after me, leaving the growler to continue its slow slide down the hill. I would come retrieve it later. I didn't want to distract Brad, and I had to know why he suddenly had decided that Ali was a killer.

The Underground was a bar that got its name from its location. In order to access the basement space, you had to traverse underground—literally. A ramp descended from street level taking us down to the basement bar. The Underground was known for its signature line of Bavarian cocktails, many of which were made with beer or wine, a rotating tap list, and the dozens of events they hosted every week from airing Seahawks and Sounders games to karaoke night.

Brad didn't say a word when we entered the dark bar and found a table, or even when I placed an order for two coffees. I was tempted to ask the bartender for something stronger like their Radler, a mix of Der Keller's lager and lemonade, or Hans's favorite, the Altbierbowle, which was a unique German drink made with Altbier, fruit syrup, and fresh raspberries. It was served in a cocktail dish along with a fork to stab the berries. By far the most popular drink with tourists was the Underground's Colaweizen—soda and Hefeweizen combined together.

I passed on the specialty drinks and returned to the table with two mugs of black coffee. "Why do you think Ali's involved with Liv's death?" I pressed.

"I don't think it. I know it." Brad sunk his head into his hands.

"Why?"

He reached into the front pocket of his ski jacket and removed a crumpled note. Without speaking, he slid it across the table to me. I picked it up and read it:

I know what you did, and you're going to regret it. I'm keeping my eye on you.

Brad watched my face as I read the note. "See? She doesn't believe me. She thinks that Liv and I had an affair."

"How do you know that Ali wrote this?" I stared at the paper. The note had been written on one of our Nitro note-pads and had been crumpled as if someone had rolled it into a tight ball and tossed it in the garbage.

"I know my wife's handwriting. Ali wrote that, for sure."

"Okay, but how does that prove that she killed Liv? This says 'you'll regret it'—that could mean anything."

Brad's eyes were laser focused on the crumpled note. "No, you don't know Ali. She wouldn't toss around an empty threat. If she said that Liv would regret it, she meant it."

"Right, but there are hundreds of interpretations—she could have meant that she planned to ruin Liv's career or call her out publicly." I realized that I was defending Ali. I didn't want her to be the killer, but obviously Brad knew her better than me. If he was convinced his wife was a killer, maybe I needed to stay more open-minded.

He took the words right out of my mouth. "No, you don't understand. You don't know Ali and what she's been through like I do. She's had a hell of a few years, and she hasn't been emotionally stable. She's done things she's re-gretted before."

That was a new detail. "Like what?" I tried to sound ca-sual.

Brad reached for his coffee. He held the mug in his hands for a moment as if he was considering whether or not he wanted to reveal more. "Like resorted to violence."

"How?" I cradled the steaming hot mug, happy to have something to take the chill out of my fingertips.

"It's a long story."

"We have time."

He dumped three packets of sugar into his cup. "When I came clean about my affair, she tracked the woman down. I don't know how she did it. She must have spent hours and hours on the phone with the hotel staff. I didn't even know the woman's full name—just her first name. We decided it would be better that way. A one-night stand no one needed to know about, no one would have regrets. But it didn't turn out like that. I woke up the next morning full of nothing but regret. In hindsight, I never should have told Ali, but I didn't think I could live with myself. Now look what I've done."

He rested his head on one hand and used the other to stack the empty sugar packets.

"What did Ali do when she found the woman?"

"She went off on her. Threatened her. Sent a private eye by her house and workplace to take photos of her and basically stalk her. I found a plane ticket in her purse. She was planning to fly out to Chicago and track her down personally. The woman is married, with two kids and a good job. I begged Ali not to do it. Why ruin an entire family? It was a stupid, drunk mistake. It was a one-night stand for both of us, but Ali was obsessed. I wondered if some of it was side effects from all the fertility medication she was taking, like the drugs were messing with her brain."

"Did she go?"

"No. I convinced her not to, but she'd done enough damage. The woman was freaked out. She said that Ali had her kids followed to school. She sent me digital photos that Ali

211

had taken of her kids on the playground, of her at a coffeeshop with friends, of her husband driving to work. It was creepy. It scared me."

"And you think Ali did something to Liv?"

"I know it." He rolled the stack of sugar packets into a tiny tube. "I broke her. I ruined our marriage. I sent her over the edge. And that note is proof."

"Where did you find it?"

"In the garbage can."

"What garbage can?"

"Liv's room."

It took every ounce of self-control not to react. What was Brad doing digging through Liv's garbage?

"Have you said anything to Chief Meyers?"

"Not yet. How can I? How can I turn in my wife for murder, knowing that I'm the cause? Ultimately, I'm the one who should go to jail. If I hadn't cheated on Ali, she would have been fine. She wouldn't have turned into this crazy woman I'm scared of."

"Brad, first of all, this note doesn't prove that Ali is the killer." My cheeks had begun to heat up in the subterranean bar and it was getting noisy as a '90s cover band warmed up on the small stage a few feet away from us.

He started to protest.

I held out my hand to stop him. "Just wait. What I was going to say is that even if it does, and it turns out that Ali killed Liv, that's not your fault. Yes, you made a big mistake, but Ali is responsible for herself. Your mistake didn't 'force' her to kill anyone."

"Maybe."

"You need to go find Chief Meyers and show her this note." I handed him the crumpled paper.

Brad clutched it tightly. "And turn my wife in?"

"Or not. But one way or the other, you don't strike me as the type of guy who could live a normal life knowing that Ali was a killer, either."

"Yeah, I guess."

I took a sip of my coffee, trying to buy myself some time to formulate my next question. I wanted to know why Brad was in Liv's room, but I also wanted to make sure I didn't spook him. Chief Meyers needed to see the note and hear from Brad.

"When did you find this?" I nodded to the note.

"The other day." He set it on the table and tried to smooth out the creases.

"Before or after the police were there?"

He was distracted with trying to fold the note. "I don't know. I was worried that Ali might have done something drastic. I spotted the door open the other morning and went in to take a quick look. That's when I found this."

Was he lying? I was past the point of being able to tell.

"Why don't I walk partway with you? I need to stop by Nitro before I head home." This was becoming a routine. The hum of electric guitars and the crashing drums were getting louder anyway. Once the band started their set, I knew there was no way we would be able to hear each other.

Brad folded the note into a tight square and placed it in his pocket. "Yeah, okay."

He left his sugar-spiked coffee untouched.

I paid and showed him the way to the police station. I had no idea if Chief Meyers had returned from Spokane yet, but I knew that any of the officers on duty would take his statement and enter the note into evidence.

As we walked in silence to Nitro, I hoped that Brad was wrong. I knew how Ali must have felt when she learned of Brad's betrayal, and as much as I didn't want to admit it, I knew that it was possible that she could have killed Liv.

CHAPTER
TWENTY-ONE

MAYBE IT HAD BEEN THE cold air or Brad's panic about Ali, but unlike earlier, Nitro felt like a welcome reprieve from my bigger problems. It also felt like a flash of déjà vu. Ali, Kevin, Jenny, Mel, and Swagger were still there—albeit at separate tables. Chief Meyers must not have given them the green light to leave.

"Hey, Sloan, I didn't think we were going to see you today. Can't stay away, can you?" Garrett teased. He stacked empty bowls of popcorn, nuts, and Doritos next to a pile of flyers for the IceFest.

Kat wiped down nearby tables.

"I see everyone's still here." I kept my voice low.

"Yeah. Chief Meyers called about a half hour ago and said she would need to detain everyone one more night. She's hoping to release them tomorrow."

"I guess it's good I came by, then. Sounds like we need breakfast again tomorrow."

"True, but we could do something simple. Bagels, toast, cereal." Garrett cracked a peanut. "I offered everyone a discounted rate for tonight but told them we wouldn't do a big breakfast."

"Smart."

"Chief Meyers said she might have the budget to help offset our cost, but I told her not to sweat it." He yawned.

"I'll swing by the store on my way home and pick up bagels and some more fruit. Do any of the rooms need fresh towels or anything?"

Garrett scowled. "Sloan, we've got this. Kat's already taken care of everything. She even left chocolates on the pillows. Isn't that right, Kat?"

Kat turned from a nearby table and grinned. "I saw it on Pinterest."

"Okay, okay." I threw my hands up. "I'll leave."

"Are you sure you're okay? Do you want to talk?" Garrett dropped his teasing tone and shot me a concerned look. He caught me staring at Ali, who was reading a ski magazine alone at the table near the front window. If I hadn't known that she was sequestered due to a murder investigation, I would have asked if I could take her picture. She could easily have graced one of Leavenworth's travel brochures, with her plush cabin socks, Buffalo plaid flannel hoodie, and thick black ski tights. The way her legs were propped on the empty chair next to her and the snow encasing the windows made for a postcard-worthy pose.

"Actually, yes. It would be good to talk through everything that's running through my head right now." I told him about my conversation with Brad and what I had discovered at the library.

He let out a low whistle. "Brad thinks she did it, huh?"

"He thinks he drove her to it."

"The old 'a woman scorned'..." As he said the words, I could tell he regretted it. "Oh God, sorry, Sloan, I didn't mean to imply—"

"It's fine. It's totally fine. Not that I haven't fantasized about punching Mac in the face every once in a while, but I'm not in danger of resorting to murder."

"No, I didn't think you were." Garrett looked at his feet. "Sorry."

"The thing is I was feeling so confident after I found the articles about Chloe's death. Taylor had to have known Lily. Why would he lie about that?"

Garrett shrugged.

"I thought I might have solved the case, but then I saw Brad stumbling around on the golf course, and in light of his revelation, I'm more confused than ever."

"This won't make you feel any better, but I had to cut Kevin off a while ago. He started to spout off about how he was glad that Lily is dead. He called her a bunch of terrible names that I won't repeat. Mel and Swagger have been keeping a close eye on Jenny."

"I'm starting to think they all did it. Wasn't there an Agatha Christie novel where that happened?"

"You should ask my mom," Garrett replied. "She's a huge Agatha fan. By the way, I forgot to mention that they're coming next weekend for IceFest. She called earlier. I blocked out a room for her and my dad and one for my sister."

"That's great. I'm looking forward to meeting your family." Garrett's parents and sister had planned to visit Leavenworth before the holidays but got snowed out by an early winter storm. Garrett had gone to Seattle for Christmas, so I knew his parents were eager to visit and see how he had transformed his great-aunt's inn. I was nervous about meeting Garrett's parents. It was silly. I felt like a teenager with a crush, but I wanted his family to like me.

"They can't wait to meet you." Garrett swept peanut shells into the garbage. "I've been talking you up for months now. They think you're some kind of beer goddess."

"Great. No pressure there." I paused for a second. Part of me wanted to tell him about Sally's visit. He had been extremely supportive when Sally and I had first gotten back in touch, but I wasn't ready. And there was no need to complicate an already stressful situation with my personal angst.

Kat balanced a tray of empty pint glasses and soup bowls. "You sort of are a beer goddess, Sloan."

"Thanks, I think." I wrinkled my forehead.

"No, I mean it," Kat insisted. "You know more about beer than anyone in town."

I hadn't come back to the pub to get my ego stroked, but I did appreciate her praise. "You don't need any help with the guest rooms, do you?" I asked, intentionally changing the subject.

"Already done." Kat turned to look at Kevin and then back to me and Garrett. "I can't wait for that group to be gone. He's such a jerk. He tells me the same joke every time

I wait on him. I think I've heard it twenty times now. Am I supposed to keep pretending like it's new?"

"What's the joke?" Garrett asked.

"You don't want to know. It gives me the creeps."

"The creeps?"

She twisted one of her curls. "Yeah, it's the same thing every time, and it's in poor taste."

"What is it?" Garrett asked again. He took a protective stance next to her.

Kat glanced at Kevin. "It goes like this: 'Why did the murderer take a shower?' The first time he told me the joke, he waited for me to ask why, but every time he's told it since, he goes straight to the punch line. 'Because he wanted to make a clean getaway.'"

"That's terrible." I agreed with Kat. Kevin's joke was in poor taste, to say the very least. I let out an involuntary shudder. Who would joke about something like that, especially given our current circumstances? The joke matched his self-inflated personality, but could his constant joking really be boastful bragging?

"And, why would he tell this joke to you more than once?" Garrett asked. He wasn't necessarily looking for an answer.

I understood his point. Was Kevin telling the joke to our young employee to make her feel uncomfortable? I wouldn't have put it past him.

"Kat, stay away from his table," Garrett cautioned. "I thought we had already talked about you letting me handle him."

"We did." Her cheeks splotched with color. "But every time I walk by him, he tries to have a conversation with me."

"Ignore him," I said, concurring with Garrett.

My cell phone buzzed. It was a text message from Alex: "On my way home. See you in fifteen."

"I'm happy to have you deal with him," Kat said to Garrett, throwing her hands in the air.

I stuffed my phone into my pocket. "I should go. I'll be here in the morning with bagels."

They said their good-byes. As I left, I passed Kevin's table. He didn't so much as look up from his phone when I walked by. I was convinced that he was trying to get under Kat's skin. Good thing Garrett was here to watch over the situation.

I couldn't stop thinking about Kevin's crude joke on my drive to the farmhouse. Who would joke about murder while being sequestered because of a real murder? Maybe someone who thinks that they've gotten away with murder?

The farmhouse was dark when I arrived. I had beaten Alex home. That was good. It gave me time to turn on the lights, turn up the heat, and put milk on the stove for hot chocolate. I wanted to tell him my news about the cottage. Fingers crossed, he would be excited, but I was also aware that the farmhouse was the only home he had ever known. He would probably be torn about moving.

While I waited for him, I whisked milk, vanilla, and dark chocolate on medium-low heat until it was frothy. When Alex was little, we would make cups of steaming hot chocolate with homemade whipped cream and chocolate sprinkles after dinner. Then we would curl up in front of the fire on cold winter evenings and read together. It had been many years since I had read aloud to my son, but we could still share the tradition of cups of cocoa and a fireside chat.

"Mom, I'm home," I heard him call as I scooped generous amounts of fluffy whipped cream onto two mugs of hot chocolate.

"You're just in time. I made hot chocolate."

"Did you make one for Dad? He's here, too."

What? I'd figured he'd just drop Alex off.

"No, but there's plenty."

Mac looked sheepish as they entered the kitchen. "I won't stay long, Sloan. Wanted to share some news with you."

A flood of panic pulsed through my body. I hadn't expected to see Mac. Not yet.

I ladled the creamy chocolate into another earthenware mug and forced myself to breathe. "What's that?"

"Dad bought a condo," Alex interrupted.

"Oh, really? The one you were looking at near Blackbird Island?" Could they tell that I was trying to hold my emotions in check? My voice sounded high-pitched and overly cheery.

"That's the one." Mac took the mug I offered him.

"Congratulations."

"It's going to be great," Alex said, sipping his hot chocolate and giving himself a whipped cream mustache in the process. "I can walk to school from there. Catch the shuttle to the ski hill. A bunch of my friends are nearby."

A bit of relief washed over me hearing Alex talk with such enthusiasm about Mac's new place.

"It turns out that I have some news, too." I told them about putting in an offer on the chalet and how Joe and Terra had accepted. Maybe keeping the conversation to our housing situation would help.

221

Alex gave me a hug. "Awesome, Mom. That's going to be so cool. I can walk to your place and Dad's." His phone rang. "I promised the guys I would help them with our math homework."

"Go ahead." I forced a smile as he answered the call and started telling his friends about moving into the village. "He seems excited," I said to Mac.

"Sloan, you're not really going to leave this place, are you?" His face was lined with concern.

"I can't do this right now, and we've already talked about this, Mac." I dug my feet into the floor.

"But, I didn't think you would do it. I thought if I was in the village—far away from here—you could keep the farmhouse. You wouldn't have to move. Nothing would have to change." I hadn't noticed that he wasn't wearing his ring any longer. The sight of his bare ring finger suddenly made everything feel real.

"It has changed, Mac." If he only knew how much it had changed.

"I know. I'm sorry for that. I just want you to be happy, Sloan. You don't need to move. I'll drive Alex home every night that he's with me."

"I appreciate that, Mac, but I want to move. I'm excited. I'm ready for this next stage of my life."

"Oh." He drank his hot chocolate in silence.

Part of me felt bad. I hadn't meant that as a slam on him, but it was the truth. I was changing, and I was ready to embrace the new me—whether that meant being a part of the Krause family or not.

CHAPTER

TWENTY-TWO

THE NEWS THAT I WAS moving sent Mac into a funk. He didn't stay long. That was fine by me. It gave Alex and me time to talk alone.

"When will we move, Mom?" He was on his second serving of hot chocolate. His teenage eating habits were all over the place. One day he would barely nibble on what I put in front of him and then the next day he would consume anything and everything he could get his hands on. I had learned to keep a well-stocked fridge and pantry.

"April thinks the sale will be fast. The inspection will happen sometime this week and then it will be a matter of signing the paperwork. Potentially we could move in by early next month."

"Cool." He rummaged through the cupboards and grabbed a box of cereal. Then he proceeded to pour himself a bowl of the cereal and milk.

"How are you feeling about the farmhouse?"

"Fine, why?" He rubbed his eyes. I had to resist the urge to smooth out his cowlick. In the past few years, Alex had lost any trace of his baby cheeks. He was taller than me, with Mac's broad shoulders and my olive skin. Sometimes when he slept at night, I would sneak into his doorway and steal a glance at my almost-grown-up kid.

"This is your home, and I know it's going to be hard to leave."

"Not really," he said through a mouthful of cereal. "I'm ready to move."

"Are you sure?" I wondered if he was putting on a brave face for my sake.

"Mom, yeah. It's cool. I swear." He plunged a marshmallow into his hot chocolate. "Yeah, this has been our house, but it's not the same now that Dad's not here."

I started to interject.

"Don't panic. I'm not saying that because I'm super depressed about it. It's just the way things are now." He had already polished off all the cereal, so he tilted the bowl in order to drink the little bit of remaining milk.

How did I end up with such a wise kid?

"I think it's going be a lot better for you, Mom."

"You do?"

"Yeah, you can't hide out here." He stuffed a couple marshmallows in his mouth. "You'll be in the village and around a lot of people. It will be good for you."

The irony that my teenager was worried about my well-being instead of his own wasn't lost on me. Alex had always been an old soul, but since Mac and I had broken up, he seemed even more astute. I just worried that he was holding too much. At some point, was he going to fall apart?

Perhaps.

I couldn't shield him from pain, I could only continue to offer a listening ear and be available when and if the loss of the life he had known came crashing down.

We finished our hot chocolates and curled up on the couch to watch a couple comedy shows before heading to bed. Deep sleep had been a challenge for me lately, some of which I blamed on my mid-forties and fluctuating hormones, but it was more likely that my restless nights were due to my erratic emotions. I had tried everything from herbal supplements to a sound machine. Even my go-to natural relaxant—dried hops under my pillow—wasn't cutting it. Tonight was no different. I could hear Alex lightly snoring as I studied the familiar bumps and marks in the ceiling. Images of Ursula and Otto plagued my brain, as did visions of Kevin lurking in the brewery and Brad's panic-stricken face. I tried a technique that Sally had taught me when I was young where I tensed every muscle in my body and then slowly relaxed. It calmed my nervous energy, but wasn't the answer to the elusiveness of sleep. Every time I drifted off, I would be jolted back awake by hazy nightmares of Ursula laughing maniacally.

The next morning I got an early start, finally giving up on my futile attempt at sleep when a pinkish light filtered through my bedroom windows. Sunrises were always spectacular in Leavenworth. I opened the curtains to allow the early morning light to flood the room. The first blush of the sun shimmered on the dormant hop vines and silver trellises, giving the newly fallen snow an iridescent shine. As beautiful as the farm looked under winter's kiss, I wouldn't miss it. That was a good sign, right?

I tugged on a pair of jeans, two pairs of socks, a long-sleeve tee, and a soft kelly green wool sweater. The color complemented my Mediterranean complexion. I moisturized my skin—a necessity during cold, crisp days like this. Then I added a touch of lip gloss and a trace of blush. I wasn't much for makeup, but given my lack of sleep, I needed anything extra that would make me look like I wasn't a walking zombie. Finally, I tied my dark hair into two long braids and pulled on a pair of lined snow boots.

I made coffee for me and hot apple cider and oatmeal for Alex, and packed his lunch before his alarm began to blare. We enjoyed a quick chat before heading out to get him to school. I'd never understood why high schoolers were forced to drag themselves out of bed and start their day so early. Alex's first class began promptly at seven fifteen. Whereas the elementary school, with its early little learners who were conditioned to wake long before the sun, didn't start until nine.

Once I dropped Alex off at school for a study group, I swung by the grocery store for bagels, juice, and fruit. I knew that at some point today or maybe tomorrow I was going to have to make a phone call to Ursula, but for the moment, I just wanted to focus on a basic task, like prepping breakfast.

Snow showers had tapered off overnight in the village as well, giving way to crystal clear blue skies. The now completely risen sun cast a bright halo on the top of Icicle Ridge, giving the mountain an angelic glow. Icy flakes glinted on the crunchy surface of yesterday's snow as I parked the car in an empty space in front of Nitro and gathered my things. As always, the pub was dark and quiet. I went through my typical morning routine—starting pots of coffee and tea, checking our fermenting beer, and prepping breakfast. It didn't take long to slice and toast bagels. I arranged them on a tray along with fresh fruit and the assorted containers of flavored cream cheese I had picked up at the store.

By the time I took breakfast upstairs, everyone was awake, including Garrett and Kat. There were puffy dark circles beneath Garrett's eyelids and stubble on his cheeks. He stood near the farthest bookcase watching over our guests like a secret service agent guarding the president.

Kat's abundant curls spilled out of her ponytail. She wore a maroon cashmere tunic over a pair of yoga pants. The color suited her youthful face. Deep dimples dotted her cheeks when she smiled and passed around packets of tea.

Garrett caught my eye, not making any attempt to be subtle. He tilted his head to the right and nodded toward the stairwell twice.

I handed the coffeepot to Kat. "You want to fill everyone's cups?"

"Sure. As long as I can fill one for myself, too." She reached for a ceramic mug that read LIFE IS WHAT HAPPENS BETWEEN COFFEE AND BEER.

I walked over to Garrett. "Did you need something?"

"Downstairs," he said through clenched teeth.

Was he upset with me about something?

"What's wrong?" I asked when we reached the bottom

of the stairs. I couldn't read his expression. His jaw muscles twitched. "Did I do something?"

He frowned. "What?"

"Are you upset with me?"

Garrett scrunched his nose, altering the serious look on his face. "No. Why would I be upset with you?"

"Never mind. I couldn't understand what you were trying to say, that's all."

"I wanted to get out of earshot from that group. I never thought I would say this, but I can't wait for our guests to depart. Maybe the B and B concept was a bad idea." He ran his fingers through his hair, making it even more disheveled than usual.

"No. I think these are unusual circumstances."

"I hope you're right." He frowned.

"What did you want to tell me, or are you simply sick of having guests sequestered here?"

He looked up the stairs to make sure no one was listening, and then pulled me into the brewery. "I think you're right about Kevin."

The cavernous space was dark. I reached to flip on the lights. "Why?"

"I couldn't sleep last night." He yawned as if to prove his point. "You know me, once I get an idea for a new beer in my head, I can't let it go. I woke up with an idea for a spring beer that I think you're going to like."

"Exciting."

"More on that in a minute, but once I started thinking about the recipe and hop ratios, I couldn't fall back to sleep, and I knew I had to write it down while it was fresh in my mind. This was around two in the morning. I came into the office to sketch out my thoughts. That's when I heard someone snooping around the tasting room."

"What?" I glanced around the gleaming stainless steel tanks, half expecting to see someone lurking behind one of the fermenters.

Garrett nodded emphatically. "Someone was up in the tasting room. They knocked over a chair. I yelled and ran up to the front to see what was going on. At first I thought maybe someone had broken in or that someone was siphoning beer from the taps."

"And you saw Kevin," I offered.

"No. I mean, I think so. I saw a guy bolt out of the front door. I'm sure I locked it when we closed, so whoever was in the taproom had to already be inside the building."

"Did you go after him?" I tried to imagine why Kevin would be in the tasting room at two in the morning and why he would run outside.

"I tried. I went outside and looked around, but whoever was in here took off fast."

"How do you know it was Kevin?"

"Because I locked the front door—I made sure of it this time, and then I returned to the office to finish my beer notes. When I went to bed an hour later, Kevin came in through the side guest entrance. He said he had gone out for a smoke, but I wasn't born yesterday. I know it was him."

"What's the connection with Lily's murder? Maybe he was getting a beer. Not that that's okay."

"Because he dropped this." Garrett reached into the pocket of his hoodie and removed a key.

"Is that the key to Lily's room?"

"Yep. The one and only key we have to Lily's room." Garrett looked triumphant.

"But what does it mean?"

He frowned. "I don't know, but it has to mean something. Has Kevin had it the entire time? Or what if he stashed it behind the bar the night he killed Lily? Maybe he was waiting for the opportunity to retrieve it."

"That's possible." I thought for a moment. "Or maybe he was trying to get into her room again. The police have searched it multiple times, but maybe he hid a piece of evidence in there that he's been trying to get back?"

"Could be." Garrett cradled the key. "Either way, I'm calling the chief right now. She can figure out the why. In the meantime, keep a close, close eye on Kevin. I have a bad feeling he's going to snap."

"Trust me, I've tried to avoid him like the plague."

"Be sure to fill Kat in, too. I already had a long talk with her last night about steering clear, but I don't want her around him." His voice was thick with concern. "Sloan, I'm worried he might be the killer."

"I know," I agreed. "And I'll make sure Kat keeps her distance, too."

Garrett went to call Chief Meyers. I tried to come up with any reason that Kevin would have had to have Lily's key. Nothing came to mind. Unless he had taken it from her the night she was killed. Why would he have been in the tasting room last night? Was he looking for something? Trying to hide evidence? Or worse? Could he have been planting Lily's key behind the bar to shift suspicion away from him? Maybe he was trying to implicate Garrett in the murder.

My theories were all possible, but none of them felt right.

What if Garrett had been mistaken? What if Kevin had been telling him the truth? Maybe Kevin had gone outside for a smoke, but what if someone else had been in the tasting room last night?

Garrett had said he had seen a man. That could have been either Swagger or Brad. Both of them were staying upstairs and would have had access to the space. Or there was a third possibility: that Garrett had accidentally left Nitro unlocked and someone had gotten in.

I wasn't sure which option was the most likely, but I agreed with Garrett on keeping my eyes open and watchful. The killer was closing in, and I didn't want to be in their line of sight.

TWENTY-THREE

CHIEF MEYERS SHOWED UP BEFORE I had had a chance to clear the breakfast dishes. She barely uttered a greeting and then asked to see Kevin immediately. Was this it? Was she about to make an arrest?

Garrett, Kat, and I tried to make ourselves scarce by working in the brewery while the chief interviewed Kevin, again, in the tasting room. I pretended to be interested in checking the gravity of our Pucker Up IPA, but I desperately wanted to go eavesdrop on the chief's interrogation. What did the missing room key mean?

"Want to take a look at my middle-of-the-night brainstorm?" Garrett asked.

"Love to." I followed him into the office, where he had sketched not one but two new beer recipes in brightly colored dry-erase pens. "You weren't kidding about inspiration striking."

"I know. It started with this one." Garrett pointed to the

left side of the dry-erase wall where he had drawn a hop cone in neon green, along with the names of ten popular hop varieties. "The PNW is such a hotbed for hops, I was thinking, why not go all in and dump as many kinds of hops into one single brew as we can? We can call it something clever, like the Hopcathlon."

I didn't respond right away. In brewing, like in baking or wine making, more wasn't necessarily better. Ten different hop strands in one beer could be overwhelming. Then again, it could be genius.

"I can tell by the look on your face that you're not convinced," Garrett said.

"Not necessarily. I'm intrigued, for sure. I don't know if that many strands will enhance a flavor profile or confuse palates."

"Hear me out," Garrett continued. "It would be an ode to PNW hops. We'd only use strands grown in Washington and Oregon. Think about it—Mosaic, Citra, Cascade, Simcoe, Chinook."

He rattled off popular Pacific Northwest hops.

"They have similar profiles. Citrus notes, good floral aromas. As long as we can balance the bitterness, it could be a cool experimental beer."

Brewers were constantly trying to push the envelope, creating unique flavors. The desire to come up with imaginative new beers had led to some strange brews, like milk stouts, tomato beer, and my personal (least) favorite—oyster beer. Garrett could be onto something with a pure PNW hop beer. He had barely scratched the surface with the first five hops he had suggested. Dozens more came to mind.

"Good point," I said to him. "I'm game. Let's try it."

"We'll do a small batch, of course." His enthusiasm waned. "Or is this a ridiculous idea?"

"No, I like it. I like it a lot. Why not? Let's get hoppy."

"Thanks, Sloan. I wasn't sure. The look on your face when I suggested it seemed less enthused."

"I just needed to think about it for a minute, but I like it, I promise. It's unique without being gross. Have you seen the latest bacon beer they're bottling in Portland?" I shuddered.

"Yeah, yuck—I'm not down with bacon." Garrett chuckled. "Cool. My other late-night epiphany was for another beer that might not fit the traditional mold." He pointed to the other side of the whiteboard, where he had sketched another recipe in pink and yellow pens.

The recipe was for a lemongrass and hibiscus pale ale brewed with agave instead of sugar. "Ooooh, that sounds like the perfect Mother's Day beer," I commented.

"Exactly!" Garrett clapped twice. "I was thinking about my parents coming to visit and remembering how my mom likes to make lemongrass and hibiscus iced tea. Then I thought, why not try that in a beer? The agave should activate the yeast, don't you think?"

"Sugar is sugar."

"Well said. Well said." Garrett picked up a brown pen and added my line under the recipe. "Sugar is sugar."

"I can totally picture sipping a lemongrass hibiscus pale outside under the blooming flower baskets. I bet this is going to be a spring hit."

"Except that we have to actually brew it first and see how it turns out."

"Sure, but we have plenty of time. We should be able to do a few test batches in order to perfect it in time for the spring line launch."

We brainstormed hop ratios while Garrett formally added both recipes to the spreadsheet he kept on his iPad. He was meticulous about keeping copious notes throughout every stage of the brewing process in order to ensure that if we came up with an amazing recipe, we could re-create it, or if we had a total flop, we wouldn't make the same mistakes again.

Chief Meyers knocked on the office door. "Got a second?"

"Sure." Garrett moved toward the filing cabinet to make room for her. The tiny office barely had enough space for the two of us, let alone a third body.

The chief stood in the doorway. "Bad news. I'm not sure I'm going to be able to release your guests yet."

"Really?" I tried not to sound too disappointed.

"What did Kevin say?" Garrett asked. "Did he confess to being down here in the middle of the night?"

She frowned. "He claims he went out the side door for a smoke. He said he heard a 'commotion' in the bar, but he didn't bother coming inside to see what it was."

That sounded in character for him.

"I'm sure it was him, Chief."

"Could be."

"Can't you take him in?"

"Not without cause." The chief stared at the high ceilings. "Too bad you don't have cameras out front. I've asked your neighbors. No one has any cameras. Might have to bring that up at the next city council meeting."

I hated that idea. Part of the charm of the village was that it was a safe place for families, tourists, and businesspeople. I understood why large cities might turn to Big Brother cameras as a crime prevention tool, but break-ins and violence of any kind were a rarity in our little Bavaria.

"You don't really think we should install cameras, do you, Chief?" I asked.

She shrugged. "Not a bad idea, if you ask me. You can never be too careful."

I wanted to respond, but instead shifted the conversation to the investigation. "Are there any other leads? Did you find anything new in Spokane?"

"Spokane was enlightening. I'm waiting for some paperwork to come in. We might be able to make an arrest today. That was my plan when I put my shoes on this morning, but that could change, especially in light of what Kevin just told me."

"You mean that he was vaping outside this morning?" Garrett asked.

The chief gave him a sly look. "Among other things, yeah."

What wasn't she telling us?

"I'll get out of your hair. I can't give you a solid window of time when I'll be able to release everyone. Hoping to have that happen later, but like I said, they may be here another night. We'll have to see how it goes."

"Thanks for the update." Garrett didn't sound particularly

happy with the news that we might be stuck with our motley crew of guests for yet another night.

"I'll be in touch." The chief gave us a two-finger salute and left.

"What do you think she meant by 'among other things'? Could Kevin have confessed something more to her?" I asked Garrett.

He doodled on the whiteboard. "I was wondering the same thing. But he couldn't have confessed, because then she would have arrested him. Did he tell her something about the murder? Maybe in exchange for leniency?"

That was an idea. Kevin was the type who looked out for himself first and foremost. If he knew anything that would put him in a better position, I didn't doubt for a second he would throw his best friend under the bus.

But what could he know?

CHAPTER

TWENTY-FOUR

GARRETT WAS EAGER TO TEST his new recipes. He went out in search of lemongrass, agave, and hibiscus. I figured he would find lemongrass and agave at the village specialty market, but hibiscus might be harder. Some of the hop varieties we intended to use in our PNW Hopcathlon we already had in stock, but I agreed to place an order with our hop suppliers for Amarillo, Centennial, and a few others. Kat took care of breakfast cleanup while I called the suppliers to see how quickly they could deliver a batch of test hops.

Operating a brewery in this region gave us an abundance of options when it came to vendors. One of our suppliers in Spokane offered to drive our order out later in the afternoon. That was going to make Garrett happy. We could have our first round of test batches brewing before the local evening crowd rolled in.

It was strange having Brad, Ali, Kevin, Jenny, Swagger, and Mel milling around upstairs. I could hear stomping feet, shutting bedroom doors, and running water. I supposed that I would get used to upstairs guests the more bookings we received. But with Lily's murder looming over us, every sound put me on edge.

"Success," Garrett announced, returning an hour later with an armful of supplies.

I had finished assembling meat and cheese trays and had put Kat to work chopping onions and potatoes for our soup of the day. We were going to make a loaded baked potato soup served with cheddar cheese, fresh dill, and a dollop of sour cream.

"You found hibiscus?"

He riffled through his reusable shopping bags and removed a package of dried hibiscus flowers. "I found them at Cup and Saucer, the tea shop. I was about to give up and then I had an aha moment. Tea."

"Of course."

"You're going to brew a tea beer?" Kat asked, grimacing.

"Hey, don't give me that face," Garrett teased. "Reserve judgment until you've tried this new brew."

"Okay." Kat didn't sound convinced. "Tea and beer doesn't really sound great, though."

Garrett wasn't deterred. "It's going to be a spring pale with lemongrass, sweet agave, and a hint of the hibiscus."

"Sounds like something my grandma would like." Kat stuck out her tongue. "I hate tea, though, so I'm probably not the best judge."

"You hate tea?" I asked. Tea was a natural relaxant for me. Simply holding a steeping mug of Earl Grey or peppermint tea brought me an instant calm. When Alex was little, he had trouble falling asleep, so Ursula had taught me how to create our own "sleepy tea" blend with chamomile, sweet orange, and hawthorn.

"Yuck." Kat hunched her shoulders. "I'm not a tea fan. It's so bland."

"What?" Tea was anything but bland in my opinion. Kat probably had never had homemade tea blends. "I'm going to make you a cup of my tea later, and we'll see what you think."

"I'll try it, but I'm telling you now I won't like it."

Garrett opened the fragrant bag of dried hibiscus. "The tea shop owner recommended steeping them in hot water, but I'm thinking we can add them directly to the boil. What do you think, Sloan?"

"Let's try it."

He unpacked the rest of our brewing supplies. "I'll go grab the iPad and then we can get started."

For our small test batches we brewed on Garrett's old homebrew system that he'd had the foresight to save and install in the industrial kitchen. His pieced-together kegs and handmade brewstand weren't fancy, but they got the job done.

I handed off the rest of the soup preparation to Kat so I could concentrate my full attention on the brewing process. Brewing isn't necessarily complicated, but it does involve multiple precisely timed steps and a constant set of eyes. If you pitch a yeast too soon or let the boil go too long, it can completely alter the beer.

"My big question is yeast," Garrett said as he pulled up the spreadsheet he had created on his iPad. "I'm leaning toward using that Omega tropical yeast we used in the IPA. It tends to have nice delicate pineapple and mango characters, especially if we ferment at higher temps. Plus, I still have a bunch in the fridge from the last brew. What do you think?"

"Let's try it. I like the idea of a touch of tropical notes to pair with the lemongrass and hibiscus."

Yeast was a critical component in the brewing process. There were literally dozens upon dozens of yeast strains available to brewers. I was always amazed at how different a beer would turn out simply based on the strain of yeast used. We had done an experiment for our brew team at Der Keller a few years ago where we brewed four batches of the same beer with nearly the same ingredients. The only thing we changed in each batch was the strain of yeast. It was incredible to watch everyone's face as they tasted the final product and realized the vast difference between the beers—simply because of one packet of yeast.

"Okay." Garrett made a note. "We'll try it, and if it's too tropical, we can do the next batch with a different strain."

The kitchen began to fill with the smell of boiling grains and Kat's savory potato soup. Much like holding a steaming mug of tea, the process of steeping hibiscus flowers and stirring the wort helped center me.

"It's already smelling good," Garrett commented as he measured agave syrup.

"Agreed. I think you might have created a winner." The scent of lemongrass mingled with the fragrant hops and grains.

Some people don't enjoy brewing aromas. We had noted

that in our listing for our guest rooms. Since we were an operating brewery, guests would often be treated to the fragrant aromas of the brewing process. The smell of grains boiling reminded me of one of Ursula's simple breakfast offerings—warm Grape-Nuts with milk and a pat of butter.

Kat poured chicken stock into the soup. "It does smell pretty good. Maybe you'll convert me after all."

I watched the boil while Garrett shook in another handful of dried hibiscus.

"That was a quarter cup," he stated, making another note.

We continued the process through the morning hours, until it was time to open the tasting room. Garrett was transferring the beer into carboys, so Kat and I offered to take the first shift. Not surprisingly, it was slow. The weekend ski crowds, excepting our guests, had returned home, and most of the villagers were at work. I caught up with two of our regular doctors who worked graveyards. Their shifts ended as we opened, so they usually stopped for a pint still dressed in their scrubs.

I chatted with them. Kat dished up bowls of the hearty potato soup to accompany their lunch—or was it breakfast?—beers.

"What the hell are we going to do all day?" Kev appeared in the tasting room with Jenny tagging after him. "Mel and Swag ditched me again. I don't know what's up with those two." He turned to me. "The Wi-Fi upstairs is terrible. I can't get a connection, and I have a meeting that I have to Skype into in an hour."

"Maybe you should try the library," I suggested.

"I'm not going to the freaking library just to be shushed

by a little old librarian. No way. If I'm stuck here, I'm having a pint."

Jenny caught my eye. Was it my imagination, or did she look skittish?

"Don't worry, Kev." She tried to pacify him. "I think that other big brewery has good Wi-Fi. We can go there for a pint."

"Fine." Kev flung his laptop bag over his shoulder. "Add this to the list of negative comments I'm going to put on your Yelp review." He marched out the door with Jenny tagging behind.

His empty threat didn't rattle me, but seeing Jenny trail after him did. I hoped she knew what she was doing. At least they would be surrounded by people at Der Keller. The sooner Chief Meyers made an arrest, the better.

Ali breezed through the tasting room shortly after Kevin and Jenny left. She was dressed in running gear.

"Off for some exercise," I noted.

"Yeah. I heard there are pretty amazing trails around Blackbird Island."

"True, but they might be hard to navigate with the snow right now." Running was a popular sport in the village in the spring, summer, and early fall, but our winter snowfall was more in line with snowshoeing than trail running.

"I'll be fine. I ran there the other day."

That was an odd comment, given her first statement about hearing there were good trails.

"You did?"

She stretched a thin pair of black running gloves over her hands. "Yeah. The trails were fine." She didn't wait for my reply. Instead she stretched her arms over her head and left.

The trails were fine? That was impossible. The trails were buried in feet of snow. The main trails that circled the riverfront park were groomed for cross-country skiing in the winter. Something didn't add up. Could there be another reason that Ali was "running" on Blackbird Island?

Part of me wanted to follow her, but duty called. A group of local workers on their lunch break came into the tasting room. Taylor was among them.

I went to take their order. Not surprisingly, they ordered bowls of loaded baked potato soup, bread, and meat and cheese plates to go along with their lunchtime pints.

After I noted their beer choices, Taylor stood and pushed back his barstool. "I can help carry our drinks."

"Thanks." I smiled as he walked with me to the bar.

"I wanted to ask you something, Sloan." He wiped grease from his hands onto his coveralls.

"Sure. What's up?"

We stopped at a high table a few feet from the taps.

"Have you seen Chief Meyers around?" He glanced from side to side as if she was about to jump from behind one of the tables.

"She was here earlier, why?"

His nails were thick with dark grease. "I'm kind of avoiding her."

"Avoiding her?"

"Yeah. She found out something pretty important from my past, and I've been trying to figure out what to do next."

What was this about?

"You know the chief as well as me. Whatever you have to tell her, I'm sure she'll be reasonable."

"No, see, that's the thing. I kind of lied to her earlier, and now it's going to look bad if I change my story."

"Okay."

"Is it weird for me to be talking to you? You're so good at listening, and everyone in the village knows that you're a vault."

"Thanks, I think."

He massaged the tops of his thighs. "No, that's a compliment. I guess I was just hoping that I could use you as a sounding board."

"You can," I assured him. "But I do have to warn you that my vault doesn't include keeping any secret that might involve evidence in a murder investigation."

"Yeah, I know. I get that." He hesitated for a moment.

Had I lost the opportunity?

"Here's the thing: I knew Lily. She and I went to high school together."

"Oh." I held my body as still as possible. I didn't want to give Taylor any indication that I already knew this information.

"We were good friends."

"Why didn't you say anything?"

"It's complicated." He knocked on the tabletop. "There was an accident. Lily, me, and our friend Chloe—we were the three amigos. We did everything together. You know what high school is like. We had some wild and crazy times."

Having a current high schooler made me flinch at Taylor's words. I only hoped that Alex wouldn't sum up his high school experience as wild and crazy.

"Chloe was the crazy one. She was always up for an

adventure. She had no fear. Lily was more cautious. She tried to keep Chloe in check, but it was pointless. Chloe never let up. She could convince you to jump off a bridge for her—literally."

I wondered where Taylor was going with this story.

"We were young. I thought Chloe's fearless streak was fun. Lily didn't. She was fed up. She wanted to break up our group of friends. She said that something bad was going to happen if we let Chloe run wild. I didn't listen to her. I should have, because she was right. Something bad— something terrible happened."

"What?"

"Chloe ended up dead."

CHAPTER

TWENTY-FIVE

I ALREADY KNEW AS MUCH, but I asked Taylor, "How did Chloe die?"

"A stupid dare. Teenagers who thought we were invincible." He wrung his hands as he spoke. Beads of sweat formed on his brow. "It was Chloe's idea. We went to the river for the afternoon, just the three of us. It was a hot day in early spring, but the water was still cold. Really cold. We had some beers and lounged in the sun. Lily and I hadn't planned to swim. Maybe splash around a little. Chloe had another plan. She wanted to see how far we could get. She wanted to swim across the river."

I knew that most of the rivers in the region were fed from mountain snowmelt. There were always warnings in the early season for boaters and swimmers to be aware of cold temps, potential debris, and swift currents.

"Chloe wasn't a great swimmer. Lily and I told her not to do it, but she jumped in and started swimming. The next thing we knew, she vanished under the water. We both went in after her, but it was too late."

Taylor started to cry. "I watched her. I watched my best friend, and there was nothing I could do. I'll never forget the look of terror on her face when she gasped for breath and went under the water for good."

"I'm so sorry."

He tried to wipe away a tear and managed to smear grease across his face in the process. "That's not the worst part, though."

I waited for him to continue.

"We left her there. We left her to die."

"What do you mean? It sounds like she had already drowned. You just said you watched her go under the water."

"Yeah. I know, but we didn't tell anyone. We left her towel and her things. We'd been drinking, and we thought we would get in trouble. Lily and I made a pact that we would never say we were there. Chloe was supposed to be sleeping over at Lily's house that night, and we decided that we would never tell a soul. Lily would call Chloe's mom and say she hadn't shown up." The conflict on his face made me want to reach over and hug him.

"That's what we did. Chloe ended up being reported missing. She wasn't missing. She died in the river that afternoon, but the entire town spent the next week looking for her. Me and Lily included. It was terrible. I couldn't look at Lily. We stopped talking. Our friendship was ruined. Both of our lives were ruined."

Suddenly I knew what Lily had wanted to confess to me the night she was killed. That's why she said she was a terrible person. She had been carrying the guilt of Chloe's death for years.

I wasn't sure how to respond. Taylor and Lily had made a bad decision, to say the least. Again my thoughts went to Alex. I could only hope that I had given him the tools and a moral compass to make a different decision in a moment like that.

"I couldn't believe it when I saw Lily here. I knew why she had come." He hung his head.

"Why?"

"She couldn't live with the guilt. She told me that she'd tried everything—changed her name, changed her look, changed her job, tried to drink, self-medicate—but every night she fell asleep seeing Chloe gasping for one last breath. I told her I understood. I felt the same, but what could we do now? She wanted to go to the police. She wanted to come clean."

That matched Lily's demeanor the night I met her. "I take it you didn't agree?"

"It's not that. It's just, like I told Lily, what would that accomplish? We weren't responsible for Chloe's death. It was an accident. It's been over ten years. Why now? Would going to the police change anything? Doubtful. We would still have to live with the fact that we watched our friend die."

"Then what happened?"

He looked puzzled. "What do you mean?"

"After Lily talked to you about going to the authorities."

"Nothing. She ended up dead. In the river. Just like Chloe."

There was something eerily unnerving about the fact that Lily had met a similar fate to Chloe's. However, if that was true, then Taylor was the most likely suspect.

I watched him try to regain composure. He didn't look like a killer. He looked like a young man tormented with guilt.

"What should I do?"

"I think you know what you have to do."

"Talk to the chief?"

I nodded.

"Yeah. I guess Lily's going to get her wish after all. The truth about Chloe is finally going to come out, and I'm the only one left to tell it." He glanced to his table of friends. "I think I'll skip the beer and soup and go get this over with. Thanks for listening."

I watched him say something to his friends and then make his exit. Why had he confessed his involvement in Chloe's death to me? Had he really needed a listening ear, or did he have another motive? Maybe he had seen Chief Meyers hanging around the pub and thought if he told me his sob story, I would defend him. Was it the truth? Or was it that Lily came to Leavenworth on a mission to right an old wrong and Taylor silenced her?

I shivered at the thought as I went to pour pints and serve Taylor's friends their lunch.

Garrett called me into the kitchen. "Sloan, you have to try this." He handed me a taster of beer. It was still warm and would need to ferment for at least two weeks, but even in its infancy the beer was like drinking spring in a cup. Herbaceous notes hit my nose, followed by a light floral front and a clean, bright finish.

"Well?" His face was expectant.

"It's delightful." I smiled.

"Maybe that's what we should call it. Spring's Delight."

"I like it." I finished the taster. "The hops will be here by late afternoon, so we can start the Hopcathlon batch tomorrow, unless you want to dive in tonight."

"Without my partner in crime? No way. I'll wait and brew with you tomorrow."

I was secretly pleased. The test batches technically didn't require two people, but I appreciated working on them together. It was easier to take extensive notes and bounce ideas off each other. And, if I was being completely honest with myself, I also enjoyed spending time with Garrett. I was nowhere near ready to think about dating yet. My relationship with Garrett was slowly evolving from a professional partnership to a friendship, and I was happy to keep it that way for the short term.

"I saw you and Taylor deep in conversation," Garrett commented as he rinsed the tasting glasses in the sink. "I tried to get your attention, but it looked like whatever you were talking about was serious."

"It was." I sighed and told him about Chloe's drowning and Taylor and Lily's pact.

"Whoa. That's dark stuff, Sloan."

"I know. It's shaken me up. I can't stop thinking about Alex. He's about the same age. I can't imagine him doing something like that, but what if I'm fooling myself?"

"You're not fooling yourself. Alex is a great kid."

I tried to smile. "Thanks. I guess it's the idea that Taylor and Lily would be so worried about getting in trouble that they could be so cavalier about a friend's death. Think of Chloe's family. Her poor parents, searching for their daughter, when she was already dead."

Garrett placed the clean glasses on a drying rack, then he walked over to me and placed a sturdy hand on my shoulder. "Alex would never do something like that, Sloan. Never."

I met his gaze. It was kind yet firm. Something inside me cracked. Suddenly, salty tears streamed from my eyes. I prided myself on my ability to maintain a steely exterior, but the weight of my looming divorce, buying the cottage, the horrific potential of Otto and Ursula's past, and Lily's and Chloe's deaths were too much. Garrett didn't say a word. For that I was grateful.

I sobbed on his shoulder. Tears spilled down my cheeks. "I'm sorry," I managed to mumble between sobs.

Garrett squeezed me tighter. "Let it go, Sloan."

His solid arms made me collapse into him more. I let him hold me while I tried to breathe through my nose and regain control of my emotions. When I finally was able to speak in a full sentence without gasping for air, I pulled away from him.

"I don't know where that came from. I shouldn't have broken down. I'm sorry."

"There's nothing to be sorry about. You can't hold the entire world up and expect not to collapse."

Is that what I had been doing? I had worked so hard to create this world, this life in the village, and it was starting to collapse. How was I going to make sure that the giant fissures in my rigid foundation didn't swallow me whole?

CHAPTER

TWENTY-SIX

AFTER MY MELTDOWN, GARRETT SUGGESTED that I take a walk to clear my head. "Go inhale that healing mountain air, Sloan. Trust me, everything is going to be okay. You are the strongest woman—I take that back—the strongest person I've ever met. I know this is going to sound bad, but I'm glad to see you show some emotion. It proves that you're at least partially human and not a total superwoman."

I tried to laugh.

"I'm serious. My mom always told me that there's nothing that fresh air and a walk in nature can't solve. Kat has the tasting room under control. Take a walk or take the rest of the afternoon."

"No, no, I'll be fine. I'll take a little walk, but I'll be back soon." I hurried away before he could see more tears starting to well. What was wrong with me?

I waved to Kat on the way out, after tugging on my snow boots and heavy coat. Hopefully, my words had sounded as breezy as I tried to make them.

Pull it together, Sloan, I scolded myself as I stepped out into the crisp air and, without thinking, turned toward Blackbird Island. The sidewalks had been cleared. Snow was piled on the side of the street. By the time I made it to the park, the pathways were deep with snow. Each step felt heavy. In some ways, trudging through the snow was a metaphor for my life. The heavy, painful burn of every movement paralleled what felt like infinite changes in my world. I knew that part of that was due to the fact that I craved normalcy and routine. I didn't blame my obsession on my years in foster care. But, those years spent in flux had shaped me for better and for worse. Since moving to Leavenworth, I had built a fortress around myself.

Every fortress falls at some point. And this was that point for me.

I didn't have a direction I was heading in. I simply plunged through the snow without a focus. Was I having a midlife crisis? Was this normal?

I wished I had someone older and wiser to turn to. Normally, I would have sought out Ursula's wise counsel, but I couldn't. I had to fix this on my own.

Time passed in a slow blur. I wandered through the snow-covered forested trails, lost in my thoughts. Tears froze to my cheeks. My toes went numb. I didn't care. I walked with a purpose, as if I could force away the self-doubt and anxiety with each mile logged. I couldn't allow myself the luxury of falling apart. I had to hold myself together for Alex. I owed it to him. I couldn't let him see me like this. It wasn't fair. It wasn't his fault.

I trekked on and on. At some point, I stopped when I realized that I was halfway to the Enchantments.

How long had I been walking? Well over an hour.

I looked up to see the sun beginning to sink behind the river.

Crap.

I was four or five miles from the village and losing light. A quick calculation of the sun's angle told me that I had less than an hour before darkness set in.

That was stupid, Sloan.

I turned around and retraced my steps, picking up my pace to more like a jog. It was tough going in my snow boots.

Why hadn't I paid more attention to where I was going? The vast network of trails that looped through Blackbird Island were challenging to navigate in broad daylight, but in the low, dusky light, I was worried that I might accidentally take a trail that led to a dead end. Then I would have to backtrack and start over again. I knew as long as I kept the Wenatchee River to my right and the mountains behind me, I would find my way back eventually, but I should have turned around long ago.

I knew the trail system well. Mac and I used to load Alex into a baby backpack and hike through the Enchantments every weekend. Some of my best memories of the three of us were on these trails. Once Alex could walk, Mac and I would take turns carrying him on our backs and then give him long stretches to run free on the narrow dirt pathways. He would stop and pick up collections of sticks and rocks. We would hike until his little pudgy legs wore out and then take a snack break under the shade of the ancient evergreen trees. I loved the smell of the baking pine needles in the summer and the way the light would filter through the canopy of brilliant green treetops.

I couldn't believe I'd gone so far without thinking about the return trip. *That's what you get for having a breakdown, Sloan.*

At least I had brought my cell phone with me. There wasn't service deep in the woods, but if nothing else, I could use the flashlight app to help illuminate a pathway home. The only other good piece of news was that I didn't have to contend with bears, since they were likely curled up in nearby caves for a deep winter slumber. This area in the summer was known to have frequent bear sightings.

Frost-filled air burned in my lungs as I jogged along the trail. Every few hundred yards, I heard the sound of hawks squawking.

Garrett and Kat had probably sent out a search party for me. That made me think of Chloe. Another wave of concern flooded my system.

In truth, Garrett and Kat likely had no idea I was semi-lost in the woods. Garrett might have assumed that I had decided to take his advice and call it a day. No one would be the wiser until later tonight when Alex started to freak out because I didn't come home.

Worst-case scenarios bombarded my head. I pictured

Alex pacing the kitchen and dining room, calling Mac to let him know I was missing.

Stop it.

This was another quality I wasn't proud of. I could leap to dozens of horrific scenarios in a matter of minutes. A therapist had once told me it was a coping strategy. That my brain tried to prepare me for the worst. I never agreed with that assessment. There were plenty of better ways my brain could have learned to cope.

I continued on, sliding over patches of ice. Branches scratched my face and arms. I ignored the pain and ran faster.

Light was fading at a rapid rate.

How far had I come?

Two miles? Three?

I had to slow my pace in order to make sure I didn't fall and seriously hurt myself on one of the many branches and limbs on the backcountry trails.

I couldn't believe that I hadn't bumped into any skiers or snowshoers. Then again, they probably wouldn't have ventured out this late knowing that darkness would soon descend.

Watching my footing became my singular focus. I couldn't risk slipping and breaking a bone. Overnight temps would plummet into the teens. I wouldn't survive alone.

Keep moving, I told myself. I had to try and silence the negative voice in my head and push forward.

Think of Alex. He's waiting for you.

I squinted to see. The sun had vanished behind the ridgeline, plunging the valley into a swath of darkness. Time to break out the flashlight app.

I pulled my phone from my coat pocket. It was like a block of ice. In order to turn it on, I had to remove my gloves and try to slide it with my numb fingertips.

The puny stream of light barely reached my feet, but it was better than nothing.

I started to shiver.

That was a bad sign.

I had been trained in CPR—it was a requirement for working at Der Keller—and I knew that shivering was one of the first signs of hypothermia. I had started to sweat from exertion, and now my sweat was cooling me off. Tiny beads of perspiration dripped down my forehead and froze on my cheeks.

What else could possibly go wrong?

Nothing. Just keep moving, Sloan, you'll be okay.

I felt grateful that the kinder voice in my head was winning the battle.

Above me in the vast stretch of darkness, the first stars of the night flashed, as if trying to light the way. Their distant glimmer spurred me on.

I trekked on for another twenty or thirty minutes with the sound of my feet crunching the snowy ground and the echo of my strained breath. Finally, in the distance I could make out the soft, hazy glow of lights from the village.

Thank goodness.

I was probably about a mile and a half out. I would be back to Nitro in less than a half hour if I could keep up this pace, maybe sooner if it wasn't too slippery.

I wasn't sure if it was the relief of knowing I was close to home, the fear of being stranded in the cold, or the physical exhaustion, but my emotions felt more stable.

That was until I rounded a corner and ran smack into Ali, who had a shovel in one hand, a flashlight in the other. She stood over a three-foot hole in the ground, stared up at me, and wielded the shovel like a baseball bat.

CHAPTER

TWENTY-SEVEN

MY BREATH CAUGHT IN MY chest. What was Ali doing?

I froze and held my arms up in surrender. "Ali?"

Her eyes were wild. "Back up. Back away!"

"Okay." I kept my hands in the air. The flashlight on my phone illuminated the deep hole at her feet.

"Don't move!" She lifted the shovel higher. "Stay there! If you move one step closer, I will hit you—hard!"

"Ali, listen, I don't know what's going on, but I can help."

"You can't help. You know what I've done." Her manic voice pierced through the empty valley.

"Know what?"

"About Lily."

I knew that I had to stay calm, but it was impossible with my shivering body and the surge of adrenaline pulsing through my veins. "What about Lily?"

"I couldn't let them get away with it. Not after what they did to my sister and my family. They ruined our lives."

"I don't understand, Ali. What are you saying?" I bounced from one foot to the other to try to stay mobile. I was already freezing. If I stood still for too long, I was worried that I wouldn't have any energy to run.

She stabbed the shovel in the air. I wondered how long she'd been digging. It must have been extremely difficult to break through the frozen ground.

"What is there to say? She killed my sister, so I killed her."

I hadn't anticipated a confession. "Your sister?"

"Yes, my sister. Don't play dumb. I know that you know. They killed Chloe. They left her there to die. I wish it wasn't you here now. I like you, and this wasn't how it was supposed to end."

Everything fell into place. Ali was Chloe's sister. No wonder she had freaked out when Brad introduced Lily as a potential surrogate. "Oh, Ali, I'm so sorry."

She recoiled. "You're sorry? Try living with your sister's death. We spent days and days searching for her. I knew there was something wrong. I could tell by the way Lily acted. I tried to tell my parents and the police, but no one believed me. They said it was a normal reaction to losing a friend. It wasn't. She covered it up. How could they have left Chloe in the river? How could they let us search night and day, knowing that she was dead?"

Ali stared past me into the darkness as if she were talking to someone behind me. I almost turned around to make sure there wasn't a scary figure looming nearby. "She might not have forced her into the river, but she left her there to die. They both did."

"You mean Lily and Taylor."

"Taylor and Lily. They were supposed to be Chloe's best friends, and what did they do? They let my baby sister drown and then said nothing. Nothing." Her words pierced the frigid night sky. "She might have been saved. How did they know? She could have drifted downriver. If they had called for help, she might be alive now, but no. NO! They let her die. She was seventeen. She had her entire life in front of her, and her best friends let her die."

"They made a terrible mistake." I wondered what I should do. Ali was distracted by her emotions and the retelling of her sister's tragic death. This might be my chance to run. I didn't think Ali wanted to hurt me, but then again, she wasn't acting rationally.

"A mistake? No. Lily told me everything. I know what they did. They killed my sister. They were murderers." She clutched the shovel tighter.

I wasn't sure I agreed, although I understood Ali's frustration. I took a step backward to test the waters.

"I told you not to move." She took a step closer. "You know what? Lily never came around after they finally found Chloe's body. She was at the funeral and then that was it. If they were such good friends, why wouldn't she have stayed in touch with my parents? With me? I left for college, but my parents were devastated. They've never recovered. How could they? I tried to move on. I got a good job, married Brad, spent years in therapy for my grief. And then fate intervened."

"You mean the surrogacy?" I could hear my words starting to slur from the bitter cold, but I had to keep her talking.

"What are the odds? I recognized her right away. She had

changed her hair and her look, but it was Lily. I don't know who was more shocked. Her or me."

"Did Brad know?" I couldn't stop shivering. How was Ali not freezing? She had to have been out here for hours digging. She should have been hypothermic by now.

"No." Ali shook her head. She hadn't loosened her grip on the shovel. "He has no idea. I made sure of that. I never thought for a second that they were having a fling. The minute I recognized her, I saw it in her face. She was riddled with guilt."

"What happened then?" I tried to calculate how long it would take me to get back to town. We were probably about half a mile from the pedestrian bridge that connected Blackbird Island to the village. From there I would have to wind along the backside of one of the bigger hotels until I got to the street. Then I could sprint uphill two long blocks.

"I formed a flawless plan." Ali chuckled. "Brad was convinced that I was distraught over the thought of him cheating on me. It distracted him and kept him from paying attention to what I was really plotting. I got Lily's number from him. He thought I was stalking her, and in a way, I was. I followed her a couple times, trying to determine when and how to strike. She caught me following her and confessed. She told me everything that happened that day. How they'd been drinking and how Chloe egged them on to get in the river. How she had watched my sister die and done nothing about it. She said she felt relieved telling me. She actually thought I had forgiven her. She told me that she was going to come here. She had tracked Taylor down, and said that it was time for both of them to come clean about what really happened to Chloe. That's when my plan really came to fruition. She had given me the perfect opportunity."

"So you followed her here?" I realized as I asked the question that nothing about the weekend had been coincidental. It was all part of a well-crafted plan. Ali had come to the village with a singular mission—to exact her revenge on Lily and Taylor. Every clue and conversation from the past few days suddenly fell into place. It made so much more sense. "I take it the romantic anniversary weekend with Brad was a ruse?"

She kicked the pile of frozen dirt at her feet. "It is our anniversary. That much is true, but that's not why I picked Leavenworth. I kept in touch with Lily. She was so self-absorbed. She had no idea that I wasn't going to let her get off easy. A confession didn't change what she had done. She wasn't remorseful. She wanted to be absolved of her sins. I had no intention of freeing her of her guilt. I knew what I had to do. What I had to do for Chloe."

Ali's body began to shake. "I told Brad we needed a getaway. He agreed. He was desperate to make amends, so I booked this weekend knowing that Lily would be in town. She didn't know that I planned to follow her here. When she saw us that night, she was shocked. I let her sweat it out. Brad went to bed, and I came back to the bar and told her I wanted to talk. We went for a walk. I told her that I wanted to be there when she spoke to Taylor. She thought it was a bad idea. She said he was likely going to be resistant. Little did she know we were headed here. The island. The river. I had stashed this shovel in the woods earlier and led her straight to it. She wasn't expecting it when I struck her on the head. Then I dragged her body and dumped it into the river. She could meet her maker in the same way my sister had."

I didn't dare respond. My face burned with cold. In the far distance, I thought I heard voices, but maybe I was imagining things.

Ali continued talking. She barely seemed aware that I was still here. *This is your chance, Sloan,* I told myself, but my feet wouldn't budge.

"Taylor was next on my list. He was harder. He suspected that I was involved. I didn't know him as well. He and Chloe had hung out at school. But I think he remembered me. Chloe and I had the same eyes. She was so pretty. So bright. So young to die."

Ali trailed off. I thought I was going to have to prompt her to finish her story, but she continued. "I think he suspected me right away when Lily's body was found. It wasn't supposed to go down like that. I had planned that they wouldn't find the body for weeks. Maybe longer. I thought she might be missing until the spring or summer. I hadn't counted on her being found so fast."

"What was your plan with Taylor, then?" Fear flooded my body as Ali's eyes drifted to the hole.

"Oh, he's going to die. He's on his way here now. I will avenge my sister's death once and for all tonight." Her voice sounded almost robotic. "I wanted him to live in fear. For days, months, maybe years. I hadn't formulated how I was going to do it, but when I did, he would know. He would know it was me."

"What changed?" I asked through chattering teeth. My

mouth wasn't quivering only due to the cold. Ali's stoic attitude was terrifying. I was fairly sure I had misread her. I needed to figure out an escape plan—now.

"I don't have a choice. I have to silence him tonight. He's going to try and go to the police. I can feel it." She shook her head in disgust. "He doesn't deserve to live."

"Ali, I'm pretty sure that Chief Meyers knows. She was in Spokane yesterday, and my guess is that she interviewed your family. She probably looked into Chloe's death. I think we should go find her now."

For a minute I thought I had convinced her, but the next thing I saw was the sharp edge of the shovel barreling down on me.

CHAPTER
TWENTY-EIGHT

FORTUNATELY, ALI MISSED. SHE GRAZED my shoulder with the piercing tip of the shovel. Pain shot down my arm. I ducked as Ali heaved the shovel in the air again.

"Help!" I screamed as loud as I could. It sounded futile in the vast wilderness of Blackbird Island.

My legs felt like rubber as I tried to run.

I could hear Ali behind me. "Stop!"

In the blur of my near miss with Ali's shovel, I dropped my phone. I stumbled forward in the darkness, clutching my shoulder.

"Help!" I screamed again—this time my voice sounded like it carried better.

But was screaming a good idea? I might attract help, but I also might alert Ali to my exact whereabouts.

Run, I willed my legs.

They didn't follow my command. My gait was shaky

on the uneven and slippery ground. I considered stopping. Maybe I could hide behind a tree until Ali gave up. But I knew she wouldn't give up. She was obsessed.

I had to get back to the village.

I had to warn Taylor.

My shoulder pulsed with a throbbing heat. Was it broken? Dislocated?

Think about that later, Sloan.

Ali's heavy footsteps thudded nearby.

My breathing sounded like it had been amplified by a dozen microphones. Could Ali hear me?

A tree branch smacked me in the cheek, almost knocking me off my feet.

I plowed forward in the darkness. A sliver of the moon and smattering of stars were my only guides.

The sound of voices brought me to a halt. "Who's down there?"

"Help! Help!" I yelled with all the force left in my body. Then I looked to the left and saw the reflection of flashlights cutting through the darkness. They were probably only a couple hundred feet away.

"Who's there?" the voices called again.

"It's Sloan!" I answered. "I need help!"

"Sloan! Stay there. We're coming to you."

I hesitated. Ali was likely close, but she wouldn't try to attack me with other people nearby, would she?

I kept moving at a much slower pace toward the flashing lights.

"Sloan, it's Garrett! We're almost to you. Keep talking."

I'd never been so happy to hear Garrett's voice. In a matter of seconds, he, Taylor, and two police officers were with me. Their headlamps were blinding. I collapsed on the ground.

"Sloan, are you okay? We've been so worried." Garrett dropped to his knees.

"Ali." I pointed behind us into the darkness. "Ali's the killer. She's out there. Probably close." I looked up at Taylor, shielding my eyes from his light. "She's after you."

Taylor frowned. "I figured."

One of the police officers stepped toward me. "Do you need us to call an ambulance?"

"No. I'm fine." I rubbed my shoulder. "I'm really cold and in some pain, but I'll be fine."

"Can you escort her back?" the officer asked Garrett.

Garrett helped me to my feet. "Of course."

The other officer radioed for support and then they both took off after Ali.

"Can you walk?" Garrett asked, placing a sturdy arm around my waist.

"Yeah. It's my shoulder. She hit me with a shovel."

"Oh God!" Taylor exclaimed. "A shovel."

We started toward the footbridge. I was surprised how close I had been to getting off of Blackbird Island on my own. "She dug a big hole about a half mile into the woods. She said you were meeting her there. It's a good thing you came with reinforcements. She was planning to kill you."

"I know." Taylor used his handheld flashlight to illuminate the path across the bridge. "I had a long talk with Chief Meyers. When I got home from work, there was a note under my door to meet Ali here."

"You didn't know she was Chloe's older sister?" I asked.

Garrett stopped in midstride. "Wait, hold up for a minute, Sloan. I can feel your body shivering with every step. Can't this wait until we get you to the police station and get you warmed up?"

"Why?" I shuddered. "We can talk and walk, can't we?"

"Sloan, you're a mystery to me. We've had half the town out looking for you for the last hour. You were attacked, and are likely close to having frostbite on all your extremities, but the only thing you want to talk about is this case?" He kept his arm secured around my waist.

"Yeah, that sums it up." I tried to laugh, but everything hurt.

"Easy." Garrett steadied me.

"Should we keep going?" Taylor asked him.

Garrett shrugged. "You heard the woman. She's the boss."

Taylor led the way, keeping a slow pace in order to light the path for Garrett and me. "Yeah, you're right, I never knew Ali. She was older than us. I thought there was something vaguely familiar about her, but it wasn't until I went to the chief with the weird note that she left me that we figured it out."

"Speak of the devil," Garrett said, as Chief Meyers's squad car zoomed past us with its lights flashing and siren wailing.

Walking up the hill toward Nitro left me winded, and my body refused to stop shivering. Thank goodness they had come along when they had. I wasn't sure how much longer I could have withstood the cold.

"Should we slow down, Sloan?" Garrett asked as we crested the hill. Nitro was less than a block away.

"No. I can make it." I tried to sound more confident than

I felt. The stress of the ordeal must have been catching up with me, because suddenly I felt like I could collapse and sleep for a week.

Kat raced from behind the bar when we entered. "Oh my God, you're okay. Oh thank goodness." She held her phone in one hand and started texting with her thumbs. "I have to send out an update. Everyone has been looking for you."

Garrett helped me into a chair by the front window. "Wait here." Then he instructed Taylor to sit with me while he went to find a blanket and Advil.

Kat brought me a steaming mug of cinnamon tea. "Here, Garrett said to drink this."

"Thanks." I smiled at her.

"I've texted everyone to let them know that you're safe." She sat next to me. "We were really worried, Sloan."

"I know. I'm sorry." I reached for her hand, but the movement sent a new wave of pain down my shoulder.

Taylor paced next to us. "I feel terrible. I can't believe she killed Lily because of me."

"Not because of you." I warmed my hands on the tea. "Ali's responsible for her own actions."

"I guess." He didn't sound convinced.

Garrett returned with a wool blanket, a heating pad for my shoulder, and a bottle of Advil. "Take these," he said, pouring a few capsules in my trembling hand. "Should we run you over to the hospital and have them take a look at your arm?"

I swallowed the pills and rested the hot, lavender-scented pad on my injured shoulder. "I think it will be fine."

Garrett made a grunting sound under his breath, but sat

down next to me. I could tell they were worried about me from the way they all surrounded me and kept checking in with one another. Fortunately, it wasn't long before Chief Meyers arrived.

She stomped snow from her boots on the front mat, and then ambled inside. "Figured I'd find you here." She came over to the table. "Thought you might want a recap."

"Yes, thank you." I huddled under the blanket while the chief explained that she had arrested Ali and was waiting for the official transport to arrive to deliver Ali to the Chelan County Jail. I didn't feel particularly relieved that the ordeal was over. The entire situation was sad.

"What's going to happen to her?" I asked the chief, taking a sip of the spicy cinnamon apple tea.

"The only thing she has going for her is that she's confessed. That may give her a bit of leverage with the court. It's always better to work with the judicial system than against it."

"But she'll do jail time, right?" I tried to ignore the throbbing pain in my arm.

"Twenty years to life," Chief Meyers said with a curt nod.

I thought of Brad. He had seemed genuinely interested in rebuilding their marriage. Would he stand by Ali now?

"Did you know it was her?" I asked, tucking my hands under the wool blanket. Feeling was starting to return to my fingertips.

"I had my suspicions. Kevin confirmed them. When I went to Spokane, I met with Ali's parents. They told me their ordeal with losing Chloe. I started putting two and two together. Thank you for encouraging Taylor to come in." She turned and gave Taylor a half nod. "You helped so-lidify my case.

Taylor still looked shell-shocked.

The chief continued. "Kevin closed the deal for us with some tangible evidence."

"Kevin had evidence?"

She twisted the volume button on her walkie-talkie. "He had pictures on his cell of the two of them on Blackbird Island that night."

"Why didn't he show you sooner? He's been complaining about being stuck here for days."

"The photos implicate him in a crime as well."

I wrinkled my nose. "Huh?"

"Hold on." The chief reached into a canvas bag she'd set on the floor. She removed several eight-by-ten glossy photos blown up from selfies. They revealed Kevin posing as he battered Lily's car with a baseball bat and splattered it with a gallon of the paint we had used for renovations.

"So that's who vandalized her car." I stared at the photos. "Why would he take selfies?"

The chief shrugged. "Your guess is as good as mine. Trying to stroke his ego. Maybe he hoped it would prove his manhood."

"I don't see Ali or Lily in these."

"Look closer."

I stared at the pictures. Sure enough, in the background there were two women at the entrance to Blackbird Island. Then I passed them to Garrett.

"We had tech enhance the images. They'll be used in

court along with Taylor's testimony and Ali's confession. It should be an open-and-shut case."

"I still don't understand why Kevin didn't come to you sooner."

"He didn't realize that in his moment of destruction, he had caught the real killer in the background."

"How did he figure it out?"

"Jenny. She found the photos on his phone. She was sure that he had killed Lily. We weren't disputing that, either, until the tech department got ahold of the photos and was able to discern that there was more than Kevin's rampage going on."

"Wow." I shifted in my chair, trying to reposition the heating pad. "So Kevin must have been the one who took Lily's room key and went through her things, too?"

"Yeah. He admitted to everything." Chief Meyers looked concerned. "How are you feeling?"

"I'm okay."

"You're pale and shivering. You've barely touched that tea. I'd say you're on the verge of hypothermia." She turned to Garrett. "Did you give her Advil? Maybe give her a couple more."

My cup sat barely touched. I didn't have the heart to tell her the reason I hadn't drunk the tea had more to do with the fact that it had gone cold in the last half hour than with my state of well-being.

"I'm right here," I replied. "And I don't need more Advil. It's taking the edge off."

We talked more about what Ali had confessed to me. Chief Meyers recorded my statement and took notes. Taylor continued to pace. I felt sorry for him. Living with the guilt of his high-school friend's death all these years must have been hard enough.

"I don't think you'll be needed in court," she said when I finished. "But there's a chance the prosecution will call you."

"That's fine." I could handle testifying against Ali. I was sorry that her grief had led her down a path of retribution, but I was also a firm believer in justice.

"Hello?" I heard a familiar voice as the door to the police station opened. Hans and Alex walked in together.

"Mom!" Alex ran to hug me. "You're okay. We were so worried. We looked all over the village. We went to the cottage, then we went home to the farmhouse, in case maybe you ended up there."

Garrett moved so that Alex could sit next to me.

"Uncle Hans and I heard you were attacked." Alex plopped into the chair Garrett had vacated.

"It's not that dramatic." I squeezed his hand with my good arm. "I'll probably have a nice bruise tomorrow." I touched the heating pad.

"Your hands are like ice, Mom." Alex looked worried.

"I promise I'm fine. A little cold, a sore shoulder, but otherwise fine."

Hans scowled. His intentionally faded brick red baseball cap made his skin tone look more pinkish than usual. "You and your need for drama, Sloan. I don't know what to do about you." He bent down to kiss my cheek "Don't do that again, okay?"

I appreciated the sweet gesture, but seeing my brother-in-law standing in front of me brought images of Otto's and

Ursula's faces to my mind. How could I face Hans? Hans had been my rock. My surrogate brother. And one of the only people on the planet who could read me.

"I have an idea to help make you feel better," Alex said.

"What's that?" I released his hand.

"Pizza. The answer to any problem is pizza. You told me that once, remember?"

"Did I?" I chuckled. Suddenly I was famished. It wasn't a surprise, given that I had walked the equivalent of a half marathon and spent hours out in the cold. Not to mention the massive adrenaline rush from escaping Ali's shovel.

"That is a great idea." Hans smiled. "What do you say, Chief? Want to come grab a slice with us?"

"Duty calls. The transport will be here soon, and I need to give the green light for our other suspects. Are the guests upstairs?" she asked Garrett.

Garrett nodded. "Yeah, I believe so. You'll have some very happy campers when you break the news that everyone is free to go."

"Except for Brad," I interjected. I couldn't help feeling sorry for Brad and even Ali. Not that I condoned her choices, but the pressure of losing her younger sister, coping with Brad's infidelity, and struggling through fertility issues had to have taken an emotional toll. I thought of my own situation. It made me even more grateful for my friendship with Garrett and the community around me. Revenge wasn't for me, but without the support of the people near and dear to my heart, I could imagine myself on a path of destruction. Maybe not to the extreme that Ali had gone, but to a place of darkness and despair.

"Right." Garrett frowned.

"I'll speak with him first. He can come have a few words with his wife before they take her to Wenatchee."

Leavenworth wasn't big enough for a jail. The Chelan County facility was located in nearby Wenatchee.

"I'll head upstairs now." Chief Meyers stood. "Thanks for your help, Sloan. Take it easy tonight." To Hans and Alex she said, "Make sure she eats an entire pie, and keep an eye on that shoulder."

"We'll make sure she doesn't leave the table until she's devoured a Bavarian." Garrett saluted Chief Meyers.

Hans wrapped his arm around my waist. "If there's one thing I know about my sis-in-law, it's that she's never afraid to eat. I concur with Garrett—an extra-large Bavarian should do the trick."

I felt my back stiffen.

"You cool?" Hans asked.

"Yeah. Fine. Just recovering from the shock."

Kuchen, the pizza shop, was famous for its German take on the Italian classic. It was located a few blocks away in a rustic three-story building complete with arched stained-glass windows and balconies. The Bavarian that Garrett and Hans referred to consisted of hand-tossed sourdough crust smothered with stone-ground mustard and loaded with brats, sauerkraut, and peppers. It was a local favorite.

Hans and Alex each took one of my arms and escorted me to the pizza shop. "Guys, I'm fine, really," I protested.

They ignored me and guided me to a red leather booth. It was cozy and warm inside from the heat of the pizza ovens. Hans ordered a bottle of red wine, the Bavarian, a meat pizza, three salads, a root beer for Alex, and a German pretzel with fondue dipping sauce for a starter.

"How much do you think I'm going to eat?"

"Chief's orders. We can't go against Meyers, can we, guys?" He looked to Garrett and Alex for support.

They shared a look of solidarity.

"No way," Alex agreed.

Garrett clapped Hans on the back. "That's right. Let's fatten her up."

I was glad that they all got along. Hans had connected me with Garrett when I first discovered that Mac was cheating on me. He and Garrett had developed a friendship when Garrett hired him to help with Nitro renovations. If Otto and Ursula really had fled due to their Nazi ties, it was impossible that Hans knew anything of their past. Suddenly the weight of digging into my roots felt overwhelming. Tiny beads of sweat pooled on my forehead. Depending on what I learned and what Sally uncovered, I wasn't just going to be destroying my stability. I was putting Hans's and Alex's futures in jeopardy, too.

For a brief moment, I thought about calling Sally and telling her to forget it.

Stop, Sloan.

You didn't do this. Otto and Ursula were responsible.

I looked to Alex. I'd always appreciated Mac's connection to our son and the fact that Alex had doting grandparents and an uncle. Now I wasn't so sure. I knew that I couldn't shield him from pain, but I had thought that I had created a foundation for success through the Krause family. Now it seemed that very foundation might be our undoing.

CHAPTER
TWENTY-NINE

AS IT TURNED OUT, I didn't polish off an entire pizza, although I did manage to devour three slices of the hearty Bavarian pie. By the end of our meal, Garrett, Hans, Alex, and I were all stuffed. I recapped the afternoon and evening's strange turn of events for them as we sipped wine and nibbled on an order of dessert pizza, put in at Alex's request.

"That's a really sad story, Mom." Alex sprinkled extra chocolate chips on top of his slice.

"I know. It's heartbreaking. I can't imagine something like that happening to you."

"Hey, what are you saying?" His face crumpled. "Mom, I would never do something like that. You know that, right?"

Garrett caught my eye across the table as if to say, *I told you so*.

"Absolutely. I just meant having you be in a position like that."

"Okay." Alex didn't sound convinced.

Hans ruffled his nephew's hair. "Cut your mom a little slack. It's her job to keep you humble."

The conversation turned to school and skiing. "You haven't been to an IceFest yet, have you?" he asked Garrett.

"Not in a long, long time. I came a couple times when I was a kid, but my memories are pretty fuzzy."

"It's awesome." Alex went on to tell Garrett all about next weekend's events, including the fact that he and his buddies had been training for the smooshing competition for weeks.

"I know I'm going to sound like I'm out of the loop, but what's smooshing?" Garrett asked.

"Basically, you and three of your friends strap your feet to two-by-fours, like skis, and race down Front Street."

"That sounds like good balance is required." Garrett chuckled.

"Yeah, and teamwork," Alex added. Then he turned to Hans. "And this guy holds the record for the snowmobile sled pull, isn't that right, Uncle Hans?"

Hans gave a half shrug. "I've done all right in the sled pull."

I knew he was being modest. Hans was a natural athlete. His carpentry work kept him in excellent shape, but on top of that he was agile and had grown up riding snowmobiles in the backcountry. The sled pull was always a flurry of frivolity with Hans, stepping outside of his more reserved personality, and hamming it up for the crowd by driving one-handed and backward during his victory lap.

I nursed my drink and watched the three of them laugh with ease. It seemed impossible that a few hours ago I had been out in the middle of the wooded island face-to-face with Lily's killer. It seemed even more impossible that my kind and intuitive brother-in-law could have been raised by Nazis.

"You look tired, Sloan," Garrett noted after paying the bill and boxing up leftovers.

"Mom, he's right," Alex agreed. "We should get you home."

I loved that Alex was always looking out for me. "Fair enough. I won't put up a protest."

Before we parted ways, Garrett demanded that I take the morning off. "I'm guessing that Kevin and Jenny and that crew are probably already halfway to Seattle, and if Brad decides to stay tonight, I'll have Kat make him coffee and toast." He paused and looked to Hans. "You're with me on that idea, right?"

Hans nodded. There was a flash of melancholy behind his eyes that I chose to ignore for the moment.

"Okay," I agreed, wincing as I tugged my coat on.

"I'm serious, Sloan Krause, I don't want to see your face at Nitro until sometime after noon. We can brew our new Northwest hops beer tomorrow and chill out."

"Okay, I already said I wouldn't come in early."

"Right, but I know you."

"Totally," Hans seconded. "She's a workaholic, to say the very least."

I scowled.

He reached out and kissed my cheek. "Not that you don't come by it naturally, sis. My parents are consummate worker bees. It's one of the cons of loving what you do."

"I get it. I promise I won't come in early." Ignoring his comment about Otto and Ursula, I waved them both away and left with Alex. I didn't remember the drive home or falling asleep.

The next thing I knew, I woke to the sound of my phone buzzing. How long had I been asleep?

I rolled over and reached for my phone. The time read ten. Had I actually slept in until ten? Waking at seven would have been a leisurely morning. I couldn't remember the last time I had slept so late.

The call was from a number I didn't recognize. I let it go to voicemail and went to shower. My entire left side was stiff. Sure enough, there was a bruise the color and shape of an eggplant that stretched from the top of my shoulder to my armpit. I was careful not to move the joint any more than I had to while getting dressed.

Alex had left a note on the kitchen island that Mac had given him a ride to school and he would meet me later at Nitro.

Per Garrett's instructions, I lingered over a cup of strong coffee and a sweet roll, along with another dose of Advil. *Die Zeitung*, our local paper, had news of Ali's arrest. There were sparse details of motive and nothing about her sister Chloe's drowning. I had a feeling that Chief Meyers was trying to protect her anonymity for as long as possible. When she went to trial, I was sure everything would come out, but in the short term, I was glad not to see my name in the paper so I didn't have to worry about being bombarded with questions about the arrest.

My relief was short-lived. The first person I bumped into in the village when I went into work after lunch was April

Ablin. She wore what I could only describe as a German princess costume meant for a three-year-old. The dress was crafted of silver and periwinkle blue tulle with hundreds of shimmering sequins. Her matching tights and white fur-lined snow boots had also been bedazzled. A fake white rabbit's fur shawl hung around her shoulders. The only thing she was missing was a wand.

"*Guten Tag*, Sloan." April waved from the gazebo where she was instructing a crew how to best position new IceFest banners with her face plastered all over them. "You've heard the news, haven't you?"

"About IceFest?"

She fumed. "Of course not. Don't be ridiculous, Sloan. About the arrest. The killer was apprehended last night, and it was quite the scene. A huge chase through Black-bird Island. They thought they might have to evacuate the village."

Classic April.

"Oh, really?" I played along with her charade. "Sorry I missed it."

"You won't believe who the killer is." She proceeded to tell me what I already knew, along with an assortment of half-truths and wild lies.

"I'm so glad that Leavenworth is safe again," I said when she finished her exaggerated version of last night's events.

"That's all you have to say?" She threw her hands up in exasperation. "Anyway, did you get a call from the home inspector yet?"

Ah. That was probably the number I didn't recognize earlier. "I haven't checked my voicemail."

"Well, please get on that. You want to close this deal, don't you?"

I didn't answer.

"Sloan, why do you have to be so difficult sometimes? Check your voicemail and call the inspector so we can get in there and see if anything is falling apart."

"Oh no, do you think the house is falling apart?" It wasn't very nice of me, but I couldn't resist messing with her.

"No, no, the cottage is in fantastic shape, don't start having second thoughts." She fumbled through another few sentences before I stopped her.

"I've got to get to work, I'll call the inspector later."

"I'm holding you to that, Sloan!" She fluffed her dress. "By the way, speaking of IceFest, this is what I mean by *derbling*. You and Garrett really need to up your game when it comes to costuming. Our guests expect to be dazzled when they arrive in the village, and you need to look the part."

"I'll get right on that, April. Don't worry." I smirked as I crossed Front Street. Preparations for IceFest were in full swing. I waved to familiar faces and headed to Nitro. The tasting room was buzzing with activity. Kat stood behind the bar.

"Hey, what's with the rush?" I asked, gingerly removing my injured arm from my coat sleeve.

She pointed to Brad, who was sitting with three men in suits. "The press was here earlier. Now he's meeting with a team of lawyers who came in from Seattle to start working on Ali's defense."

"Is he still staying here?"

Kat shook her head. "No, he said he'll be leaving in an hour or two. He's going to Wenatchee to be closer to Ali."

I helped Kat with orders. The rest of the crowd consisted of locals who had stopped by for the gossip. Brad came up to the bar to close out his tab.

"Hi, how are you doing?" I asked.

"Not great." He glanced at the team of lawyers. "I've hired the best defense team in the state, but I don't know what else to do."

"That's probably all you can do. Ali's lucky to have you."

He looked as if he had aged a decade overnight. "I'm sticking by her side. I won't let her go through this alone. Some of it is my fault."

"It's good to hear that you're going to be there for her, but you can't take responsibility for her actions."

He scribbled his signature on the receipt I had printed for him. "I know. It's just terrible. I can't believe I'm the one who reconnected her with Lily. If I hadn't done that, she wouldn't be in jail right now."

"You don't know that. She has obviously held on to a lot of grief, sadness, and anger. My bet is that she would have tracked her down eventually."

"Maybe." He folded the receipt and stuck it in his wallet. "Thanks for your help. I heard what she did to you last night. There's no reason for you to be kind to me. It means a lot."

"I'm sorry that it went down like this." My hand instinctively went to my shoulder.

"Me too."

He left. I wondered what would happen to their relationship. It was valiant of Brad to stick by Ali, but if she ended up in prison for life, that could change.

Garrett and I spent the afternoon working on our new beer, which was a relief because I had summoned the courage and called Ursula. I was due to meet them at Der Keller for dinner. I wasn't sure if I could have contained my nervous anticipation if it weren't for losing myself in the brewing process. The citrusy scent of our Northwest-style hops and steeping grains made Lily's death less glaring. I concentrated my energy on new thoughts and what lay ahead. The Bavarian IceFest would bring happy crowds to the village, we had our spring line of beers to focus on, and I was about to move into a charming cottage that I could make completely my own. Things were changing. The thought of redefining my life was daunting, but as I snuck a sideways glance at Garrett, who was trying to see through steamy brewing goggles, I knew that there was one major difference in my life—I wasn't alone.

CHAPTER
THIRTY

WHEN I HAD CALLED URSULA about getting together, I had gone back and forth about meeting somewhere private versus public. Ultimately I landed on Der Keller because it was midweek and the restaurant shouldn't be crowded and because if the conversation didn't go well, I could easily bolt.

I said my good-byes to Garrett and Kat, zipped up my hooded parka, and left Nitro. My heart thudded in my chest as I made the short walk toward Der Keller. Thankfully Hans, Mac, and Alex were having a guys' night out at the Festhalle, where there was a Warren Miller film playing. Different versions of what I intended to say rang through my head as I turned onto Front Street. Der Keller sat at the far end of the block directly across from the Festhalle. I could see the twinkling balls of string lights dangling from Der Keller's wood-beamed rafters in the distance.

You can do this, Sloan.

I gave myself a pep talk and squared my shoulders.

Once inside the brewery, I was greeted by more tiny white twinkling lights, German flags and banners, and the delicious scent of simmering goulash.

"Hey, Sloan. You here to meet the Krauses? They have a table in the back." One of the bartenders pointed me in the direction of a cozy collection of tables behind the bar.

I spotted Otto and Ursula at a booth. My stomach flopped, and my heart beat even faster as I approached their table.

"Sloan, we are so happy you called. Sit. Sit." Ursula pressed her hands together as she spoke. She wore one of her signature hand-knitted shawls.

I slid into the booth.

Otto nodded at the stein of beer waiting for me. "Dis is our newest batch. It is a new recipe. A dark IPA. Not our usual German-style. Mac, he has been convincing us zat we need to break free from only ze German beers. You must try, *ja*."

The ale was opaque black. I held my glass to the light, barely able to see through it. Then I took a sniff.

Otto grinned in approval. "Zat is our girl."

I breathed in through my nose. Despite its dark color, the beer had a light and bright scent, with notes of resin, chocolate, and berries. I took a sip. It had a nice balance of fruitiness mingled with a touch of spice, and a hoppy finish.

"This is nice," I said, taking another taste.

"*Ja*. I zink it is very nice for ze winter." Otto held his stein of the dark IPA up in a toast.

I couldn't even fake a smile. "I think you both know why we're here." I set my glass on the table. "I don't want to prolong this, and I can't pretend that everything's okay right now."

"We understand." Ursula placed a hand on Otto's leg. "We are happy zat you are willing to sit with us. We will tell you whatever you want to know."

A waiter started to approach our table. Ursula looked to me. "Should we wait to order?"

"No. Now is fine." The fewer interruptions, the better, as far as I was concerned.

Otto and Ursula ordered schnitzel and potato soup. I opted for the goulash. As soon as the waiter was out of earshot, I leaned closer.

"Before we even get into what you may know about my mom, I need to tell you that I know. I know about your past. I know about your real names."

Ursula let out a small gasp.

Otto put his arm around her.

I wished I had brought the files that Sally had given me, because for a moment, I didn't think they were going to respond.

Ursula dabbed her eyes with a napkin. Otto stared at his beer.

We sat in silence for what felt like an eternity.

Finally, Otto broke the awkwardness. "*Ja*, it is true. We had hoped zat we had left zat all behind us when we came here, but we knew at sometime ze truth it would come out. Ze truth, it has a way of following you and finding you."

So it was true? My stomach dropped.

"Have you told ze boys?" Ursula said through tears. "I do

not know how zey will handle ze news. It will be terrible for zem."

"It's terrible for all of us. I don't understand. Why? Why would you lie? And why Leavenworth?"

"It seemed like ze best place for us," Otto offered. He kept his arm firmly secured around Ursula. "At ze time, it was new and fresh and very far away from our homeland. It was perfect because we knew no one. No one would find us here, and it had so many good feelings of our village back in Germany. It is not ze same as living in Germany, but it was close and familiar, and we zink zat would be easier for raising ze boys. We could give zem a taste of Germany if we could not live zere and live near our family anymore. It was a big sacrifice to come here, but we made it work, and we found friends and created our own family."

I had no idea how to respond. The way he was talking made it sound like they were the victims. "A new life?" I couldn't stop the disgust in my tone. "Think of all of the people who don't have an opportunity to flee their past and start over. You completely erased your past. You lied to your children. You moved here under false identities. I don't understand, and I don't have any sympathy for you."

Ursula sobbed louder. Luckily, the section of the restaurant we were seated in was otherwise empty.

"It was horrible, Sloan. I know you have not known your family, which is a tragedy, but it was also a tragedy to be forced to leave ze country you have loved. Forced out for no reason. Do you zink zat we have enjoyed living a lie? No. Of course we have not. It has been in my head every day since

Mac was born. What would he do when he finds out. I had hoped zat would not happen until after we were gone, or if we were very lucky, maybe never."

I took a long, slow sip of the black IPA in an attempt to steady my feelings before speaking. This wasn't how I had imagined the conversation would go. "It's going to be worse than just Mac and Hans learning that you've been living a lie. The entire community is going to find out. You could be going to jail."

The color drained from both of their faces.

"What are you saying?" Otto looked confused.

"You've been running from the law for what—forty-five years? The crimes that you're involved with are catching up to you. The FBI is involved now, and you want my sympathy? I'm sorry. I can't. I feel like I don't even know you." My cheeks warmed, and my neck flushed with heat as I spoke.

"Crimes? What is she talking about?" Ursula turned to Otto.

"We have not been involved in any crimes," Otto said to me. His eyes were bright with surprise. "What is zis crime you are talking about?"

Before I could answer, our food arrived. I pushed my bowl of goulash to the side. The hearty scent of beef, paprika, red wine, and vegetables usually made me polish off an entire serving and consider seconds. But tonight I had no appetite.

Neither Otto nor Ursula touched their dinners either. They gazed at me with wrinkled brows. "Sloan, maybe we are talking of different zings. We are not criminals."

"I saw the files. I saw your real names. You've admitted

that you fled Germany and created new personas here. What do you want me to say?"

"What files?"

"The files that the FBI have on you. I should have brought them with me. They're at home. You are both labeled as being dangerous and having deep connections to Nazi leaders, including Otto's uncle."

They recoiled in unison. It was as if they were deflecting my punch.

"No, no. Zis is a mistake. You do not understand. We are not Nazis. My uncle, he was no Nazi. He had ze unfortunate luck of sharing ze same name as one of ze men from ze regime, but zat is it."

"But you just said you fled Germany."

"*Ja. Ja,*" Ursula chimed in. "Because it was too hard to zink about raising children in ze shadow of ze war. Otto was worried about his name because so many war crimes had been committed. After occupation, many war criminals, zey would steal names like Otto's family to escape conviction. Times, zey were very dark. Deutschland had external peace but internal strife with ze Red Army, kidnappings, terror attacks. Zis was ze height of ze Cold War when we left."

I wanted to believe them. Their story lined up with my gut feeling about the Otto and Ursula who had adopted me as their own daughter and invited me into their family many years ago. "Then why change your names and remove any trace of your past when you came here?"

Otto answered. "It was a different time. Germany was trying to rebuild after ze war, but our country did not have good relations with ze rest of ze world. It is understandable, *ja*. During ze war, many, many families like ours did not support ze efforts and worked to help harbor and protect our Jewish friends and neighbors. When we decided we wanted to try for children, we knew we needed a fresh start. We didn't want anything to be attached to zem and us zat could be bad or associated with ze war. Maybe it wasn't a good idea, but by ze time we would want to tell Hans and Mac, it is too late. We have been living as ze Krauses for their entire lives. Why would we ruin zat for zem? Why would we make zem question us?"

Ursula stirred her soup. She lifted her spoon as if to take a bite, and then returned it to the bowl. "Sloan, we should have told you. We should have told Mac and Hans. I can only tell you how very sorry I am, and I promise zat we made a choice to create new lives out of love. Zat is all." Tears flooded her light eyes.

I reached my hand across the table to console her.

"You believe us, *ja*?" Otto asked.

I inhaled deeply. "Yes, I think I do. I want to. I love you both. You've been the only family I've ever known, but I still have so many questions, and I don't understand how this connects to you not telling me about Marianne."

Otto removed a handkerchief from his jacket pocket and handed it to Ursula. She dried her eyes. Then she bent down to pick up her purse. "I have something to show you." She took out a folded sheet of paper and placed a trembling hand over the top. "It is true zat I have kept ziz from you, but as you will see from ze note, she asked me to do zis."

She slid the paper to me.

I opened it to discover lovely cursive handwriting on the page.

> *Otto and Ursula,*
>
> *You showed me kindness many years ago, and I'd like to ask a favor. Sloan is dear to my heart, and while she might not know it, she is in danger. There's not much more I can say, other than I ask you to keep watch over her. She's safe with you. Please never share this with her, it's better and safer if she doesn't know. If you should ever need to get in touch with me, you can send a message to the PO box below.*
>
> > *Kind regards,*
> > *Marianne*

A PO box in Spokane was listed at the bottom of the note.

"What is this?" I asked, clutching the letter.

Ursula shrugged. "We do not know. It was waiting for us under the front door the night you and Mac were married."

"Did you talk to her?"

Otto shook his head. "No. Zis is the only zing we have ever received in all of ze years we have known you."

"Did you ever try to contact her?" The room started to spin. Wavy lines blurred my vision.

"No. We never had a need. Like she said, you were safe here. We do not know why she came to us with zis, but she must have been keeping watch over you to know that you were here and that you were marrying our son."

Why the secrecy? I asked myself. My mother (if Marianne was my birth mother) had been here in Leavenworth on my wedding night? Why wouldn't she have come to the wedding? And what possible danger could I have been in? It didn't make sense.

Ursula nudged Otto. "She does not look so good. Sloan, you are very pale."

"I'm okay." We all knew that wasn't true.

"Do you want to eat?" Otto suggested, pointing to my bowl. "Ze goulash, it is good for ze soul."

"I need to go." I folded Marianne's note in half and stood. The floor felt like it might fall out beneath me.

Ursula gave me a pleading look. "I am so sorry, my dear Sloan."

"I know." I leaned down and kissed her wrinkled cheek. "Thank you for this." I held the letter tighter, not that there was any likelihood that she would try to rip it from my hands, but the letter was the first tangible piece of proof I had that someone outside my small world here in Leavenworth knew me. "I need to be alone for a while."

"*Ja.*" Otto blew me a kiss. "Go. We will be here when you're ready."

I left my dinner untouched and my stein nearly full. The twinkle lights blurred together as I stepped out into the cold. Any relief from hearing Otto and Ursula's side of their story was lost in light of Marianne's letter. Who was she? Why had she been watching me? Why had she never made contact?

Questions swirled through my head like the tiny snowflakes erupting from the dark night sky. I wasn't going to be able to answer any of the questions tonight. I wasn't even going to try. My plan was simple—for the first time ever, I had a starting point. I had an address. Marianne might have lived in the shadows, but that was about to change. Tomorrow my search for answers would begin in earnest, and I had no intention of stopping until I learned the truth.

Read on for an excerpt from

THE CURE FOR WHAT ALES YOU—

the next installment in the Sloan Krause mystery series—
available soon in hardcover from Minotaur Books!

CHAPTER

ONE

THE SCENT OF CITRUS ENVELOPED the brewery as I dumped a bucket of Lemondrop hops into the brew. The new hop varietal had become an overnight sensation, with its notes of lemon, mint, melon, and green tea. Garrett Strong, my brewing partner, and I were using the new style of hop to enhance the fruit profile of one of our spring ales—the Lemon Kiss. Our first batch of the light and refreshing beer had been a huge hit. It was unlike anything we had brewed to date, thanks to the unique hop profiles. In addition to the Lemondrop hops, we had added two of the most popular varietals in the region—Calypso and Lotus—along with lemon zest and fresh squeezed lemon juice. The result was a bright and tangy IPA that reminded me of sipping iced lemonade on the back porch. It was perfect for spring. The only problem was keeping it on tap.

Luckily we had planned ahead for this weekend's Maifest and brewed enough for the tourist crowds that would pack into the village for the traditional Maipole dance, Sip and Stroll, chainsaw carving, fun run, and outdoor spring markets. I knew that I was biased, but there really wasn't a bad season to visit Leavenworth, Washington. Our charming version of Bavaria tucked into the northern Cascade Mountains was worth the trek through the Snoqualmie Pass in the dead of winter when everything was draped with a crystalline blanket of white. The trip through the winding narrow passage with spring in full bloom was the stuff of dreams.

I had recently moved into town after years living in a farmhouse with a small hop field on the outskirts of the village. Not a day passed that I didn't feel a deep sense of gratitude for my decision to move. My "commute" to work now involved a short walk past the miniature golf course and rows of German-inspired buildings with their sand and limestone walls, tiled rooflines, half-timber framing, and balconies with window boxes overflowing with vibrant trailing geraniums, petunias, and ivy. No restaurant, delicatessen, shop, or hotel spared any expense when it came to colorful floral displays for Maifest. The abundant blooms dripped like a cascading waterfall from one story to the next.

Nitro, the nanobrewery where I had been working for nearly a year, sat just off Front Street, the main thoroughfare. I loved the scent of boiling grains and working up a sweat on brew days. Today was no exception. Garrett and I had gotten an early start. Maifest activities kicked off later this afternoon, which meant the tasting room would be buzzing with activity by early afternoon.

With that deadline in mind, I turned my attention to the brew and used a large metal paddle to stir the hops.

Garrett tugged off a pair of rubber boots, placing them on a shoe rack next to the stainless steel tanks. He had finished hosing down the equipment. Prior to learning the trade myself, I had always thought brewing was simply like baking or cooking, where you mixed a few ingredients together. But I had come to understand it was so much more. At least 75 percent of our time in the brewery involved cleaning. "Man, it smells amazing, Sloan. I think this batch is going to be even better than our first round," he said with a crooked grin.

That tended to be true. Garrett, like many brewmasters, took meticulous notes during each stage of the brewing process, from how long to steep the grains to ratios of hops and yeast. There was no way to identically craft the exact same beer each time. Often in second and third iterations of a beer, we would make minor adjustments to pull out specific flavors or reduce the bitterness. It was a constant tweaking and one of the reasons that brewing had turned into my dream job. It might be hard, physical labor, but it was never boring.

Garrett mopped sweat from his brow and removed his chemistry goggles. "I think that's it. Not bad for an early start. Now I need a coffee—or a pot of coffee."

I smiled. Garrett and I had opposite rhythms, which worked well in our professional relationship. We had recently transformed the upper floor of the building he had inherited from his great-aunt Tess into "beercation" suites. Four guest rooms, themed after the four elements of beer—water, yeast, hops, and grains—offered visitors a unique immersive experience that included a beer-infused breakfast, brewery tours, and complimentary tastings. We had officially opened for guests in January and had seen steady bookings ever since. There wasn't a weekend between now and Oktoberfest that we weren't sold out. Garrett had wisely decided that it was time for another set of hands at Nitro and had hired two college students who were home for summer vacation, Casey and Jack, to help pour pints, wait tables, prep pub fare, and wash dishes. Our permanent hire, Kat, had taken on a larger role building out our social media presence, managing guest reservations, and being our go-to person in the taproom. She had mastered how to pour a perfect pint and the subtle nuances of each of our beer profiles in a short amount of time.

I finished stirring the hops and climbed down the stainless steel ladder. "I wouldn't turn down a coffee. Kat should be done with breakfast cleanup. Then she and I are going to review the special Maifest weekend menu and make sure Casey and Jack are ready for the onslaught of beer enthusiasts."

"Sounds good. I'll go wash up and get ready to open the tasting room." Garrett tossed his chemistry goggles into a bucket of cleaning solution. "After I down a cup of coffee."

"I'm right behind you." I chuckled, kicking off my boots. Then I wiped the paddle with cleaning solution and hung it on the rack on the far wall. I stopped in the bathroom to douse my face with water. My olive-toned cheeks were pink from exertion. I cooled them with a splash of cold water and retied my long dark hair into a high ponytail. I found myself staring in the mirror a minute too long.

I knew why. I was hoping that my reflection might hold the key to who I was.

Everything I had thought I knew about my past and my family here in Leavenworth had come into question recently.

I had grown up in the foster care system. Being bounced

from house to house had come with challenges, but it had also made me the strong, independent woman I was today. When I met Mac, my soon-to-be ex-husband, the experience of feeling like it was me against the world had shifted. His family—Otto, Ursula, and his younger brother, Hans— had welcomed me without judgment or expectation. For the last two decades, I had been a Krause. Otto and Ursula had become my surrogate parents and doting grandparents to my son, Alex. Then everything fell apart. I caught Mac cheating on me with the beer wench at Der Keller, the Krause family brewery and Leavenworth's largest employer. The shock of Mac's infidelity was nothing compared with what I had learned about Otto and Ursula. The sweet German couple who adopted me as one of their own and taught me their brewing legacy had been living a lie.

Sally, my caseworker from my foster care days, had un- covered information that linked the Krauses with Nazi war criminals and flagged them as potential Nazi sympathizers. She had been convinced that Otto and Ursula had been funneling funds from Der Keller to Ernst, Otto's uncle and one of the last living members of the Nazi regimes who had escaped to America after the war. I had confronted them im- mediately. They admitted that they had changed their names when they fled Germany in the 1970s. However, they in- sisted their move to Leavenworth wasn't because of any Nazi ties. The exact opposite. Otto's uncle shared an unfortunate connection—the same name as a former member of the re- gime wanted for atrocities so dark it was impossible to fathom. I had wanted to believe them, but I had lost trust.

Fortunately, thanks to Sally and a friend of hers in the

FBI, the Krauses had been exonerated. It had been a huge relief when Sally called a few weeks after my heart-to-heart with the Krauses to tell me the news.

"Sloan, I have an update for you," she had said, her voice breathless and rushed on the call. "I was mistaken. We've been able to track down a cousin of Otto's who is still living in Germany. The Krauses are telling the truth. Ernst, who has since passed away, was cleared of any misdoings. He did not fight with the Nazis. He had the misfortune of sharing a name identical to a war criminal and nothing more."

I had told her it was a great relief to know that the surrogate parents who had taken me in and made me feel like one of them, and who had helped me raise Alex, were the people I believed them to be—kind, empathetic, and caring.

Sally had apologized profusely for her mistaken logic. I didn't blame her. Her theory had been solid. The Krauses were connected to my personal past. Ursula had received a letter from a woman named Marianne, who had visited Leavenworth in the 1970s with a young girl who bore a strong resemblance to me. According to Ursula, Marianne and a man named Forest, claiming to be her brother, arrived in the village under the guise of buying Der Keller. At the time, the brewery was just getting off the ground. Forest offered them a lucrative cash buyout, something that Otto and Ursula considered strongly. Only the offer was a scam. Forest had no intention of purchasing Der Keller. He had a history of swindling people like the Krauses who were new to the country and still learning the lay of the land and the language.

Marianne had taken off with me and vanished. Shortly

afterward, I was placed in the care of the state. Sally had found incomplete pieces of my old case files and discovered that an agent, whose name was redacted, had been responsible for putting me in care. She had theorized that Otto and Ursula's story about Forest was fake. That the real reason Marianne and Forest had been in Leavenworth was to provide surveillance on the Krauses. She had believed that Marianne was responsible for making sure I was protected.

Of course, none of that turned out to be true, which left me with a new mystery—who was Marianne?

On the night that Mac and I got married, Ursula discovered a note from Marianne on their front porch. It said that I was in danger, but I'd be safe in Leavenworth, and should Ursula ever need her help, she left a PO box number in Spokane.

Ever since, I had been writing weekly to the PO box with no response. Sally had tapped into her resources as well, with similar silence. It was a long shot. The letter had been written sixteen years ago; what were the odds that the PO box still belonged to Marianne? Lately, another thought had been creeping into my head. What were the odds that Marianne was even alive? If I hadn't heard from her after all these years, maybe there was a reason.

There was one looming problem. The Krauses still hadn't told Mac or Hans about their past or the fact that their family name wasn't even Krause. I had been stuck in the middle. Ursula had begged me for more time, and I agreed. Maybe it was the wrong choice, but it wasn't my story to tell.

Stop, Sloan. I splashed more water on my face and tried to center my thoughts.

For the past few weeks, I'd been starting to feel like I was

305

losing it. I would wake up covered in sweat from nightmares I couldn't remember. My memories of my time before foster care were fuzzy at best, but that hadn't stopped me from trying to recall every tiny flash of a memory until my brain hurt. On more than one occasion, I had thought I had seen a woman who resembled Marianne around the village—near the gazebo, at Der Keller, on Blackbird Island. I had always prided myself on my ability to keep my emotions in check. Suddenly, that was in jeopardy, along with everything else.

I let out a long sigh and went to the kitchen. Garrett had left a coffee cup, a spoon, and carton of cream next to the pot. It was the simple things that made me wonder if perhaps our working relationship might turn into more at some point. Leaving the coffee ready for me, checking in on how my search for answers was going, always being game to try any of my brewing ideas, and listening, really listening to what I had to say. Or maybe I was interpreting his kindness differently because of my past with Mac. Not that Mac hadn't cared about me. His style was grander—big gestures, expensive gifts—and a tiny piece of his attention.

I poured myself a cup and took another moment to ground myself in reality.

"Hey, Sloan," Kat called, coming into the kitchen with a tray of breakfast dishes. "How did brewing go? I can't believe Garrett was up before nine. That must be a record."

"Good. We're done. Now we wait." I raised my cup of coffee. "How are the guests this morning?"

Kat set the tray next to the sink. Her bouncy curls bobbed as she plunged the dirty dishes into soapy water. "Easy. They loved the beer-battered breakfast potatoes and devoured the entire platter of apple strudel."

"That's what we like to see. Empty plates."

Kat grinned, revealing deep dimples. "Empty plates mean easier cleanup."

"Do you want coffee?" I took a sip of mine.

"No. I'm good. I'm saving myself because I have to meet April Ablin at Frühstück, remember?"

"Oh, that's right. Sorry." I grimaced. "Thanks for taking one for the team." Poor Kat, she was due to get an earful at Frühstück, a popular breakfast spot known for its traditional morning spread of rye toast with marmalade, nougat cream, and thinly sliced meats and cheeses. April Ablin was Leavenworth's most annoying resident. She had a penchant for finding ways to showcase the tackiest Americanized versions of German culture, from her rotating collection of dirndls to cheap plastic flags, nutcrackers, and other kitsch that she insisted each business owner in town display. Garrett and I were thorns in her side. We refused to succumb to the pressure. Like the rest of the village, the exterior of Nitro resembled Bavarian architecture, but we preferred to keep the interior modern with exposed ceilings and a clean beer chemistry vibe. Visitors who came to town to join in the revelry at our rotating festivals often dressed in German attire, but those of us who lived in the village year-round (excepting April) rarely donned lederhosen or a barmaid's dress with a plunging neckline.

"Hopefully it will be quick," Kat said, rinsing the dishes before arranging them in our industrial dishwasher. "I just have to get our assignments for tomorrow's parade, and she said she had some extra 'materials' for us to put on display."

"That's code for something ridiculous," I replied. "I'm envisioning Maipole bobbleheads, don't you think?"

Kat laughed. "Yep. That sounds right. Don't worry. I won't bring back anything with ruffles or an apron for you."

"And that's why you'll keep your job," I kidded.

While Kat finished the dishes, I reviewed our menu for the weekend. Since Nitro is classified as a nanobrewery, we serve a very small bar menu including a daily soup, meat and cheese platters, and a beer-inspired dessert. When I had woken up with a nightmare the other night, I couldn't go back to sleep, so I'd tried to relax myself by flipping through a magazine. A recipe for a British trifle caught my eye and gave me a spark of creativity.

"Okay, you want to hear my crazy idea for this weekend's special dessert?" I asked Kat.

"Of course."

"I'm thinking a beer trifle. We'll make a lemon pound cake and soak it in our Lemon Kiss beer. Then we'll layer it with lemon custard, fresh strawberries, and whipped cream. What do you think?"

"Delish. Yeah, that sounds amazing."

I'd never made a beer trifle, but if a traditional trifle could be soaked in liquor, why not craft beer? It was worth a shot.

"I want to be like you when I grow up, Sloan." Kat finished loading the dishwasher. "You're so fearless."

Yeah, right. I wish. To Kat, I smiled. "Maybe outwardly. I promise, inside I'm a total mess."

She dried her hands on a dish towel. "No way. I don't believe it. You treat life the way you treat brewing and baking—

308

fully diving in. Maybe I should tell April that you're my hero. How do you think that will go over?"

"Now, that is an idea I can get behind."

Kat grabbed her phone. "Wish me luck. I'll be back soon unless I can't escape April's clutches."

"Stay strong," I called after her.

I checked the clock. It was after ten. Garrett would open the tasting room in an hour. I had time to pop over to the market to get the ingredients for my beer trifle as well as for a spring soup I wanted to serve in honor of Maifest—a fresh pea with bacon.

Garrett came downstairs freshly showered. He wore a pair of khaki shorts, a Nitro T-shirt, and a pair of hiking sandals. We kept it casual in the pub. "That felt good." He returned his empty coffee cup to the sink. "I can't believe I'm going to say this out loud, but there is something rewarding about having a new batch of beer done before noon."

"Does this mean I'm going to convert your night owl tendencies?"

"No way. Not a chance, but with so much going on this weekend, it is a relief to have that done." He opened one of the cupboards and took out bags of pretzels and Doritos. "I'm going to get the front prepped. Casey and Jack will be here in about thirty. Let me know if you need either of them to help out in here."

"I could definitely use a hand, but first I need to run to the grocery store and grab a few items."

"Sounds like a plan," Garrett said as we walked to the front together. I left him at the long exposed-wood bar, and headed for the front door.

Warm air greeted me as I stepped outside. Blue sky stretched to the top of Wedge Mountain and the Enchantment Plateau streaked with the last remnants of winter's snow. Waxy green leaves rippled in the trees and pastel ribbons and banners hung from streetlamps and balconies. When I turned onto Front Street, I was greeted by the sight of dozens of vendors setting up tents in the park. The aroma of grilling brats and roasting nuts made me pause. Was it too early for lunch?

There was no denying Leavenworth's charm. Every shop and storefront was designed to resemble a quaint German village. The brightly colored buildings with balconies and exposed timber framing were painted with unique murals like a cascading waterfall and a goat farmer shepherding his flock. Nesting dolls, gorgeous cuckoo clocks, beer steins, and Hummel figurines in the storefront windows made it easy to forget this wasn't Rothenburg or Schiltach. A wooden gazebo flanked by a massive weeping willow tree had been adorned with more flowers than most wedding venues. Keg barrels lined both sides of the street. They had been repurposed to display even more spring blooms. Each overflowed with fragrant hyacinths, primroses, tulips, and camellias.

The giant blue and white Maipole stood upright in its post. Tomorrow it would take center stage in the Maifest parade, where dancers in colorful pinafores and lederhosen would perform the traditional Maipole dance. Beautiful silk ribbons would stretch from the top of the pole to each dancer's hands. They would weave around the pole in a seamless rhythm, ducking under ribbons and creating a magical pattern of rippling colors. It was the highlight of the parade.

I continued past the gazebo, which had been adorned with

six-foot-wide flower baskets filled with deep purple and lilac blooms. Nearly every shop and restaurant had propped open their front doors to welcome in shoppers and hungry tourists. Der Keller, the Krause family brewery, sat at the far edge of Front Street. The building itself was a sight to behold, with its sloped A-frame roofline, hand-carved trim and wooden shutters, and iron accents. Der Keller's outdoor patio had been decked out for the festival with strands of twinkle lights, strings of baby blue-and-white-checkered flags, topiaries, and more hanging baskets. Staff wearing *Trachten* shirts placed menus on the outdoor tables while a German oompah band warmed up.

The Festhalle was directly across the street from Der Keller. Throughout the busy weekend, a variety of bands and musicians would perform on the stage. An outdoor fruit and flower market took over the grounds next to the Festhalle. Rows and rows of long tables had been constructed where local farmers and artisans were selling hop starts, flowering currants, blueberry bushes, heirloom fruit trees, and fresh cut flower bunches.

The excitement was palpable. Plenty of tourists had already arrived. I enjoyed watching them delight at the sight of the bustling village and the sweeping alpine views. A couple was trying to take a selfie at the end of Front Street in order to get the view of the gazebo, village, and the jutting Alps behind them and yellow balsamroot blooming on the building next to them.

"Would you like me to take your picture?" I asked. It was commonplace for those of us who called Leavenworth home to stop and offer to snap photos for tourists. It didn't take any extra effort on my part, and it was one simple way (unlike April's in-your-face style) to make our guests feel welcome.

"That would be great. Thank you so much." The young woman handed me her phone. I took a few shots, making sure the Maipole and snowcapped mountains were centered behind them.

After I returned her phone, I was about to cross the street toward the flower market when a flash of movement caught my eye. A woman sprinted out of a narrow alleyway between the coffeehouse and wine shop on the opposite side of the street. She caught my eye. Our gazes locked on one another.

I froze.

I knew her face. I'd been carrying around a picture of that same face for months. She looked exactly like Marianne. Her silver hair flapped in the breeze. Her dark brown eyes were wild with fear.

My legs wouldn't move. I stood in the middle of the town square, unable to make sense of what I was seeing.

She broke eye contact first. Her manic stare drifting behind me.

I started to move toward her, but she bolted back down the alleyway.

"Wait!" I called, running after her.

She vanished.

When I made it through the alleyway, there was no sign of her. Where could she have gone?

Or did I need to ask myself a different question?

Was she real?

I blinked hard. Were my eyes playing tricks on me? Or, worse, was I really losing it?